Tales of Hardooth 7

REFLECTIONS
AND
BEGINNINGS

Dara J. Carr

Tales of Hardooth 7

REFLECTIONS
AND
BEGINNINGS

Dara J. Carr

Harrison House Publishing

Harrison House Publishing
www.theharrisonhousepublishing.com
info@theharrisonhousepublising.com
ISBN: 978-0-9996147-6-1
Library of Congress Control Number: 2019909715
Harrison House Publishing and the "HH" logo are trademarks belonging to Harrison House Publishing.

PRINTED IN THE UNITED STATES OF AMERICA

This story is fictional. No actual person or event is depicted. Any similarity with any person, living or dead, or any event, is entirely coincidental and unintentional…and seeing as how we're talking about mutated people from other planets, it ain't too practical either!

TXu 1-969-328

REFLECTIONS AND BEGINNINGS

1

Soolchakan sat there pondering many things. He was sitting in his "throne room" in the "other" apartment. There were now fifty-one thrones in this room. There were only five of the original twenty-eight among the ones in this room. He had dismantled and removed the thrones that had been "uncomfortable" or had started to fall apart from age. He had wondered, for a long time, why the women were so generous in giving him all of these thrones until he found out that each one of them had kept five or six for themselves. Each of the ones they kept were all more comfortable and ornate than anything he had in this big room (big surprise). Most of them were better looking as well. Now he knew why they were so generous - he was getting the leftovers they had turned their backs on and turned their noses up in disgust. Still... the thrones were, for the most part, rather good looking and very expensive...and he could sit on the one that he felt like sitting on, whenever, or whichever was the most comfortable. Plus when he dismantled any of them, there was always some gold, silver or other precious metal inlay along with precious stones and some other substances from the planet of origin.

He turned the computer on and pulled up his memoirs. For some strange reason, when Nagasoom was the *Voice of Power,* he had ordered everyone to start writing a daily log of what had happened. Soolchakan was not sure who was supposed to read the silly things, however, the *Voice* had spoken and no Owlamite could refuse and no other *Voice* had changed that rule. The only ones he could imagine reading these things were his children.

He looked in disgust at what had been originally written. While Nagasoom and Plothok were in power, Soolchakan had been drinking heavily and what words were spelled correctly were nothing but rambling nonsense. It was not until Neenatha had made him stop the constant *self-medication* that he started writing intelligent sentences and accurate renditions of what he had seen and experienced (even though a lot of it was very repetitious).

He quickly scanned through the pages until he got to Xadorm. That mass battle where they had to defeat that pesky Alliance had been the glorious time for Xadorm. He had lasted another 537 years after that epic war was over, for a total of 648 years in power. Here came another enemy from outer space called the Cheendoz. Another 312 Owlamite names were added to the list of the fallen after this horrid battle.

All of the Owlamites were thrown into a bit of a quandary because in the initial attack, Xadorm and his entire Staff were wiped out. The top nine on the list were all dead in an instant. There was a scramble by everyone to get to their list and find out who was number 10 on the list. It turned out to be Officer Leader, Hrombisk. Unfortunately, he was giving a report to the Staff when the attack hit and he was killed as well.

Number eleven was Officer Grade 1, Plykatha. Here she was, suddenly, the new *Voice of Power* with no experienced members of a Staff to assist or advise her. She was the thirteenth one to obtain the *Power* and only the fourth woman to end up there.

She had to make some very quick decisions in order to gain control and find out anything that she could about this new pestilence. They had more new technology that the Owlamites eventually "obtained" when they wiped this new enemy out.

New (and more) sensors were put in place to act as guardians. These new sensors did their job...for another 381 years. A very new, dangerous and resilient enemy called the Skax came in and, like many of those frustrating enemy, ignored all of the guardian sensors completely.

When Plykatha was killed, Booxo took over as the fourteenth *Voice of Power*. He had to fight the Skax during his entire term of 378 years. 222 Owlamites were killed in the initial attack by the Skax and another 184 while Booxo continued to lead the fight against them.

When Booxo was killed, Kloob became the fifteenth to reign over the Owlamites and take over trying to gain peace from the chaos perpetrated by the Skax.

Kloob tried a different approach. He made several attempts at negotiations for a peace treaty with the Skax. It seemed that they were not going away any time soon and he hoped that some kind of treaty would bring order out of the chaos. He tried to negotiate with them for 326 years. It was not until another devastating attack that killed Kloob and another 737 Owlamites that they realized that the Skax were using the negotiations in order to realign their attack ships and obtain more intelligence data in order to try a full scale attack that would end the war in one battle with Hardooth.

Officer Grade 3, Zebenee ended up being the sixteenth *Voice of Power*. She was not even the Team Leader for her Team. She was under Officer Grade 1, Amahay on Team 114. It had been some time since she had commanded anyone, however, she did have some experience to fall back on and used it in order to fulfill her new obligation in the number one position.

She had no intentions of making a peace treaty with anyone as deceitful as the Skax and she simply ordered that they be destroyed completely. All of the Owlamites that had died over 675 years of Booxo and Kloob was totally unacceptable. End this nonsense by totally annihilating the Skax without remorse. Easier said than done…however, it was eventually accomplished.

There was a wonderful period of 477 years of peace… followed by, yet another, marauder from outer space. Zebenee, and over 300 Owlamites, were killed in the initial attack by the new enemy, the Zalkansan. Junrud took over as the seventeenth *Voice of Power*. He did not prove to be a capable leader and during his short two years in power, he was killed by the Zalkansan along with more than 400 more Owlamites.

Pextow took over as the eighteenth top leader of the Owlamites. He did everything that he could to battle this terrible nuisance, however, he only lasted for one year before falling along with 140 more Owlamites.

Civilian Farmer, Thes, one of the few surviving farmers, became the nineteenth *Voice of Power*. This only seemed to add more problems to the current chaos because no one had ever expected any of the civilian farmers to reach the lofty title. He had not even been a Team Leader. He, like all of the farmers, was listed last in rank on the Team that he was on. Now he had the roll of ultimate leader when he had never led anyone in anything except proper farming techniques. He relied heavily on his new Staff. They came up with the idea of treating the Zalkansan as if they were a hoard of insects that were there to devour your crop. Thes enemy was finally defeated by the only way that the Owlamites knew to completely end a war – genocide. What else would a farmer do with a bunch of bugs that want to destroy your entire crop?

Thes is a very good-natured man and turns out to be a relatively good and congenial leader. There is another time of peace…that lasts for 236 years under Thes…until another attack by a group called The Tiserion Society. Thes, along with another 311 Owlamites die in the initial attack and Gorral takes over as the twentieth *Voice of Power*.

The Tiserion Society is another persistent pestilence that plagues Hardooth during the entire 173 years of Gorral being in charge. Another 302 Owlamites die…along with Gorral. Now comes the sixth female and the twenty-first *Voice of Power* - Sleea.

Under Sleea, the Owlamites get back to basics and use all of their fantastic powers against the Tiserions. Finally that enemy is nothing but part of history as well. Gorral had tried to use some kind of finesse in order to take out the Tiserions and that had only turned into disaster. Sleea did not like finesse. She had one tactic/ strategy: Just blast them, wherever they are, and their home planet and get rid of them.

Soolchakan sat there disgusted. It seemed that most of the history was nothing but boredom until someone comes along and attacks Hardooth, causing all kinds of destruction and death.

While Sleea was in charge, there was one bright light in the history of the planet though. Kiyalee went to Sleea and her Staff and, once again, informed them of the horrible plight of the vegetation on Hardooth. All of those attacks from above were having a terrible toll on the plants and the soil. Sleea liked the idea of new crops and plants being brought to Hardooth...from anywhere.

For the next seventy years, the Owlamites were bringing plants from all over the galaxy. They brought plants, trees, flowers and crops from other dimensions as well. The only plants and crops that were indigenous to Hardooth that were still flourishing were the plants the Owlamites were cultivating in the hydroponics gardens on all of the captured ships floating around in dimension #45. Kwatha and all of the ingredients for *Tuzine* were abundant in the spaceships along with some tasty fruits and nutritious vegetables. The Owlamites never hesitated to bring seed and cuttings back to Hardooth to keep those plants around.

He smiled as he remembered how pleased all of the races of Hardooth were when they each discovered some new fruit, vegetable or grain crop that was nourishing to all. He thought of some of the huge trees that were now growing along the edge of the gorge. They helped shade a large portion of the area where the apartments were located, thus keeping things a little cooler in this humid tropical environment.

The peaceful time with Sleea in charge lasted for 367 years. A new enemy called the Mypoth show up and now Sleea is killed. Eeleeg is now the new *Voice of Power*. When it came to finding tunnels dug by the enemy and blowing up those tunnels while the enemy is still in them, Eeleeg is second to none. When it comes to leading the Owlam nation against an outworld enemy, he is severely lacking. He lasts barely one year in the battle against the Mypoth.

The next man to take the lead position was Panatorm. He is number twenty-three and like Eeleeg, he is not very good at leading the entire Owlam nation. Panatorm lasts less time than Eeleeg. Under those two men 231 more Owlamites end up as battle fatalities.

Another civilian, Malapi now becomes the twenty-fourth *Voice of Power*. She, once again, gets the Owlamites back to basics and the Mypoth are demolished.

76 years into the tenure of Malapi, the alarm bells go off in regards to an unidentified single space ship entering the star system. Team 7016 is called upon to investigate this new invader…because of some duty roster that shows that it is their turn. Once again they grudgingly obey the order to be the first one

on scene. The result is very different than any of them could have ever expected.

Soolchakan checked the message to find out where the "unknown" was located. According to the message, Officer Grade 5, Thoyneesa, of Team 194 spotted the thing while on patrol. It was located just inside the orbital path of Makatindi and was heading towards the central area of the star system. He grunted in disgust as he read the coordinates.

He shook his head. "Why couldn't you have investigated that thing while you were there?" He scoffed in disgust again. He headed for his fighter. "**Ladies, we are headed for the planet Makatindi. Somewhere around that planet is a... strange new spaceship...in our system**."

Chyning came back sounding just as disgusted. "**And, of course, there's no one else who can do this**!"

Kiyalee came in. "**What'd you expect**?"

Bonarain sighed. "**Is it going to be the standard investigation tactic**?"

Soolchakan chuckled. "**What else**?"

The four of them got in their fighters and pulled up a picture of one of the three moons orbiting Makatindi. They all landmarked on one of the many craters on that moon, hopped to Spy and Jumped to that location. Once there they joined in formation to look for the *unknown*. After several moments of seeing nothing unusual, they split up and started doing some sweeping grid searches around the planet.

"**I've spotted it**," sent Bonarain.

'Finally,' thought Soolchakan.   He looked around. "**Okay...where are you**?"

"**I'm turning my rotating light beacon on**," she sent back.

Soolchakan turned his ship around until he saw the pulsating light in the distance coming from Bonarain's fighter. He gunned his engine and headed for her. He arrived at her location at the same time that Kiyalee got there. As usual – Chyning was last to get there.

He sighed. "**You're the one who spotted it...so... lead the way**."

Bonarain hit her throttle and the other three followed behind her. They went a little bit of a distance before any of the others saw it.

Kiyalee frowned. "**Uh...kinda small for an attack ship, ain't it**?"

"**No wonder we didn't spot it when we first got here**," sent Chyning.

Soolchakan was confused as well. "**So...what do you think? Maybe a crew of...four or five**?"

"**Unless they're *sticks* like the Zizzys**," sent Chyning.

"**Then it could be a crew of thirty...or more**," sent Kiyalee.

They all moved forward slowly and cautiously.   The

strange ship was a cylinder that was only 45 taja in length and 12 taja in diameter. Seeing as how their fighters were each 11 taja in length, things could get a little crowded inside the ship. There were no visible markings on the outside of the ship. There was also a complete lack of any kind of porthole for anyone inside to peer out of the ship. Soolchakan looked down at his monitor and saw that this ship was traveling a very leisurely speed.

"**Whoever it is, they're in no hurry**," sent Soolchakan.

Kiyalee huffed. "**I'm having a very hard time keeping my fighter going this slow.**"

Chyning snickered. "**Maybe they believe that if they don't go to fast…we'll trust them…or not see them.**"

He shook his head. "**Let's go inside and…find out… who they are.**"

"**And what they want**," sent Bonarain.

Soolchakan headed for the nose of the ship. Kiyalee headed for the area that she guessed was the engine room. Bonarain and Chyning were between the other two. When they entered the ship they were even more confused at what they found.

"**Either they're all asleep or they're stone blind**," sent Chyning.

"**There's no one aboard**," sent Bonarain. "**I'm not sensing or reading any minds…except us.**"

Kiyalee switched her light beacon from "pulsate" to "on". Her light alone lit up the entire interior of the small ship. There was one small conventional engine in the rear. There were a few computer monitors that were currently showing no sign of being active in the central part of the ship. There was a small navigational computer in the nose. There was no living creature on board. There was a rather large, cylinder-shaped transparent glass case that took up the entire central part of the ship.

Chyning grunted in frustration. "**Okay...now what**?"

Soolchakan sighed. "**Find out where this thing is going...and just exactly...*what* is in that glass coffin**?"

Chyning turned her beacon on and started going back and forth on the container. "**It looks like...floating around inside there is...a bunch of necklaces and...daggers of some type...in sheaths.**"

"**They're not floating around in it**," sent Bonarain. "**Someone made this case out of glass by getting the glass so hot that it turned to liquid. Then they shoved those things...inside the big thing and...let it harden with them inside.**"

Kiyalee frowned. "**Why would anyone want to do that**?"

"**I don't know**," sent Soolchakan. "**I wasn't on that committee!**"

Kiyalee gave Soolchakan an obscene gesture.

"**Four necklaces and four sheathed daggers encased in that thing**," sent Chyning. "**Should we get them out**?"

Kiyalee scoffed. "**How**?!"

"**I'm gonna try it in Ghost**," sent Soolchakan. "**I'll see if that can get me in there…and find out what is so special about those things**."

Bonarain giggled. "**Go for the necklace with the red stone…it looks like it matches your shirt**."

The other two women snickered.

Soolchakan grunted in disgust. He hopped to Ghost and slowly made his way into the interior of the glass case. He was trying to decide which one to go to first and shrugged as he went with the suggestion to get to the gold necklace with a red translucent stone. He saw that the other three stones were blue, yellow and green. He chuckled inwardly as he thought of basic colors that were used most of the time. Blue, red and yellow were the basics and green always seemed to show up fourth as an afterthought. He reached for the red one and took hold of it. He hopped it to Ghost and pulled it out of the area where it was encased.

All three women gasped.

Bonarain reacted first. "**Did you see that**?"

Soolchakan looked around for the three women. He remembered that he was in Ghost and that they were in Spy so he could not see them at this time. "**See what**?"

"**The…rock**," sent Bonarain. "**When you…touched it…it sparkled for just a heartbeat**."

"**It did**," sent both Kiyalee and Chyning!

Soolchakan rolled his eyes. He wondered what kind of a trick they were trying to pull on him. "**I didn't see any light**."

"**It did light up**," sent Bonarain. "**Just for a brief heartbeat**."

'Right!' he thought. 'It's helping in celebrating one of the holy celebration days.' He made his way back to his fighter, got back in the cockpit and hopped it back to Spy.

Bonarain sent to him in an admonishing manner. "**The stone lit up...but the dagger didn't!**"

He looked over at Bonarain. 'Dagger? What dagger,' he thought? Then he looked down. In his right hand was a red stone that looked as if it had once been part of a small sphere that would fit inside his fist. The gold chain hung down from the stone. He could not see any form of setting that showed how the chain and stone were linked together. In his left hand was one of the sheathed daggers that had been encased in the glass. He was sitting there rather baffled (and a little scared) because he did not remember going for, or grabbing hold of and taking the knife with him. He nervously cleared his throat. "**Okay, Bonarain, why don't you go for the blue one? I guess that one will match *your* shirt**."

Bonarain hopped to Ghost and headed into the glass. She moved towards the blue stone. She took hold of the stone and hopped it to Ghost. She did not see any illumination from this stone.

"**It lit up as well**," sent Kiyalee.

"**It did**," sent Chyning!

"**I saw a sparkle that time - a blue light**," sent

Soolchakan.

Bonarain chuckled uneasily. "**I didn't**." She pondered what had happened. 'He didn't see the red one light up when he grabbed it and I didn't see the blue one light up when I grabbed it. Interesting,' she thought! She made her way back to her fighter. She got back in, hopped to Spy and decided to take a closer look at her stone. It was then that she noticed that she had one of the sheathed knives in her left hand and could not remember grabbing or hopping the knife. She sat there confused and a little frightened. **"Uh...Kiyalee, why don't you...go for the yellow stone**?"

Kiyalee retrieved the yellow stone...and a knife...with the same results. The stone lit up for a brief moment. Kiyalee did not see the light – the others did. She got back to her fighter without any recollection of grabbing one of the knives.

Chyning had the same experience with the green stone... and the fourth knife.

There were now holes in the glass that were the exact shapes of the stones, chains and knives that he had just rescued from the large glass tomb.

Chyning sighed. **"What do we do now**?"

"Yeah," sent Kiyalee. **"We have to tell our Supreme Commander something!"**

Soolchakan sighed. **"We've pilfered the ship of the riches. Is there anything here, that anyone can see, that might be useful...to someone else**?"

Bonarain pointed to the computer consoles. **"Look!**

There are those consoles. Right there in the middle. It looks like some kind of storage box for...whatever these people used for computer discs. Maybe, take a couple of consoles...and the discs and...turn them over to Sankiki and Tula."

He shook his head and sighed. "**I can't think of any better idea. Let's grab two...or three consoles and...the discs...and get out of here**."

They looked over the computers and all of the connections. When they disconnected the equipment from the ship they heard no warning klaxons and saw no other strange lights. They all looked at each other and shrugged. They got back in their fighters with the newly acquired equipment and Jumped back to Hardooth to report to Malapi.

Five days later Sankiki and Tula were making their report to the Staff. Team 7016 was asked to be there as well.

Tula gave a rather boring speech about how the computers were nothing but very basic computers that had no real value here in the gorge. All of the computers that were here were all far more sophisticated and capable of much larger memory on their hard drives.

Sankiki gave a different briefing. "I found that there was some very puzzling illustrations on those discs. That ship was designed just to hold that big glass coffin and then just according to the navigational settings...fly right into our star Holgotho... according to the trajectory of the ship. Whatever is being held inside that glass coffin, it is a bane to them…uh…whoever *them* is, and they want it destroyed. Flying it into a star…any star, will definitely do the trick."

Malapi raised her eyebrows and smiled. "Exactly what is in that glass coffin?"

Sankiki shrugged. "I have absolutely no idea. We can't see through that black glass. I mean the glass is so dark and thick that light won't shine through it."

The four members of 7016 all looked at each other completely confused. When they had been on board that ship, the glass was totally transparent. They could not understand how it had darkened so completely after their theft.

Master Officer, Filfaya cleared her throat. "Should we allow that ship to continue into Holgotho?"

"We have plenty of time to think about it," said the physicist Itchami. She snickered. "At the current speed that thing is going, it'll take at least eight years before the ship is near our orbit…then another two years before it gets to Holgotho. I don't think that any of us have to worry about coming up with any hasty decision."

"I still don't like it," said Malapi. "If…whoever built that thing…wanted something destroyed…why didn't they run it into their own star?"

Master Officer, Strinta sat there drumming her fingers. "Is there any clue as to what is in that coffin?"

Sankiki huffed. "The only word that we can come up with, from the illustrations, that describes the contents is: Oppositions…

if we are translating any of the words correctly."

Master Officer, Ribatha frowned. "Oppositions to… what?"

"It just indicates oppositions, Sir," said Sankiki. "Apparently there is something…or some *things* in that coffin that…they don't like. They want them destroyed and running them into a star…should definitely destroy just about anything."

Master Officer, Sheekog shook his head. "Why don't we just throw the ship into dimension 45 and that'll give us all kinds of time to study it and…maybe find out what is in there? We could make an educated guess from there."

Strinta looked up. "Wait! Why are we having so much trouble translating? Officer, Bonarain is here and she has had no trouble translating languages before. Why can't she do it now?"

Bonarain stood up. "This is different, Sir. When I was translating those languages, I was listening to them being spoken, or thought. There is no one on that ship who is speaking the language. It is only written. I can't do the same thing with just the written language. I have to hear it, either spoken or read a mind."

Strinta leaned back and sighed with a sour look on her face. "Noted!"

"Okay," said Malapi. "Hop that thing into 45 and we'll… discuss it later."

Team 7016 was back in their apartment looking at these strange goodies they had taken from the coffin ship. Each one had a stone and a sheathed dagger sitting in front of them. They all looked at each other apprehensively. Not one of them was exactly sure what to say about these stones on the necklaces or the knives they had purloined from the coffin ship.

Soolchakan shook his head. He sighed, sniffed, reached down, picked up the gold necklace and put it around his neck. The stone hung just around the middle of his chest. "It does match the shirt…perfectly," he said flatly.

The three women sat there without moving, just staring at him with concern on their faces. Bonarain shrugged, picked her necklace up and put it on. The other two women did the same. They all looked down at the stones on the chain and all were a little amused by the fact that the stones were almost the exact shade of their shirts. The same kind of shirts used to indicate status on a Team, even after all these centuries.

Suddenly all four stones started glowing. Four Owlamites sat there with their eyes, and mouths, wide open in shock. The four stones pulled towards each other and the four people were yanked forward by the pull of the stones. The four stones merged together over the middle of the table and became a perfect sphere that turned a bright translucent golden color. Gold colored rays of light started shooting out of the sphere, lighting up the entire room. The four Owlamites felt no pain. They were all too stunned to make any attempt at pulling away from each other. Then just as suddenly, the light show ended, the four pieces separated and turned back to their original color and the four Owlamites fell back into their seats. Soolchakan and Bonarain were able to catch themselves on their seats. Kiyalee and Chyning ended up toppling backwards with their chairs.

Chyning stood up and was panting nervously. "What... just...happened?"

Soolchakan gave her a stunned but nasty look. "Just exactly *how* should I know? We're all four experiencing...*this*... whatever happened...for the first time."

Kiyalee swallowed hard. "Maybe we should put these things away...and...try to find out more about them...before...we do anything else with them."

The other three nodded in agreement. They all four grabbed the stones and started to pull the necklace over their heads. They all froze, when they all had an unexpected dread of taking the necklaces off. The thought of taking the necklaces off was now terrifying to them. They had to keep them on. They could not understand why.

"I can't...take it off," said Soolchakan with fear on his face.

"I can't either," said Bonarain looking rather confused.

Kiyalee just looked around at the other three.

Chyning handled the stone, looking at it in a curious manner. She let it drop.

Soolchakan let go of the stone and let it fall. He picked up the sheathed knife that he had pulled out of the coffin. He looked it over a little more thoroughly than before. It did not seem to weigh very much at all. The hilt looked like some kind of nondescript metal. There was no pommel stone. The hand guard was a simple square bar at the business end of the hilt. There was a small leather-like strap that held the knife in the sheath. The sheath itself was just some kind of nondescript, black leather. He pulled the strap off and pulled the knife out.

Now there was another incredibly strange phenomenon that none of them were prepared for. As he pulled the knife out, the double edged blade started glowing bright red. As he pulled, the blade kept on coming out. It was impossibly long for the length of the sheath. When the blade finally cleared the sheath, he was staring at a sheath that was approximately one taja in length and a blade that was just over four taja in length. For the size of the blade it seemed incredibly light. The red glow of the blade made everything in the room appear to be one shade or another of red. The entire room and the four Owlamites were all red. He swallowed hard and decided to see if the thing would fit back in the sheath. He carefully placed the tip of the sword in the sheath and slowly pushed it back in. The entire sword fit back in a sheath that was only one fourth the length of the blade. As soon as the last part of the blade disappeared into the sheath, all normal color was restored to the room.

The three women were all staring at the thing in his hand with shock and horror on their faces. All four glanced around at the others nervously.

He chuckled in a strained manner. He saw that there were two small belts on each end of the sheath. He placed the sheath against the outside of his right calf. He wrapped the upper and lower belts around his calf and strapped the thing to his leg. He then leaned back in his chair. "I think that…right now…that is the best place for this thing…until we can figure out what it…really is."

Bonarain gave him a frightened smile. She picked her sheath up, released the strap and slowly pulled her blade out. She was having the same results, as far as the length of the double-edged blade, however, this one turned the entire room different shades of blue. After putting the sword back into this magical sheath, the strapped it to her right calf as well.

Kiyalee did the same thing with her blade and (surprise) it was yellow. She followed along with strapping the thing to her leg.

Chyning sat there with a disgruntled look on her face. She sighed, sniffed and picked her knife up. She pulled it only half-way out. It turned the entire room different shades of green. She shook her head, slammed the sword back in the sheath and then strapped it to her right calf.

Kiyalee grunted in disgust. "So how do we find out about these…bizarre things? It may be a little difficult going to Tula… and asking her about them."

Bonarain sighed. "I…got hold of one of the computers… and…" She looked up trying to act innocent. "…we have copies of the discs here…as well."

Chyning smirked. "So, are you going to try to translate them yourself…and figure out just exactly what we got hold of?"

Bonarain gave her a patronizing look. "I was hoping that…maybe, just maybe…I could get a little assistance from the three of you…in any attempt at translation."

"We'll definitely work on that," said Soolchakan. "I won't promise any results, but…we'll assist…in any way that we can."

All four of them continued staring at the stones that the others were wearing. Occasionally their gaze went down to the sheaths on the legs. Not one of them could come up with anything intelligent to say or ask about these odd relics. They sat there in silence until finally someone suggested dinner.

2

Bonarain was sitting at one of the tables eating a melon when the other three members of the Team walked in. She looked up just after stuffing a large piece in her mouth.

"Looks like you've got something on your mind," said Kiyalee.

"**I do**," sent Bonarain trying to get around the mouthful of melon.

"Well spit it out," said Chyning. Then she started laughing at her own joke. She looked at both Soolchakan and Kiyalee for backup, however, received none. She stopped laughing and cleared her throat with a disgusted look on her face. "Okay, what's bothering you?"

"**It's been five days and they haven't asked us a thing about any pilferage of that ship**," sent Bonarain with a worried look on her face.

Kiyalee chuckled. "They haven't asked us because they don't think there was anything to pilfer on that ship...unless there is something in that black glass coffin, they can't see."

Bonarain finally swallowed. "They read the stuff about the oppositions. Suppose that these stones and...very strange swords are...the oppositions."

"Suppose they are," said Soolchakan. "Have you taken that…necklace off…just once since you put it on and the *chokwad* things did that crazy…joining?"

Bonarain sighed. "I…can't take it off. Every time I try…I get this…horrible dread of losing it on my mind. I've been naked in the bathtub at least eight times…except for the necklace. I don't wanna take it off. I can't seem to take it off."

"Same here," said Kiyalee dejectedly. "Taking it off…the thought of that just terrifies me."

Soolchakan noticed that half of a melon was sitting on the bar. "Are you going to eat the whole thing or can anyone claim that other piece?"

Bonarain waved her hand at him to let him know he could have it.

He picked up the melon half and a spoon. He walked over to where Bonarain was seated and joined her at the table. "I think that we should just wait…until they ask us about any goodies that we…might have obtained off of that ship," he said flatly. "If they don't ask us, they don't need to know where these things came from."

Chyning scoffed. "Every time I come across anyone else…I stuff the stupid thing down inside my shirt. I don't think that any of the others have ever seen this rock. Have any of you showed your rock…to anyone?"

Soolchakan now had a huge mouthful of melon. "**You put it inside your shirt as well? I've done the same thing**."

He shook his head. **"So we agree to keep our mouths shut about these rocks**."

"What about the knives," said Chyning? "Don't you think that someone might ask something about a big lump under one of our cuffs?"

Kiyalee gave a nervous chuckle. "I've...been asked about that. I told the ones asking that...since a lot of technology has been blasted off of this planet by those *chokwad* outworlders... carrying a weapon on our person just seems to make us fit in better. Someone who is carrying or wearing a dagger or sword...is not very uncommon out there...in this day and age." She shrugged. "Think about it! It has been over 6,500 years since the firestorm attack. We've faced off against fourteen different outworlders on numerous occasions and...most of the targets by the outworlders, on their initial attacks, have been against any form of technology they find on the planet. This planet has been practically blasted back into days prior to the discovery of electricity."

Bonarain snickered. "Maybe we shouldn't be so paranoid about the necklaces. If it is becoming normal for people to carry antique weapons out there, then why would it be so crazy to be wearing some kind of jewelry...in the open?"

Soolchakan held his stone up. "Look at these things. Each of our chunks look like they're part of a busted orb of some kind. When they joined...the other day...they did form a perfect sphere. Now, each one looks like a piece of broken glass...again. That doesn't sound like some fancy piece of jewelry that you'd want to show off."

Chyning smiled smugly. "So we tell them that we're wearing them more for the gold chain rather than the busted glass."

Kiyalee looked thoughtful. "That actually sounds...crazy enough to work."

Soolchakan shrugged in acceptance and went back to work on the melon.

201 years later, yet another outworlder came on the scene. Once again most of the security sensors were bypassed and over 650 Owlamites were killed in the initial attack – including Malapi and the top two members of her Staff: Filfaya and Strinta. Sheekog (who was also on the Staff) became the twenty-fifth *Voice of Power*. He started the counter-attacks against this new enemy called the Vashasnog. The attacks are somewhat successful, however, the Owlamites lose another 150 of their people during the two years that Sheekog was in power...included in the fatalities - Sheekog.

Melming takes over as the twenty-sixth *Voice of Power*.

While Soolchakan was perusing his notes he was also looking at some of the notes left by others who had been the *Voice of Power*. He blinked his eyes and looked at the other notes. He wondered why such a mistake had been left, or even written, in the logs of anyone.

"Bonarain, this is Soolchakan, can you hear me?"

Bonarain looked up from polishing her silver. **"I'm here... what'd you need**?"

"Could you get to your computer and look something up real quick?"

She put the candelabra down and huffed. "**Why**?"

He snarled. "**Just get to your computer and look up Melming.**"

She sighed and headed for her computer. She turned it on. "**It'll take a little while to warm up. I haven't had this one on for several days.**"

"**That's all right. Just let me know when you have the information on Melming on your screen.**"

She waited for all of the beeping and clicking to end. She pulled her logbook up and went to the information on Melming. "**Okay, I've got it…now what?**"

"**Now get into the logbook left by Salgim and look up his notes on Melming…and read a few of them.**"

She shook her head in disgust and pulled the other logs left by Salgim. She pulled up the information on Melming and started reading. She stopped abruptly and sat there looking shocked. "**What's all of this…he, his and him stuff? Melming is a woman.**"

"**I know! I'm wondering what Salgim was thinking…when he put all of those masculine pronouns in there…on Melming.**"

"**He did have a few problems talking to women. Do you think he had…some kind of really bad psychological problem with it?**"

"**Hard to say, but...he messed up bad in gender identification here.**"

Bonarain frowned. "**Hold on...let me check something else.**" She ran through some of the other parts of his entries. "**I think he did have problems with women. He referred to Malapi as male...also Sleea. He has nothing but masculine pronouns for Zebenee...Plykatha... Wymini as well. He also wrote about Neenatha and Holla in the masculine...as well. I think he did have problems with women.**"

Soolchakan shook his head in disgust. "**That must have been a royal headache for his three Teammates.**"

Bonarain sighed. "**No doubt!**" She backed away from her computer. "**Are you suggesting that we alter his notes...and change all of those erroneous pronouns... to feminine?**"

Soolchakan hung his head. "**The last thing that I want to be is some kind of historical revisionist...on our own writings. We'll just have to admit that he had a problem. I kinda wonder if he's the reason that Stra went crazy. She was on his Staff.**"

Bonarain groaned. "**That could explain...something.**"

"**Yes it could.**"

Soolchakan went back to his entries. The Vashasnog had been some very persistent adversaries. They had killed Malapi, along with over 650 Owlamites. They killed Sheekog two years later along with 150 more. The next one that came up had been Melming and she only lasted for one year, in which another 149 Owlamites died. Yod came up next and though he only lasted for one year as well, he did finally find the home world of the Vashasnog and had it destroyed before a remnant of their forces killed Yod as well.

Yod had not been that good at leadership. He was not one of the Team Leaders, he was just a member of the Team. He had been too close to the action and that was what got him killed. Four Supreme Officers had been killed by that bunch.

Then came the total misogynist Salgim, who was the twenty-eighth top leader. He led that final counter-attack against those wretched Vashasnog. There was a general sweep up implemented by him to find the remaining enemy ships and it was finally successful in completely wiping out another deadly enemy after only eight years with Salgim at the top.

Six years after Salgim was sure that all of the Vashasnog were gone, he called his Staff in for a special meeting to implement a new plan. He called the meeting to order. "I've decided that we need to have more of that diversion in order to...give us a little time to see some of these enemies...should any more show up. What we're going to do is take some more of the older and more worn out spaceships from dimension 45 and slam more of them into the side of Niygool that never faces Hardooth. We need to make even more wrecks on Niygool. Really litter the entire landscape of Niygool with all kinds of spacecraft. Since Zhagool rotates, they just might see some of the wreckage and start asking some rather difficult questions. If they never see them on the far side of Niygool...then no one on Hardooth will ever see them to ask that question."

Master Officer, Chreeker looked a little confused. "How is this...extra crashing of ships going to be a diversion...especially since we've already been doing just that?"

Salgim smiled. "The outworlders will come in from the outside and see all of that wreckage. It could slow them, as far as attacking Hardooth. That could give us some valuable time in order to be able to get ready for them...and suffer far less fatalities than we have in the past."

Master Officer, Doolatsa shook her head. She chuckled a little. "How can you be sure that it'll work...this time...or even get their attention?"

Master Officer, Stra huffed. "Even if they do see the crashed ships...they'll know that all of them are new crashes. I don't think that someone can fly 500 light years to get here and not be able to determine that the crashes all happened recently."

Salgim snarled at her. "I have been informed by one of our physicists, Officer, Bookbor, that if we spread a little indigenous dirt on some of the crashes, it'll give the appearance that they've been there a lot longer than just a few days or years. The more dust that we throw on them, the longer it'll appear that they've been there."

Master Officer, Soomootana gave him a friendly smile. "All right, we crash a few more ships. How do we determine which ships to crash on Niygool?"

"That's easy," said Chreeker. "Which ships have we cannibalized the most parts off of them? We simply install the worn out parts on the derelict...hop it back here to dimension 1 and then push it into Niygool."

Doolatsa shook her head looking a little worried. "Even the oldest and most decrepit of those ships...still has a good hydroponics garden. We're using all of them for that."

Salgim nodded. "And in one year, we're creating more food than all of us could eat in ten years. Some of it is going to waste because of all of the excess. We can plant some of the excess in areas around Hardooth, giving local populations something to eat, and then crash the ship."

Soomootana still looked skeptical. "How do we cover some of them with indigenous dirt? I mean...if someone comes along that is that intelligent...they'll see areas of the ground that are disturbed. How do we hide that?"

Salgim looked up in thought. "I suggest that we use the thrusters of our own fighter craft, flying low over a crash site to stir up the dirt. It might take a while for the dirt to settle, but, I don't think that anyone will look at the ground that closely. They'll be more interested in the wreckage than where it hit." He looked back down at the Staff. "If we think of any other little oddities like that...we'll correct them as we come to them."

Stra shrugged. "So how do we decide which ships are in the worst condition?"

Salgim smiled. "Who is the best mechanic that we have?"

Kiyalee looked at the written order from the Staff. She closed her eyes, hung her head and groaned.

Chyning snarled. "Why can't the rest of you be a lazy *chogo* like me? They always choose us…because of the expertise of you people." She headed for the closet to pull her spacesuit out. "Why can't they leave us alone?"

Bonarain snickered. "Maybe the reason is to keep you out of trouble. There are rumors that you've been stealing goodies from some other Teams in the gorge."

Chyning huffed. "I have never done that…yet!" She pondered for a moment. "That does sound like a good idea though." She looked at the shocked faces of her Team. "I'M JOKING! If I ever did anything like that…some of them might come here and try to take our stuff. I wouldn't like that. I know that you wouldn't. I won't steal from them!"

Soolchakan shook his head. "We may have to keep an eye on her."

"No," said Bonarain. "I believe her. If she takes something from any of them, it'd justify all of them coming here…and taking from us. I remember…several Leaders ago…that they said that it was all right to take any and all goodies from the enemy. I don't know if anyone is as competent at pilferage as *she* has become."

He nodded. "And once you have it in your possession, if someone wants to trade for it…that's up to the new owner."

Kiyalee sighed. "Come on, we've got some hydroponics

gardens that we have to move…and some ships to crash."

After crashing twenty-nine ships on Niygool and pushing dirt up on them with reverse thrusters, they decided to hold off for a while. Allow these ships to become part of the Niygool landscape. Then they would go in and crash a few more. Salgim gave the order (using *Voice of Power*) that another ship should be crashed onto Niygool every 300 to 500 years. The more wreckage, the more variety and the long times between crashes should make the disguise work rather well.

They could not be sure if the planned diversion worked or not. 35 years later another bunch called the Inzikoon attacked. Salgim was killed in the initial attack…along with 939 Owlamites. After this attack, the population of the Owlamites dropped below 16,000. The second eldest Owlamite, Doolatsa was one of the fatalities as well. That put Master Officer, Stra in command as the twenty-ninth *Voice of Power*.

Stra was now in command and things could not have been worse. Yes, the Owlamites were beating the Inzikoon back with humiliating defeats and the old process of blowing up the light speed engines internally. Yes, the enemy was avoiding Hardooth until they had a mass armada, which by the time all of them got there the Owlamites already had their defenses in place to destroy (or capture) all of the ships.

The main problem with Stra in charge was that she suffered from depression. Being the *Voice of Power*, her depression was contagious. There were several Owlamites who committed suicide because of her problem.

Doctor Aneensa of Medical Team 226 was the one who figured out what the problem was after about twenty suicides. She went to Stra and confronted her with the problem. Aneensa attempted to analyze Stra and get the problem fixed. The bigger problem in trying to fix the depression was that Stra was the *Voice of Power* and almost had the greater impact on Aneensa.

After 56 suicides, Stra was finally convinced that she was a bigger problem than those outworlder Inzikoon. After nearly one year of causing the suicide problems for the Owlamites, Stra forcefully gave out one last order: **"Don't follow me!"** Then she committed suicide.

Chreeker now became *Voice of Power* number thirty. He immediately started doing everything he could to lift the spirits of everyone and battle the Inzikoon at the same time. He did this successfully. Less than one year after the death of Stra, the Inzikoon were destroyed and their empire (along with their home planet) was cleaned out.

One thing that was really discussed (with great frustration) was the question of how each new outworlder would come in with technology, that made the stuff that the Owlamites already had, look totally archaic. Each new one brought new technology that was more sophisticated and shielded against the technology that had been previously obtained. They discussed it at great length in Staff meetings and put the question to every Owlamite everywhere to try to determine how the new attackers always had the upper hand in the initial attacks. Seeing as how there were no idea people among what was left of the Owlamite population all they could do was vent frustration and come up with nothing productive.

149 years after Chreeker took power, the frustration was no longer his problem. Another race called the Siyveschon attack and Chreeker, along with 975 other Owlamites, are killed in the attacks. It seemed as if being the *Voice of Power* was a kiss of death.

Officer Grade 5, Banbora now assumes command as number thirty-one. It is a shock to all Owlamites that a Grade 5 is the eldest. There is still a group of Grade 2, 3 and 4 Officers, however, it is a Grade 5 who is the eldest – how? Banbora is not the Team Leader of her Team. Her Team Leader is Officer Grade 2, Donava.

Banbora informs everyone that she was bypassed for promotion numerous times because she refused the bed of many superior ranking officers. It took her a long time to go from Grade 7 to Grade 6 and even longer to obtain Grade 5. The strange *Power* that goes to the eldest has no prejudice other than going to the eldest. It does not concern itself with gender, attitude, mental health or someone who was passed over for promotion. It only goes with age.

While she does have a few vindictive attitudes towards men, she does her best to remember that all of the officers, who kept her in the lower echelon of rank, all died in the firestorm attack. None of those sexual predators are still alive and even if they were, considering the fact that all male Owlamites are impotent, she has nothing to worry about now regarding sexual playthings.

She is able to lead a successful counter-attack against the Siyveschon and defeat them utterly. Her victory celebration is rather short-lived when just six years after taking over, a new race called the Whimich came in and killed Banbora along with 163 other Owlamites. Another new race who came in and bypassed all of the guardian technology.

Surprise, surprise! Another civilian becomes the *Voice of Power*. Sumik becomes number thirty-two to obtain the *Power*. Like the other civilians he is listed last in rank in the Team listings for his Team. Unlike the other civilians - Thes and Malapi - he is a nursing assistant on Medical Team 223. Doctor Gramhana, Doctor Kolokoko and Nurse Ishakana are all above him in the Team rank structure and none of those three women have any military leadership experience or capability. Sumik assumes command and must rely heavily on personnel from outside of his Team for military tactics, strategy and policy.

There are several counter-attacks on the Whimich that send them reeling with heavy losses. For some reason, they keep coming back for more with new technology and determination. The Owlamites are not able to find the home world of the Whimich because they are spread so far and wide. This war rages on for the entire 114 years that Sumik is in power.

There are a few times of peace between major battles, however, and during those times the Owlamites do what they can to improve their position, both on and off the planet.

36 years after Sumik takes over, Bonarain goes to a Staff meeting and makes a rather strange suggestion. "Sirs, I've been thinking of how thin we are spreading ourselves, with defending Hardooth from outworlders and at the same time defending High Country from invaders. It seems that a lot of the races here on Hardooth want some of the fertile tropical soil that we have to grow crops as well as have the high cliffs that surround this country as a defense. If we could get the local Heyyah more interested in this defense in a way that…scares off any intruder…maybe we could focus in only one direction."

Master Officer, Chasikaya scoffed as she leaned back in her chair. "What are we supposed to do? Do you suggest a propaganda effort where we appeal to their good nature? They're all a bunch of cowards."

"I wouldn't call them cowards," said Master Officer, Mivisk as he looked at Chasikaya in a scolding manner. "They just don't have the military skills. Most of them are farmers, ranchers, merchants, business owners, tavern owners and the like. There are also a lot of them who are judges, lawyers and constables. There are very few with any good military experience."

Master Officer, Meechee shook her head. "The local Heyyah feel that the cliffs will do most of the work for them. They really don't believe that anyone could or would bring an entire army up here."

Master Officer, Quonbaya huffed as well. She then snickered. "From what we've seen, there are a few that have tried…from land and sea. We're the ones who stopped those invaders. We destroyed their ladders, elevator and pulley systems. We're the ones who made it so costly to the invaders that they just gave up."

"ENOUGH," shouted Sumik! He gave all of his Staff an admonishing glare. "Before we say anything nasty, let's at least hear her out."

Chasikaya shook her head. "I agree! Let her talk. I need a good laugh."

Bonarain stood there tight-lipped. She looked around the table, cleared her throat and started up with her idea. "In dimension 120, there is a planet that has a great deal of different types of reptiles. There is one specific breed that…is capable of flying. I've been working around these beasts for a while and I found that we can do a little bit of mental manipulation with them…where we can domesticate them. I suggest that we do some…mental manipulations with the Heyyah in High Country and…get *them* to utilize these reptiles as a…flying defense force."

Senior Officer, Silsaya laughed out loud. "How do you control some…flying reptile…from the ground? We might be able to do it with our telepathy but…you're talking about Heyyah. How are they supposed to control the beasts?"

"By raising them from birth and riding on them," said Bonarain flatly.

It got very quiet in the room.

Bonarain saw that she had the attention of even the most skeptical. "Yes, there are some of them that are so small they fit in your hand. Yes, there are those who…are only ten taja from the tip of their nose to the tip of their tail. BUT…there are many who are large enough to put a saddle on them and be ridden…much like many people ride on the backs of equines."

Senior Officer, Hollondok sat there scratching his chin. "Let's say that you do bring the big beasts here. Now, how do you plan on getting the Heyyah interested in flying on them…and defending High Country with them?"

Bonarain smiled sweetly. "We lead them into thinking that it will be a great honor to be a part of the Dragon Defense Force."

"Oh, now they're dragons," said Senior Officer, Niynansa with a smirk on her face. "I thought you said that they were just… big flying lizards."

Senior Officer, Dintasama shook her head. "Once we've got this…bunch of dragons in place…what will stop the upper echelon bunch, here in High Country, from using this force to invade and conquer other countries?"

"The Heyyah of High Country will be keeping it a secret… that the lizards are *not* dragons," said Bonarain. "They are to be used only for defensive purposes. To take them out conquering… would only give away the secret that they are not that great a weapon to begin with. They cannot be used for conquering. We'll have to instill into the mind of every sovereign and every leader at every level of High Country that the Force is for defenses only.

They don't sign any kind of pact or treaty with another country or kingdom for offensive purposes."

Sumik sat there pondering. "For defensive purposes only." He nodded in approval. "That would keep them here...keep the secret...and could very easily keep outsiders from trying to get up those cliffs."

Quonbaya looked at him in utter contempt. "How? How could a few reptiles keep an invader out?"

Mivisk grunted loudly. "The primary way to set up an invasion is through stealth, secrecy and diversion. The only way to get to High Country is to climb the cliffs, set up a series of ladders or elevators and then bring all of your equipment and personnel up the cliffs. If there's a flying force that patrols the cliffs – north, south, east and west – any enemy loses any and all forms of surprise. The High Country ground forces could push them back over the cliff easily because all of the supplies of the invader are down at the bottom of the cliff and they're going to be outnumbered by ground forces, flying forces and if necessary... *us*!"

Sumik shrugged. "It is...definitely worth a try. If it works, we have a few less headaches. If it doesn't work...at first...we can refine it until it does work. Either way I think it is a project that is worth attempting."

Hollondok shook his head. "It's going to take a lot of mental manipulations of the Heyyah in order to achieve this lofty goal."

Dintasama snickered. "That'll give us all a lot more

practice at doing the mental manipulations on others. Some more practice at it won't hurt any of...us."

Sumik nodded. "All right...here is what is going to happen. First, we get together and create a constitution or...a set of laws for the Heyyah. It has to be a system of where and how they utilize this defensive force. There has to be a set of rules for...training the..." He cleared his throat as he snickered. "...dragons..." He gave Bonarain a silly look. "...training the riders as well as any support and administrative personnel. It may require setting up an entirely new government."

Quonbaya looked at Bonarain inquisitively. "I take it that these...dragons are carnivorous?"

"Yes, Sir, they are," said Bonarain.

Quonbaya looked back at Sumik. "That'll mean that we'll have to have a much larger bovine, ovine and porcine industry here in High Country...in order to feed the beasts."

Sumik nodded. "That is definitely another step in the process. We need to figure out just exactly what is going to be needed to support this...Dragon Force."

Silsaya looked around. "Are we going to do it here...while we're trying to take on and defeat the Whimich?"

"No," said Sumik. "We're going to set up a few Teams...I suggest in those meeting bells that the Alliance introduced us to. Figure out all of the needs and laws supporting the Dragon Force. We'll also have to set up guidelines for training both rider and beast."

Niynansa sniffed. "What Teams are you suggesting for this project?"

Sumik licked his lips. "At least one Medical Team. One Team of physicists. Dintasama, you're on one of the Science Teams...so you'll have to go there as well."

Bonarain raised her hand up. "May I suggest the Architect and Construction Teams as well?"

Meechee grunted in disgust. "What are you planning on building?"

"There has to be a hatchery," said Bonarain. "They have to have some location where they have the females lay the eggs, then hatch them and then train the hatchlings along with their riders. We have to have...probably a very large box canyon of some sort in order to achieve this."

Silsaya gave a grunt of disgust as well. "And how do we explain to a bunch of Heyyah...how this box canyon suddenly appeared...where there was no canyon before?"

"More mental manipulations of the Heyyah," said Hollondok with a smug smile. "After one or two generations...all will accept that the box canyon has always been there."

Ten Teams head to the meeting bell ship in #45 in order to set up a new government in High Country that includes this Dragon Defense Force. The bell has not been used in a long time so it smells a little musty, even after getting rid of all of that nasty, high alkaline Doolood water.

All Owlamites are asked to give some input as to what the new constitution of the government should be, especially since they are all going into a new territory with the flying reptiles. They also look at different constitutions, laws, and regulations of current governments in order to get some of the ideas about this new government.

Once the debate (and sometimes some very heated arguments) are over and the new constitution has been written, along with instruction manuals on raising and training the hatchling and handler, the Owlamites must now go all over High Country and put the thoughts about the Dragon Force into the minds of all of the Heyyah, along with integrating the beasts into the society. They have to look for candidates for riders, support personnel, administrators, and doctors for both man and beast.

They came up with an entirely new rank structure with insignias, emblems, symbols, flags and uniforms.

The Architect Team and Construction Teams built a box canyon where they created caves, tunnels and rooms that make up the dragon hatchery.

Certain Administrators have to be put in place that are convinced they were the ones who discovered the strange breed of reptiles in this box canyon and set up the entire thing through decisions of their own.

Once all of the paperwork and ideology were in place, now they have to bring some of the dragons from dimension #120, large and small, male and female.

They have to set up standards on how the dragons are

measured. They took the current sovereign of High Country and determined that the dragons will be measured in sizes, each size measurement established by the length of the ruler's hand going from the wrist to the tip of the middle finger. It turns out to be 8 decitaja. The eggs that are laid and the dragons that hatch from them will go by this standard for as long as there is a High Country and as long as the Dragon Force is the defenders of the land.

The primary mistake that the Owlamites did in setting up the entire thing, which they found out about later, was that they put a rule in that the Supreme Commander would be the one with the largest dragon. They forgot to put leadership capability and experience in the equation, however, since this entire thing is a ruse, they did not think that military and leadership experience was that necessary.

Once the plan was put into action, the three other countries that were part of South Chilamte: Falamin, Joktel and Peegruch, began spreading the story of the Dragon Defense Force of High Country. Most people on other continents and island chains did not believe it until their emissaries were sent to Joktel and Peegruch to witness the phenomenon for themselves. In less than one year after the dragons started flying, the entire world was aware of the High Country dragons and were astounded at the speed in which this kind of force had come up from…what?

Surprisingly the Whimich are also aware of this new episode on the planet that they are attempting to conquer. For some strange reason they decide to leave the Dragon Force alone in order to study it further…once they are in total command. Through spying on some of the high command of the Whimich, it is found, they are going to use the Dragon Force in a carnival back on their home planet. People would pay greatly in order to be able to ride on one of the larger beasts. Great fun and profit for the conquerors...if they could somehow figure out how to finally conquer this stubborn planet.

It takes a total of six years to set the entire thing up. It takes another two years for the Owlamites to convince the Heyyah in High Country that it was their idea and that they are all proud to be part of this new situation.

During the entire time that the Owlamites were establishing the Dragon Defense Force there were no attacks by the Whimich. Two years after that they find out why. The Whimich came back and attack with a new vengeance...and new technology. Even though the Owlamites have captured and are using some of the Whimich technology for their sensor guardians, the Whimich bypass the guardians as if the things were not there at all. The Owlamites are finally able to destroy the new attack armada. They still have not found the home planet or know just how many planets the Whimich have claimed in their empire.

114 years after Sumik took over, the Whimich come back and start another massive attack, once again, with new and improved technology. Sumik and another 300 Owlamites end up dead in that battle.

Sumik had been the lowest ranked member of Medical Team 223. Upon his death, the new *Voice of Power* ended up being another civilian. Coincidentally, Londarid, the new *Voice of Power* number thirty-three, is the lowest ranked individual in Medical Team 222. He is another nurse assistant (as well as a farmer) under Doctor Voolatha, Doctor Heemaha and Nurse Chaysheea. He has virtually no military skills or leadership skills. His total experience is in farming and medical. He ends up getting killed in less than one year by this new technology along with over 1,130 Owlamites. They still have not figured out this new technology.

Another new *Voice of Power* number thirty-four is now in charge and, once again, it is a woman who was bypassed for promotion several times because she refused to obtain promotions in bed on her back. Officer Grade 5, Manifana is now in charge. Unfortunately because of her lack of leadership experience (and a few prejudices about listening to any man) she ends up getting killed in under one year along with over 1,340 Owlamites.

This new technology that the Whimich has is devastating.

The new *Voice of Power* is yet another woman who refused to obtain rank by existing on her back. Officer Grade 5, Nepnep is now number thirty-five. She is also the third in a row who is in power less than one year and is labeled as a "one-year-wonder", the first time this term is used, however, it ends up being historically applied to all of the top Leaders who served one year or less. When Nepnep is killed, over 1,380 Owlamites have died in the devastating clashes with the Whimich.

After Nepnep, Officer Grade 5, Snewap becomes the new *Voice of Power.* It is now discovered that it was not just women who suffered the pangs of bigotry when it came to favoritism as to the ones who were promoted quickly and those who were held back when Snewap, a male, is now the eldest even though there are still several who wear the rank of Grade 2, 3 or 4.

It is also under Snewap that, finally, the Owlamites discover a weakness in this new Whimich technology and start to exploit it.

Usually, the plan had been to place a bomb of some sort in, or next to, the light speed engines. The bomb would detonate and then the engine would detonate as a result of being thrown out of balance. Catastrophic consequences for the ship the engine was in. The Whimich were able to get the bomb out before it detonated, even if it was only a few heartbeats away from discharge.

The Whimich are also able to chase the Owlam perpetrator even though they hop into a different dimension to attempt an escape. It is now found out that the Whimich technology allows them to trail, trace and even follow the Owlamites into the other dimension. Once in the other dimension, the Owlamites thought they were safe…until they were attacked and destroyed by the Whimich. Unfortunately, the ones who realized this horrible effect were killed before they could report it.

Teams 235, 6975 and 7016 are in an attack formation to attempt a sabotage against one of the big attack ships of the Whimich. Team 235 under Officer Grade 2, Tossosi is leading the attack. Her Team members: Grade 5, Mamoa, Grade 5, Aljor and Grade 7, Whenno enter the ship in Spy dimension. All four go in, drop a hand held bomb near the engines that has been hopped into Home dimension and then fly out of the ship still in Spy.

Somehow, some of the Whimich fighters are able to follow them into Spy and start blasting them out of the sky. Teams 6975 and 7016 were to cover the escape and attempt killing any enemy that might try to follow Team 235. Instead they find themselves under fire from other Whimich fighters that are also, somehow, in Spy dimension. Teams 6975 and 7016 are now fighting for their own lives instead of covering Team 235 (which by now has been totally obliterated).

Chyning sent a mental message. "**I'm not gonna die out here in outer space. If I have to die, I'm gonna do it in my favorite place**!" She then Jumped to the planet Beasties in dimension #10.

Bonarain decided to do the same. "**We can't fight this many enemy ships**!" She then Jumped to dimension #120 to the planet where she had discovered the Dragon Force.

Kiyalee did not send any messages. She just Jumped to a place she liked to go in dimension #143.

Soolchakan sent a mental message to Officer Grade 5, Koosasa, the Leader of Team 6975. "**If you don't want to die here...find a favorite place and go there**." He then Jumped to dimension #30 to one of his favorite planets.

Team 6975 all Jumped as a Team to dimension #192. There was a star system that was 16 light years away from the current location in that dimension. Officer Grade 6, Doyvoma of Team 6975 had been the one who discovered dimension #192 and the Team had been exploring it to see if there was anything there that they could use or enjoy.

All eight members of 6975 and 7016 survive without anyone following them. Koosasa and Soolchakan send a mental message to Snewap and the Staff about the Jump being a better form of escape. A new Staff meeting is called.

Snewap looked around at his Staff. "We have lost Master Officer, Tossosi in that last attack. In order to keep the chain of command as it is supposed to be…Senior Officer, Sankiki, you are now promoted to Master Officer and will take full command of Sector 2. I have called Officer, Uhnita from Team 272 here to be promoted to Senior Officer and will take the position that Sankiki just left as Vice Commander of Sector 1." He hung his head. "Tossosi and her Team did not die in vain." He looked up. "It was discovered - albeit an accident, that the Whimich cannot find us if we Jump. We can hop to any dimension and those murderers find us. We Jump…and we leave them far behind."

"That's good for escape," said Master Officer, Dintasama. "What about attack?"

Snewap sighed. "If someone can come up with a better attack plan…I'm ready to listen. All that we know now…we *can* escape."

Master Officer, Pabia smiled. She chuckled lightly. "If we can Jump out…we can Jump in."

Snewap narrowed his eyes. "What are your thoughts?"

The smile on her face got bigger. "Recently, one of the Teams under my command, Team 3406, reported to me that they got a little frustrated with not being able to bomb the light speed engines. Officer, Sondeea and her Team entered one of the ships in Spy, each one dropped a hand-held bomb in…different places around the ship. They then *also* Jumped out of there. We didn't put the two together at first. Now it makes sense. Because they were able to drop a hand-held in another area…it seems that the defenses against us dropping any weapon in the engine room… are *only* in the engine room. All four of the hand-helds that they dropped went off and did significant damage and the ship was powered down for almost half a day while they repaired it."

Master Officer Pensesk looked up from his notes. "Another thing that I found is that…they don't start tracking us…until we hop in. We can come up there to any of their ships and follow it… all day long. If we don't hop any weapon into Home dimension to attack them…they don't know that we're there. So…we take a bomb…much larger than a hand-held, hop it into an area near the engine room, Jump out and let it go off. If it works, then… maybe…just maybe, that bomb will upset that precious mixture in the light speed engines…and we can get total catastrophic results on that ship…and eventually the entire armada."

Snewap nodded his head. "I hear some good plans here. Let's get them going immediately and…see if we can get these monsters off of our back…and star system. Meanwhile, have those spy Teams made any gains on…finding the home planet of the Whimich…or how many planets they are currently occupying?"

Senior Officer, Chavak hung his head. "Not much more information since the last report. We've found a total of 122 planets that they occupy…but none of them could be called their home planet."

Snewap pounded his fist on the table. "The time for pride...should have been over...long ago. Team 7016 seems to have a special talent for finding home planets of...any adversary. Get them on it...and they do nothing else until they find that filthy place. Any questions?"

Chyning once again sat there with that churlish look on her face. "I hate being called on...whenever it's time to find the garbage. Why can't someone else do it?"

Bonarain huffed. "You should be proud! They've finally admitted that we're something special. Plus, this could take us out of the fighting for a while."

Kiyalee giggled. "We also know just how to get out of trouble...quickly."

Soolchakan sighed. "Right. Just Jump out of there and... leave those *bimyocks* wondering what happened." He downed the last of his juice. "Let's get to it!"

Chyning just snarled. "In defeating the enemy, there is profit. No battle – no profit. Everyone else will be getting all of the goodies."

3

By not giving away their presence in any of the ships Team 7016 was able to observe several rituals the Whimich performed on a daily basis. Bells were a large part of the rites. They had pictures of bells everywhere. There was an overabundance of pictures of bells.

One day, Bonarain finally noticed that all of the bell pictures, which were in every room of the ship, were all pictures of the exact same bell. There was a slight imperfection at the top of the bell and it was in all of the pictures.

Kiyalee compared several pictures for her own satisfaction. "Okay, so they're all the same bell. What do we do with that knowledge?"

Chyning got up close to one of the pictures. "What is this…down in the bottom corner of the picture? It shows up in all of the pictures as well."

The four of them each got a picture and all started staring closely at the bottom corner.

Soolchakan shook his head. "That can't be!"

Bonarain looked up. "Can't be…what?"

He sheepishly looked up from his picture. "Those tiny little objects…at the bottom of the picture…are…Whimich people!"

"That's ridiculous," sputtered Kiyalee!

Bonarain pulled a magnifying glass out. "No…it is *not* ridiculous. He's right! Those are…Whimich people. I'd recognize that sickly yellow skin anywhere."

Chyning looked up in shock. "If that bell is that big… it…"

"It *is* our landmark," said Bonarain triumphantly!

Soolchakan chuckled nervously. "If that bell is that big…I don't think that these people are going to make more than one… or two at best." He scoffed. "I've seen smaller mountains than that…thing."

Kiyalee gave a sullen look. "Are we going?"

"Yes," said Soolchakan. "Let's…each take a picture…get in our fighters and…we landmark on that…*monstrosity* and…. Jump."

They all were sitting in the cockpits of their fighters concentrating on the big bell.

Soolchakan finally sighed. "Is everyone ready?"

The three women all responded affirmatively.

"Go to Spy and…in formation…Jump!"

They found themselves in a large dry desert area. They opened the canopies on their fighters. They found the picture had been incomplete. The bell was definitely there, however, it was suspended above the ground. They were able to see that as much metal went in to making the bell, the four-legged contraption that was used to suspend it above the ground used even more metal in order to hold the bell up without bending. To the right was another suspension contraption that had a very large rod hanging from it.

Kiyalee was the first to think. "**What is that thing off to the side**?"

"**I think they use that big rod to ring that thing**," sent Bonarain.

Soolchakan saw the big rod being pulled away from the bell. "**If it is, I think that we'd better hop to Observation. If that thing starts chiming…we could all end up with busted eardrums…and or shattered skulls**."

They all made the hop to Observation. They watched as the giant rod was released and swung toward the bell. It bounced off of the bell and in just a few moments they all saw that the sand around them was vibrating slightly and coming up off of the ground a little before settling back. Closer to the bell, entire sand dunes were totally flattening because of the vibrations. Once the shock wave subsided the wind started reforming the dunes and blowing sand across the flat desert again.

Chyning shook her head. "**Do you think that is the way they call their gods**?"

"**If it is, then those gods have to be totally deaf by now**," sent Kiyalee sarcastically.

"**If it takes something that loud to get their**

attention, I don't think they care very much about their people," sent Bonarain.

Soolchakan looked down at the monitor in his fighter. "I don't know if any of you have looked at your monitors but...we're 25.6 kilotaja away from that bell. If it can make the ground vibrate at this distance, no wonder no one else lives around here. If there was any kind of structure in this area, it'd be shaken to pieces in no time at all."

Chyning opened her visor. She grunted in disgust. "Oh, h'oolyach! It's hotter than...it's HOT!" Her breathing appeared to be a little labored.

Bonarain opened her visor. "OH! It is...hot. It's stifling."

Soolchakan opened his visor and the first breath was almost a chore because of the heat. "It makes sense. If you're gonna have some kind of monstrosity like that...it'd be best to put it in a place where no one lives...or could live. That way you don't upset anybody by making them move...by flattening their house with vibrations."

Chyning wiped some sweat from her forehead. "Can we try to find someplace on this planet...that's a little cooler? This place is horrible."

Soolchakan chuckled to himself. "Good idea. We need to find some more landmarks on this planet...in order to find a good target area to blast these chokwads into history and out of our hair."

The four closed the canopies on their fighters and took off. They each went a different direction, mapping as they went. They flew around the planet for two days doing the mapping.

Soolchakan looked at all of the results. Four major continents, three minor continents. Forty-one island chains. One capital city in a centralized location on the largest continent in the southern hemisphere that has a population of over nineteen million. The population of the planet was over 8.6 billion.

Bonarain interrupted his thoughts. "**If we did attack this planet...and cut it in half like we have with other planets, I don't like the idea of that...bell...floating around in space. Do you realize what that thing could do to...any planet it might come in contact with**?"

"**That's a frightening thought**," sent Kiyalee.

"**It'd be too much trouble to steal that thing**," sent Chyning. "**Where would you put it**?"

He smiled. "**They put it in the middle of a desert... we could put it in the middle of the Desert planet. The population of that planet still hasn't discovered those flood doors from the ships that we placed there**." He chuckled. 'A bell that big gives them pause. Floating around in space, it could cause massive damage,' he thought. 'What about two halves of a planet...floating freely?'

Bonarain huffed. "**That still doesn't help with the final solution for this planet. We'd have to get close enough to that thing to Jump it and because of how big it is, it could take several people touching it in order to** perform a Jump with something that heavy."

"That, is a problem for the Staff to figure out," sent Soolchakan.

"I don't see how we're going to use our planet killer ships," sent Bonarain. "These people have a network of guardian sensors that surround their planet. I don't see how they can launch a ship from the surface of the planet...without colliding with one of the things on the way out."

"They keep on talking about basics," sent Kiyalee. "We did a little basic attack with that plan of yours. We hopped all of those guardian pulse weapons into Ghost and when they fired at our hand-held bombs...nothing happened. Maybe we can get back to basics on that."

"Yeah," sent Chyning. "All of the others who kept on trying those complicated plans...and all it did was get more of our people killed. Get back to our basic attacks that work and we do just fine...and eliminate enemies."

"There's still a lot of the firestorm weapons at our disposal," sent Kiyalee. "Don't you think that we could use them to poison the whole atmosphere of this planet?"

"It takes a LOT of those things to do that," sent Bonarain. "I don't think that we have that many left."

"I don't know," sent Soolchakan. "These *doovofts* have a whole bunch of those things stockpiled here.

We could always use their arsenal against them."

Bonarain shook her head. "**Again, something for the Staff to decide. Do we have all of the information that we need**?"

"**I think so**," sent Soolchakan. "**If we don't need anything else here...I suggest that we...go back home and...get ready to end this war...hopefully by getting back to the basics and ruining the lives of these *doovofts*.**"

Snewap looked at the report. "I don't think that their firestorm weapons would be attacked by their guardian attack sensors." He sighed. "Of course, we'd have to experiment with a few of them in order to find out. Maybe grab a few of them and see if we can set them off...inside their atmosphere."

Pensesk shook his head. "I still can't believe it. I'd have to see this bell myself...in order to believe that thing is as big as Team 7016 says that it is."

Pabia laughed. "Didn't you look at the bottom of the picture? They have some of their yellow-skinned Whimich people standing there...and you can use that as a comparison."

"I'd still have to see the thing myself," muttered Pensesk bitterly!

Snewap nodded in agreement. "I agree with the thought that...it would be a horrible waste to...destroy something that big. It should be...somehow taken apart or melted down and all of the pieces could be used to make something else…that is a bit more useful to anyone else." He huffed in anger. "That much metal in one…bell, not to mention the thing that is being used to suspend it above the ground…and that giant hammer that's used to ring it."

Sankiki giggled. "What if we steal that bell and tell the Whimich that we're keeping it hostage. The fact that we could steal something that big, hide it in another dimension, that they can't get to…without our help, it just might scare them away from us. If not…then we can always do that other thing…hop their guardian sensors into Ghost and blast their planet."

Snewap sighed. "And hope that they don't send all of their power after us. I mean, we already know of at least thirty planets they've added to their empire and they have a large military contingency at each planet. It just might irritate them badly enough to send all of that power after us."

Dintasama smiled. "But, if their guardian sensors don't go after their own firestorm weapons, we can steal their entire arsenal of those things and use all of them against their ships as well. I'm looking at the count and according to what Team 7016 found, there are 88,602 of those things stored on the Whimich home planet… that we know of. That is a huge arsenal and can do all kinds of damage…to anything, anywhere."

"You're right," said Snewap. "Use one of the firestorm weapons on a Whimich ship first. Then we'll know if they attack their own weaponry with their own guardian sensors. Then we steal that bell…and inform them that it is a hostage that will not be returned unless they leave us alone…*permanently*!"

One of the firestorm weapons was placed in the cargo hold of one of the Whimich war ships. The timer was set so it would not go off for at least half of one day. When it finally did blow up and take three other warships in that armada with it, the Owlamites found out that it was only foreign weaponry that the guardian beacons, in and outside of a ship, were looking for.

There was another test on the Whimich home planet to determine if that was correct. A major city was blown up and the Owlamites observed for ten days to see if the Whimich suffered the same problems that Hardooth had. No new species were formed by the explosion and that told the Owlamites that it was time to set off some major catastrophes for the Whimich. All it did was irritate many of the Whimich High Command, attempting to determine exactly who had detonated that bomb.

First, the giant bell was stolen along with the giant hammer. It did cause all kinds of consternation among the Whimich when they realized that the main symbol of their deities had disappeared. It did not scare them it just irritated them. They brought all of their power to the battle against the Owlamites, because no other planet had caused them so much grief.

With the giant bell sitting in the middle of the huge desert on that planet in a different dimension (which the Whimich had never been to), the bombs that the Owlamites had stolen from the Whimich were used against them and another race disappeared from the cosmos. Again, someone who could not listen to reason was wiped out.

4,332 Owlamites died fighting against the Whimich. Now Snewap declared peace since that horrid enemy had been exterminated.

Now Snewap decided that the Owlamites needed to add on to the apartments in the gorge. No one understood why, however, he was the *Voice of Power* and he was to be obeyed. Now there were a total of 575 apartments on all 12 levels in the gorge. Snewap said that 6,900 apartments would serve as an initiative for the doctors to figure out why the Owlamites could not procreate and maybe then, they would be able to fill all of the apartments and add on again. The doctors did not share his enthusiasm. They had been experimenting and testing for over 7,200 years and still had no positive results, even with the idea of cloning. Making a few new apartments just did not seem to add any new kind of incentive. However, the *Voice of Power* had given instructions and the instructions were obeyed without question.

Snewap lasted for 162 years. Then another new enemy showed up – the Hesh. Over 1,700 Owlamites died in the initial attacks along with Snewap. Officer Grade 5, Umeso becomes the new *Voice of Power* number thirty-seven. He becomes another one-year-wonder and during his time over 900 more Owlamites died.

Officer Grade 5, Kenchom becomes number thirty-eight. At first he had some success in beating the Hesh back, however, in just twenty-six years, he becomes a fatality as well along with another 1,000 Owlamites.

Officer Grade 5, Shaffani becomes number thirty-nine. She is another one who was victimized by prejudice. Once again it is becoming more and more painfully obvious, the favoritism that went into a lot of promotions and personnel that were being passed over. Of the last nine who held the *Power*, two were civilians and seven were all Officer Grade 5, again, even though there were still a lot of Grade 2, 3 and 4 who were still alive.

Shaffani defeats the Hesh and she lasts for fifty-two years…until the Konvong show up and attack Hardooth. When the Konvong attack, the Owlamites lose another 1,088 of their badly dwindling population.

Another Civilian takes over as the *Voice of Power*. Tachter becomes number forty. He is not very responsible. He would rather sit and drink, tell tall tales or hear tall tales, rather than get down to business and fight back against the Konvong. He somehow lasts for 43 years in the top position. His death comes about from an act of stupidity…his own. 956 more Owlamites die because of his irresponsibility and failure to act against the enemy.

Surprise! Another Officer Grade 5 takes the top position in the Owlamite race. Klup takes over and becomes *Voice of Power* number forty-one. Under him, the Owlamites are able to destroy the Konvong. He lasts for forty-six years…until another enemy comes along – the Erbor. Almost 950 more Owlamites are killed in that initial attack.

Another Officer Grade 5 takes over as number forty-two. She is Seetaya. She is in charge of battling the Erbor for 142 years before she is killed along with 1,070 more Owlamites.

Another civilian takes over as number forty-three. Halalua is on a Science Team and like the other civilians, she is listed last in rank on the Team. She finally gets everyone working in order and the Erbor are eradicated completely.

Halalua does not like barren land. She likes to see all kinds of vegetation growing everywhere. She gets another crusade going, to get all kinds of new plants growing on Hardooth. Plants from anywhere and everywhere no matter what planet or what dimension. Once again, the doctors have to step in and remind her that there are plants that have symbiotic relations with certain rather dangerous creatures (including microorganisms) that no one wants to see let loose on Hardooth. She listened to the doctors and now there were certain limitations on some of the plants. The Owlamites are still able to replenish vegetation all over the planet.

Halalua lasts 213 years…until the Pantan show up. Halalua and another 900 Owlamites perish.

Officer Grade 5, Pirem becomes number forty-four. He is able to defeat the Pantan. In the 119th year of his tenure, the Owlamites celebrate anniversary number 8,000 since the firestorm attack that changed them from Heyyah to Owlam. Forty-five years later, a new enemy attacks, called the Aldima. Pirem and 550 more Owlamites perish.

Officer Grade 5, Voostoo becomes number forty-five. During his reign, he realized that the guardian sensors were primarily aimed in one direction. They are aimed at the direction that the old Alliance had come from. He introduces the Owlamites to the fact that outer space is all around them…in every direction. Even though the sensors are tethered and in a different dimension, they do not look in all directions simultaneously. Someone has to actually turn them. Go to the south pole and look up and you see stars in outer space. Go to the north pole and look up and you see stars in outer space. Go anywhere on the planet at any time of the year and look up...you see stars in outer space.

Even when Team 7016 was mapping the stars, they only mapped in a limited direction. Now, using what limited resources the Owlamites have they must do some more mapping – in all directions. These horrible conquering enemy can come from any direction. The Owlamites have to copy what the Whimich had done and have more guardian sensors put in place...aimed in all directions from Hardooth.

Voostoo lasts for 103 years until another enemy sneaks in, called the Zhozhick. Once again all of the guardian sensors are ignored by the enemy and the Zhozhick attack, killing Voostoo and another 440 Owlamites.

Yet another Officer Grade 5, Wunteer becomes number forty-six and another genocide is performed against the Zhozhick.

During his time as the *Voice of Power*, a new island is found on Hardooth that none of the Owlamites were aware of before. Each Owlamite spends some time on the strange island in order to experience this bizarre phenomenon.

In time, Team 7016 finally gets their chance at exploring the island. They did not have to wait as long seeing as how there are only 273 Teams still alive that consist of 1,092 Owlamites.

They get the landmark of a small sandy peninsula on the north end of the island. Using one of the small shuttlecraft they have *obtained* from one of the extinct enemy armadas, they Jump to the peninsula in the craft. As soon as they got out of the shuttle they all were hit with some sweltering humidity, telling them that this was definitely a tropical island somewhere near the equator. They all pulled a cloth out of their pockets for wiping the constant sweat off of their foreheads.

Chyning scoffed. "Doesn't look like much from here. All I see is some crumbling walls."

"They might appear to be crumbling but they're still pretty tall...and strong," said Kiyalee.

"According to Officer, Itchami, the walls, depending on where you are in the compound, are between thirty-seven and forty-five taja high," said Soolchakan.

Bonarain was looking at a small map. "According to this... we have to walk around to the west side of the island in order to find the entrance."

Soolchakan sat there and nodded. "And according to everyone who's been here before, you can't Jump in - you have to walk."

Chyning giggled. "Walking a long distance is going to be something totally different for us. I don't remember having to do that for some time. Usually all we do is...Jump."

Bonarain sighed. "So let's hop this shuttlecraft into Spy and...get walking."

The shuttlecraft was hopped and nothing was visible except the marks the landing pads left in the sand. The four of them started walking towards the west side of the fortress they had heard so much about. When they got close enough to touch the walls they realized that these walls were not crumbling. The walls did look old, however, they were not made of concrete, they were made of stone. Very large pieces of stone that had been put in place and fit so precisely that mortar was not needed.

Soolchakan stopped near the end of the peninsula. "Aren't you women listening?"

Bonarain turned back and looked at him. "To what?"

"I tried to...mentally send a message to the three of you," he said frowning.

"I didn't get anything," said Kiyalee.

"I didn't either," said Chyning.

"Try sending something...mentally," said Soolchakan.

The three women all closed their eyes and stood quietly for several moments. Each one of them opened their eyes and looked around at their Teammates.

Bonarain smiled sheepishly. "Did...any of you...get anything from me?"

Kiyalee shook her head with her mouth hanging open.

"This is eerie," said Chyning.

Soolchakan cleared his throat. "Uh...yeah! For... over 8,150 years...we've been able to communicate...mentally.

Now...*here*...nothing!"

Bonarain looked at her hands. "Do you remember that...Kalash trick? It was the one with the...electrical fingers. Remember? You can shock...an opponent."

Soolchakan shrugged. "Let's give it a try."

The four of them now stood there rubbing their fingers attempting to make the electrical charges appear. They went through all of the mental imagery processes in order to make it happen. Not one crackle of electricity came from any of their fingers.

Kiyalee threw her arms tightly down at her sides. "Okay, this goes beyond peculiar. It is a total void...for any form of powers."

"I agree," said Bonarain while staring at her fingers.

Soolchakan cleared his throat again nervously. "Let's go find that entrance...and take our tour of this...unusual place."

They now increased their pace. They all wanted to get in, look the place over, get out and then get back to their form of normalcy, or what could be considered normal for an Owlamite. It was much further than they thought. They were perspiring profusely the entire way.

"I don't think anyone could attack this place...easily," said Chyning.

Kiyalee was confused. "Why not?"

"Look at the distance...from the high tide line...to the

wall," said Chyning pointing at the gentle surf that was washing up on the sand. "In some places...the high tide line...it's only about five taja in other places...maybe as much as fifteen taja. You couldn't get any kind of large equipment on the beach."

Soolchakan chuckled. "Are you planning on attacking this place...any time soon?"

She turned and gave him a dirty look. She then threw her arms up in exasperation. "Oh yeah! You can't receive any mental communications...here."

"I'll bet you tried to send something really nasty," giggled Kiyalee.

Soolchakan gave Chyning a dirty look. "So why don't you say it out loud?"

"Never mind," said Chyning dejectedly. "I usually don't say anything like that...out loud."

Kiyalee gave Chyning a dirty look and scoffed. "Right!"

They continued on. There were three places they had to go single file and hug the high wall in order to *try* keeping their boots dry. In one of the spots they were totally unsuccessful at keeping dry.

They finally arrived at the entrance. They stood there huffing and puffing a little from the long walk. They looked around at the way the entrance had been designed. The corridor going up to the door was about fifteen taja wide. It was some forty taja from the beach to the door. The door was nothing more than a door you would find on a normal house, other than the fact that it was made of metal.

"I don't think that any large equipment could go through that doorway," said Chyning sarcastically.

"That might be why it was designed that way," said Bonarain.

"I wonder…if you could fly over it in one of those Teltermak kites," said Kiyalee.

"The kites don't work on any…magic," said Soolchakan. "If you had enough…of a momentum to get airborne…you could fly in." He scoffed. "That's the problem though, getting the momentum to go high enough…in a very short distance."

Bonarain chuckled. "Getting out wouldn't be a problem."

"No, it sure wouldn't," said Soolchakan as he looked up at the high walls.

"Once again," said Chyning. "I don't think that any large equipment would be able to make it. You could bombard anyone and anything…with anything from up there."

Soolchakan took a key out of his pocket. "So…let's go take a look inside…and see what we see about this unusual place."

Kiyalee shook her head in disgust. "Why did Wunteer bother putting a lock on the place? If no one is here…who would stop anyone from getting in? All you'd need is a bunch of ladders."

"Or something that could bust that padlock and chain off the door," said Chyning.

"Wunteer said it should be there…it is there," said

Soolchakan emphatically!

Bonarain chuckled. "Other than ladders...or kites, this door is...the only way in or out. Very strange! Whoever designed this place, that is one very tiny door for a compound this big."

Kiyalee shrugged. "We could use the shuttlecraft or our fighters."

Chyning nodded.

Soolchakan inserted the key and opened the padlock. "Shurmook said that we would need to oil this thing constantly... in order to keep it from rusting."

"I know," said Kiyalee. "That's why I brought some oil... that I was told to bring."

After giving the padlock a virtual bath in the oil, they opened the door and entered the compound.

Kiyalee scoffed. "Next time, I'm going to bring some grease. It'll last longer than the oil because it won't drip off."

Once inside the compound they realized just how large the place was. The entire interior had no buildings in the middle. Any form of living quarters were all along the interior of the wall. The massive central area was nothing but plants, saplings and shrubs.

"Wunteer ordered any farmers that were left here to come here and plant anything that is edible," said Bonarain. "I see that they've got plenty of room to do it."

"There aren't any trees...fruit trees anywhere," said Chyning.

"They just got planted less than a year ago," said Bonarain. "Give them time to grow and then…they'll be a few huge orchards in here."

"I can see some vines for all of those different melons over in the south area," said Kiyalee.

"Looks like there's a lot of grain crops over on the east side," said Soolchakan. He chuckled. "There's plenty of room for…all kinds of food in here…grain, vegetable, fruit, tuber…and kwatha."

"Must be some really fertile soil in here," said Bonarain.

Kiyalee looked back at the high wall. "Of course! None of that salt water can get in here. Only rain water. That helps keep the soil from losing any fertility from the salt."

"I wonder where…the people who built this place lived," said Kiyalee.

"According to this stuff from Officer, Tuyasa, she said that most of the living quarters, where they found old skeletons, were in the northern part of the fortress," said Bonarain.

"Yeah," said Kiyalee. "A bunch of crumbling bones."

"Twenty-two skeletons," said Soolchakan. "Bones that were so old…according to Shurmook, those people died over 3,000 years ago. The fortress has been…vacant ever since."

"Weird," said Chyning!

Bonarain wiped sweat off of her forehead. "Shall we go see the living quarters?"

"You go ahead," said Soolchakan. "I'm going to try something else." He started walking directly towards the east side of the complex.

All three women shrugged and headed for the area where the inhabitants had all passed away. It took quite some time to get there and they were all rather tired when they got there. The only place to sit and rest were some very uncomfortable stone benches. After sitting for a while, wiping sweat off of their faces, they entered one of the domiciles. There were eight rooms in each of the places. There was no furniture of any kind that was left. The only room that they could distinguish from the others was the kitchen because of a rusting stove that still had some soot and a partial chimney over it.

"If we ever come back here...I suggest we each bring a huge bottle of water with us," said Chyning as she stood there panting.

"Shurmook said that there were several big basins for catching rain water...all over the place," said Kiyalee.

Chyning looked up. "Good! Let's find one!"

They were able to find one of the massive basins and each got a long healthy drink, before and after dunking their heads in the tepid water. The water was rather warm, however, it was wet. They splashed fresh water on their bodies during the process of rehydrating.

"There's not much else to see here," said Chyning. "If you want to do some more exploring...go ahead. I'm heading back to the main door...by way of any other water holes."

"I'm with you," said Kiyalee.

Bonarain shrugged and followed the other two women.

The trio arrived at the door and started scanning the compound, looking for Soolchakan.

"He's coming back this way," said Bonarain. "He's coming back from the east wall. I wonder what he found…other than crops."

They waited for him. He appeared to be concentrating on something, however, it eluded the women as to what he was doing. They all looked at each other and shrugged. Just wait for him and then find out exactly what he was doing. He kept on coming closer without any eye contact with the women. He looked like he was taking very deliberate steps as he walked along. He ignored all three women until he got to the door and stopped.

Soolchakan turned to the women shaking his head. "It is exactly 7,455 paces from the door to the east wall." He let out a bit of an exhausted puff. "I'm very glad that, between here and there…I found three different water holes. Without that fresh… albeit warm…water, I don't think I could've made it."

Bonarain chuckled. "With this humidity…you need a lot of water."

Kiyalee looked over towards the south wall. "Do you think that the south wall is just as far as…what'd you say…7,455 paces…from the north wall?"

Soolchakan huffed. "Do you want to go pace it off?"

Kiyalee held her hands up shaking them as if in surrender.

"No, no, no, no, no! I'm curious…but not *that* curious!"

"Yeah," said Chyning. "It does look further…but…I'm not that curious either."

Soolchakan shook his head. "Not much else to see here… unless you're farming. Those fruit trees…not a one of them is over four taja in height. It's gonna be at least six or seven years before any one of them are producing a real fruit crop."

"I agree," said Bonarain. "We've seen the place. Let's get out of here…to someplace that is a little cooler."

"A *LOT* cooler," said Kiyalee!

They exited the door and replaced the chain and padlock. They took the long trek back to the shuttlecraft. Once inside the craft, they turned the temperature on low and the dehumidifier on high. Inside the craft and all sat there wiping the remaining perspiration off…with some different dry towels.

"When we get back…these uniforms are absolutely going to need to be washed," said Bonarain.

"My neck is too," said Kiyalee. "It ain't just sweat dripping down my back."

"Same here," said Soolchakan.

"Let's get out of here," said Chyning. "For once, when we get back, I'm not going to take a hot bath. This one will be a lot cooler, so I can cool down."

No one argued.

4

Every Team gets a chance to go back to (what is now called: Fortress Island) the island and assist in the growing of crops. Since it seems that no one else is exploring the island, they seem to have a wonderful opportunity to grow crops for themselves without ever having to worry about anyone pilfering their crops, even though they can plant anything they want in the special areas of the ships floating around #45.

Several of the Owlamites are wondering why they have to lock the door when, so far, they have seen no evidence of anyone else being there at all.

During one of the *visits* by Team 7016, Soolchakan walked the entire perimeter of the compound. When he came back to the one entrance, the three women were there glaring at him angrily.

Chyning stood there with her arms folded across her chest. "Did you have fun in your little walk? I mean, we're here to gather some fruit and vegetables for our Team...and all you do is walk around aimlessly."

"This is the third time we've been here," he said calmly. "I just noticed something that...seems very odd about this place."

Bonarain scoffed. "What new oddity is that?"

"Inside the walls," he said as he looked around. "There are

no…staircases…to the top of the wall. When you're inside *you are* inside and…there's no way to *see* out. All you can see is the sky. There are no ramparts. There are no high walkways. What kind of a fort is that? You can't see any enemy coming in from the sea. There are no high towers for a lookout or…anything."

The three women started looking around confused.

"You're right," said Bonarain. "All the times we've been here…I never thought of that. We only came here to…look at all of the crops, care for the crops and do some fruit picking."

Kiyalee chuckled. "And no one else ever made that observation before…did they?"

"They did not," said Soolchakan emphatically! "I'm going to…report this oddity to Wunteer…and see what he thinks about it."

"Him and the Staff," said Kiyalee.

Bonarain sighed. "Enough of the oddities of this place, let's get moving back to the shuttle. This fruit will start rotting rather quickly in this heat, now that it has been picked, if we don't get it refrigerated."

They all grabbed hold of the handles of their wheelbarrows and started the long trek back to the shuttlecraft.

Wunteer and the Staff were all amazed (and embarrassed) that no one had ever made the observation about the lack of staircases or high walkways before. Once again each member of the Owlamite race was ordered to go back to the fortress and see if there were any remains of a staircase that might have been there before…at some time or another.

After numerous observations, the only conclusion that could be drawn was that any staircase that might have been there before had to have been made of wood. Since the skeletons were several thousand years old, any trace of the wooden scaffolding or staircases must have rotted away to nothing a very long time ago. It left them wondering why no high walkways had ever been made of stone since, in most cases, all castles had walkways and ramparts made of stone that were usually part of the main structure.

Officer, Roosook of the Architect Team was instructed to look into the possibility of building a staircase and walkway around the inner perimeter. When he informed the Staff of how all of the lumber would have to be carried in from elsewhere and that they could not Jump or hop anything in there, and how much lumber it would take, the Staff suddenly realized the monumental task that would come from attempting to build it. The idea was shelved until someone could come up with a way to get it done without all kinds of heavy labor that they were just not used to any more.

386 years after Wunteer became the *Voice of Power*, Hardooth was attacked again. This time it was a race called the Pah-Hapick. Wunteer and over 500 more Owlamites perished.

Officer Grade 5, Groff became *Voice of Power*, number forty-seven. He turned out to be another one-year-wonder. Almost 400 more died during his short reign.

Officer Grade 5, Porompet became number forty-eight. The Pah-Hapick are finally defeated (through genocide) and once again peace is obtained.

While Porompet is in power, it is observed that the vast majority of different types of animals on Hardooth have been lost forever. He starts a new campaign (with what is left of the Owlamite race) to repopulate the planet with animals from other planets and dimensions. Now the Owlamites have to be really careful in what they bring to Hardooth. They need to make sure that any animal brought in does not become the absolute top of the food chain…such as the giant swimming brown beast that eats giant pink sand snakes that are over 100 taja in length. There were a lot of tough decisions that had to be made because there were some symbiotic relationships as well as some diseases that certain creatures carried. In order to bring one creature they had to, in some cases, bring almost an entire ecosystem. There was one situation where a certain very large edible plant was brought to Hardooth and they had to bring a special little flying rodent along with the plant. The plant could only be pollenated by the flying rodent and the diet of the rodent was only the nectar of that specific plant.

The research and search took almost 180 years to accomplish. Thirty-two years after they finished searching out animals, a new enemy from outer space showed up – the Toozisk. Porompet and 114 more Owlamites die, leaving just 57 Owlamites still surviving out of the original 28,064. Ten males and forty-seven females.

The remaining Owlamites were able to use more of the enemy firestorm weapons to defeat and destroy the Toozisk. Even in the victory over that latest enemy, the Owlamites were not sure how they could ever totally defeat another enemy with what few remaining personnel that existed.

Officer Grade 4, Joogdam became *Voice of Power* number forty-nine. He was the Drey Sssorg of an empire that had set up 28,007 funeral pyres. Those who had not been blasted to atoms in outer space or disintegrated by some powerful pulse beam had been cremated in funeral pyres and their ashes were spread out over the original location of the city of Owlam.

Joogdam decided that rank was not really that necessary any more. There were two Grade 3 women that were still living – Boolala and Tah-Mink, however, they were number 6 and 8 in line. He decided that the rank should be where they stood in line from the eldest to the youngest.

Team 866 had three surviving members. There were seven Teams who had two survivors. Team 7016 was the one and only Team that was still intact from the beginning. All other survivors were the only survivors of the Team they were affiliated with.

Soolchakan found himself fifth in line behind Joogdam and three women: 2, Tooktoy, 3, Weenda and 4, Stahama. Bonarain was number 15 in line. Kiyalee was number 36. Chyning was shocked to find out that she was number 55. There were actually still two other surviving Owlamites younger than she: 56, Vivip and 57, Tontani.

They all started looking at the occupancy of the 6,900

apartments in the gorge. Twelve lived on the first level, six lived on the second level, two lived on the fourth level, eight on the fifth level, one on the sixth level, three on the seventh, six on the eighth, two on the ninth, seven on the tenth, two on the eleventh and eight on the twelfth. All personnel who had lived on the third level were gone.

Joogdam addressed his people. "I have made a suggestion…to several other Drey Sssorg before me. None of them listened. Now that I am the *Voice of Power* I don't need to ask for any permission to make someone listen. One of my observations of these…all of these outworld enemies…is that they were all fascinated by the mineral content of the planet Bri. Since all of them were so mesmerized by that planet…we are going to move about 2,000 guardian sensors to that planet. We will install them on the planet in Spy dimension. Hopefully this will give us a better…and earlier warning…about any new outworld enemy that…happens to come here and attempts to enslave us." He sighed. "This is not a suggestion. This is an order! We will begin…and when I say *we*, I mean *all* of us…will begin installing guardian sensors on Bri…today!"

The audience all sat there somewhat surprised. It did sound like a wonderful idea. Having all of the sensors on Hardooth only let them know the moment the attack occurred. Bri was a perfect place to put the sensors. It was way out there with only two other planets outside of the orbit of Bri: Afkoth and Denhahbon. They all collectively wondered why other Drey Sssorg had not executed this plan before.

Setting up the 2,000 sensors on Bri took just over one year. They also added a few sensors to the five moons orbiting Afkoth. It was further decided to add a few more sensors in a more interior orbit. They chose the sixth orbit where Chabayo and Ragath were always on opposite sides of the star. Several sensors were placed on the moons of the two gas giants.

Now they had guardian sensors all over the star system. They hoped and prayed that they would never be surprised again. With only fifty-seven Owlamites remaining, they absolutely felt that they could not afford to lose any more of their tiny population.

One thing that all of them were grateful for was the fact that the Dragon Defense Force that Bonarain had come up with was really popular in High Country. Now, the Owlamites did not have one single concern about guarding High Country. They could place their entire attention on outer space and any outworld intruder.

Fifty-five years after the sensors were all activated, the ones on Bri lit up. An unknown outworlder had arrived and was ogling the mineral wealth of the planet.

Number 47, Uvansa was watching the screens while enjoying a big mug of kwatha. She had just filled her mouth with a few large lumps when she saw the activity on the monitors.

"Number 1, Joogdam, this is Uvansa! Can you hear me?"

Joogdam came back in a rather sullen manner. **"Yes I can hear you. This had better be something important!"**

Uvansa clenched her teeth. "**There are ships, of unknown origin, orbiting Bri. I've never seen the likes of them**."

Joogdam let fly with several curses and made a full callout to all Owlamites in regards to the message.

All Owlamites responded and were in there fighters rather quickly. They all hopped to Spy and Jumped to Bri. They discovered that there were forty-one ships of unknown origin. Forty were all cylindrical and approximately two kilotaja in length. One was almost four and one half kilotaja in length.

Joogdam did a quick assessment. "**Team 7016, get inside that big one and see if that's a control ship or a troop transport. All others, standby to see which one we attack first**."

Chyning sent a private little message to the rest of the Team. "**Notice how he always talks about everyone else in the lineup but us? It's Number 2, Tooktoy or Number 6, Boolala. But when it comes to us, we're always a Team**."

"**We're the only Team that is still intact**," sent Bonarain. "**Considering what we've been through I think that that is something rather extraordinary**."

Chyning just huffed. "**Team 866 still has at least three people left in it**."

"**That doesn't count**," sent Soolchakan. "**Remember that Number 4, Stahama and Number 48 Leemiya were** originally on that Team. Number 30, Tandehoy was originally on Team 1372, but moved to 866 when she was the only surviving member of 1372. There are now only two original members of Team 866 that are still around."

Chyning huffed again. She sulked as she aimed her fighter for the central portion of the big ship just like the normal reconnaissance plan called for.

Kiyalee flew into the engine room and started her assessment. Soolchakan and Bonarain went to where they estimated the bridge would be. Chyning started looking for anything that she could pilfer.

Joogdam sat there in his fighter impatiently waiting for any report of this enemy. "**What is taking so long**?!"

Soolchakan started getting a little tired of the constant badgering from Joogdam. "**This is NOT any kind of instantaneous thing! We have to get into their minds and listen for a while. Your interruptions are only slowing progress**."

Tah-Mink broke in. "**Number 1, Joogdam, you can't rush it. You need to learn some patience**."

Joogdam scoffed. "**Excuse me NUMBER *EIGHT*, Tah-Mink! You were an Officer Grade 3...and yet you're younger than seven others...only one of which was an equal rank to you. We know how you got your rank so fast. Don't tell me anything about patience. I had to EARN my rank!**"

Finally Bonarain had the situation figured out. She waited a little while longer because Joogdam was still having a temper tantrum and giving others a load of guff as he vented. Finally there was a little silence in the mental communications and she broke back in with her information.

"This is Number 15, Bonarain. This bunch of invaders is called the Rimrooshk. They have every intention of exploiting the mineral content of Bri and also going in and taking over Hardooth in order to come up with a few billion slaves. This *is* a totally hostile invasion with full intent of forceful conquering and no form of negotiation."

Joogdam sat in his fighter with an evil grin. **"All personnel…start killing the enemy. If you find something that you want, don't take too long in obtaining it. Let's get rid of these monsters…quickly!"**

All of the Rimrooshk ships started calling into the flagship of the operation. They were reporting all kinds of equipment and personal items that were suddenly disappearing from their ships. The High Command in the flagship found that the same strange things were going on in their ship. The High Commander was a little confused as to whether or not he should put everyone on emergency alert. He was more of the thought that this was just some kind of superstitious reaction to being in a new star system and not some pilfering by unknown entities. He was figuring that some of the personnel had forgotten where they put things and were now trying to blame it on ghosts or some other kind of thing that goes *bump* in the night.

Then it was too late. After Chyning reported back that she had absconded with anything she could find that was valuable, Kiyalee dropped a hand-held into the core of the light speed engine and the flagship was now nothing but floating debris. Shortly after that, the rest of the ships started blowing up as well.

They did not know if a distress signal had been sent out by the flagship or any of the others. Now all they could do was wait and see if another armada flew in the system from points unknown. Joogdam had placed the sensors on Bri to get an early warning about any intruder, however, there was nothing to indicate exactly which direction they had come from. All that could be ascertained was whatever information was taken prior to the explosions.

Over the next three years, there were several more task forces that came into the star system from the Rimrooshk. Each one was scrutinized for as much information as possible and then blown to atoms.

When the fourth task force arrived, the Owlamites were finally able to get a landmark on the home planet. This time, when the Rimrooshk were threatened, using the ever popular Multifastidigeous Thonlock Communicator. They listened. Especially since they had been so militarily weakened they only had enough power to defend their home planet. They had to call all ships in from previously conquered planets and use them to defend the home front. It would be many centuries before they would be any form of a galactic power again.

103 years later, another intruder was seen entering the star

system. This time they were able to see the direction that this
enemy came from. Once again all Owlamites were put on full
alert and all of them did a Jump to Bri to watch the intruders ogle
the minerals on that big planet.

Team 7016 had to guess which one was the flagship of a
task force of 33 ships. Once again it was the largest. Standard
Operating Procedure took over as Chyning headed in for booty,
Kiyalee headed to the engines while Soolchakan and Bonarain
headed for the Bridge to gather intelligence data and translations.

Soolchakan was doing his normal routine, figuring out what
tasks were performed at each station. Bonarain was attempting
to figure out the language in order to ascertain their intentions.
Chyning was ripping off anything that she could get her hands on
that looked valuable. Kiyalee was already bored – the light speed
engines were so very similar to all of the others that she had seen
before. Apparently there is a system that works and until you can
improve on it - you do not change it. No one can bypass the laws
of physics.

Bonarain had been translating and sending the information
to her Teammates when suddenly she just froze and gasped in
shock. She stood there on the Bridge with a look of total horror
on her face.

Soolchakan was very worried. **"Bonarain, what's the
matter**?"

Her expression did not change. She slowly turned to him.
**"Those...rotten *chokwads*...we let them live...and...all
this time...again...they've been still giving information**

on us."

He frowned. **"Who...what...I don't understand... what're you talking about?"**

She closed her eyes and clenched her teeth. **"What these people, the Honchamik said, and I quote: Those talking fish were right about this mineral planet. All this time... the Doolood have been giving intelligence data on us to any and all marauders...still. I know because they also said something about the talking fish warning about all of our guardian sensors on our home planet."**

Joogdam had listened in on that conversation and was seething with anger. **"When was the last time we sent anyone to the Doolood planet...to check on them?"**

Boolala answered. **"Because of our shortage of people...we don't send anyone there...except maybe once every 300 years."**

Joogdam sat there even more boiling mad. He had to arrange his thoughts in order to set up any kind of a plan. He clenched his teeth, fists and eyes, counted to ten and then started thinking. **"Let's blow the other ships up. Let's keep the flagship. We toss all of the inhabitants of that flagship into...outer space...I don't care which dimension...we get as much intelligence off of that ship as we can...and then we go pay a long overdue visit to our old friends... the Doolood!"**

Six of the Owlamites started Jumping from one ship to another, placing hand-held bombs in the light speed engine core. In a very short time the only ship in the area was the flagship. Before they could attempt to activate their engines and run, Kiyalee had disabled all of the engines with some intricate sabotage. They were helpless.

All the rest of the Owlamites were on board the flagship, tossing all personnel into outer space…starting with the highest ranking ones. It took quite a while to toss 3,155 Honchamik personnel into outer space, however, none of the enemy were able to accomplish anything, seeing as how they were all waiting for orders from higher ranking personnel…who were no longer with them.

Joogdam sat in the Commander's chair on the Bridge. **"Let's start learning everything about this ship that we can…as quickly as we can. Then once we've learned all that we can…we go pay a visit to our old friends… the Doolood. We just might be visiting them…using our reliable planet killer ships."**

Kiyalee looked up in surprise. **"Sir, those ships haven't been serviced in…a long time…because of the lack of sufficient personnel."**

Joogdam stood up looking as if he wanted to shout something in anger. He checked himself and slowly sat back down. **"Number 36, Kiyalee…I think that it is time to service them…and prepare them for use. If you need help – take it! Let me know when they're ready. In the meanwhile, we'll be gleaning as much information off of this ship that we can obtain."**

Kiyalee thought for a few moments. "**Number 23, Moonta, Number 41, Pawa, Number 44, Dayeta, Number 50, Inxa and Number 54, Oilayla, I need your help in servicing the planet killers**."

Before anyone could protest, Joogdam followed up. "**The ones that Number 36, Kiyalee has called…go with her NOW**!" He leaned back in the chair looking at the Commander's console. 'We let those fish live…and this is the thanks we get,' he thought. 'Time for a massive fish fry!' "**People of Owlam! Let's hop this Honchamik flagship to dimension 45 and park it along with the rest of our captured ships…NOW**!"

The hop was accomplished immediately. The ship was now another trophy in their huge collection in dimension #45. Now they could look it over carefully without having to worry about any more Honchamik coming along and attempting to reclaim it. It was parked between the two planet killer ships for convenience. Everyone who was still on board was looking through every personal log and any other data in order to find the Honchamik home planet and see exactly what had been obtained from the Doolood.

Number 49, Beejani found an encrypted program that was soon broken. In it they were able to find all of the information that the Doolood had given to the Honchamik along with information that the Doolood had been giving all of this information to all other invaders of the Hardooth star system for many centuries – because they confessed to this act. All of those invaders had been forewarned by the Doolood in regards to all technology that had been obtained from previous invaders. That was why they had all been able to defeat the previous sensors that were guarding the planet. None of them had dreamed that the sensors would be placed on any of the outer planets - in another dimension.

Joogdam looked over the information feeling his anger growing. "All this time and...our greatest outworld enemy... was the Doolood." He took a deep breath and let it out slowly. He shook his head. "No more! As soon as the planet killers are ready...we boil that Doolood planet."

Number 7, Moncoll walked up to Joogdam. He felt a little nervous. "Uh...Sir, as I remember...the Doolood...are on two different planets...still...I think."

Joogdam turned to Moncoll. "Then we boil both planets," he said in a quiet, sinister manner. "We make sure that those fishies never give out information again." He chuckled. "We don't have to destroy the planets...just get all of that water boiling hot."

Moncoll smiled and nodded. "Yes, Sir...that's...very prudent."

It took six days to get the two planet killers ready. When they took the ships to the Doolood home planet, Joogdam manned one of the 459 cannons himself. The next day, the second planet occupied by the Doolood was boiled.

After looking over more of the information in the Honchamik data banks, they found the location of their home planet. The Honchamik home planet was then destroyed completely.

5

For the next 75 years, the remaining Owlamites were bullied by Joogdam. As a matter of fact, they were bullied the entire 246 years that he was in power. The main victims of his torment were the two women who had been Grade 3 – Boolala and Tah-Mink along with Team 7016. He harassed the two women because he had originally been an Officer Grade 5, who was older than the two women while they were both Officer Grade 3. It did not matter to him if they had actually earned their rank properly, he kept on hinting that they had, in all probability, obtained their rank laying on their backs. He could not stop reminding them of the fact that while they were Officer Grade 3, he - Joogdam along with Tooktoy, Weenda, Stahama and Soolchakan were all older than those two women. Moncoll was also on the list as older than Tah-Mink.

Team 7016 was harassed because it was the one and only Team that had remained intact. Do not forget the fact that this Team had received all kinds of accolades and recognition because of the individual accomplishments of the Team. This Team had discovered more dimensions than any other Team. This Team had the primary translator. This Team had someone who could teach anyone just about anything. This Team had the best mechanic and electrical expert. This Team was wealthier than any other because Chyning had a knack for finding and obtaining many of the most valuable treasures. Soolchakan had come up with several ideas that had helped the Owlamites in their defenses and every time they strayed from his ideas, numerous Owlamites had ended up dead.

All other Teams had lost most of their membership. Teams 269, 866, 2498, 6128 and 6957 all still had two original members of their Teams alive. It was said that 866 still had three members, however, Number 30, Tandehoy was not an original 866. She was originally from Team 1372. Team 7016 was still the only Team that was intact from the beginning.

Of course, as with any bully, it absolutely was *not* his fault that he was a bully. It was the fault of his victims because they forced him to *show them the error of their ways*. They were at fault for being bullied. Since they were so imperfect, he had to constantly remind them of just how flawed they were…in his eyes…and how dare they find any fault in him. That was grounds for more *corrective* action (primarily known as bullying). Most of the Owlamites grew to hate Joogdam, however, there was nothing they could do because he was now, the *Voice of Power*.

Then one day, Joogdam decided to explore all of the apartments that were being utilized by Team 7016. He was curious about the many treasures they had obtained over the centuries and wondered if he should add any loot to his collection. Upon arriving in the liquor locker of Soolchakan, Joogdam discovered the fifty-six cases of Golden Age Liquor and nearly went into shock.

Joogdam looked angrily at Soolchakan. "All these years…

and you haven't shared that...treasured liquor...with *anybody*?"

Soolchakan gave him a blank stare. "I was ordered by...I think it was Neenatha...or Holla...I don't remember. I was usually too drunk but...one of the women ordered me to stop drinking. I had it then...and...she ordered me to not partake of another drop of any alcoholic beverage. I haven't touched it...or even thought of it since then."

Joogdam shook his head. "Something...as wonderful as that...being kept from all of the other Owlamites! That is disgusting! A symbol! Something that existed before those rotten firestorm weapons went off. Something manufactured in the city of Owlam and...because of your greed, you've deprived all of us from even setting our eyes on it."

"I didn't even think about it...because of the order from Neenatha...or was it Holla," said Soolchakan with a shrug. "I didn't know of anyone else who wanted it because I never heard anyone mention it."

Joogdam got right in Soolchakan's face and glared at him angrily. "No one mentioned it because no one thought that there was any of it left!"

Soolchakan frowned and remembered. "Wait, Jahong knew about it. I think it was Jahong. He...came to me and... requested a case of it. I gave him a case."

Joogdam huffed. "Neenatha! Jahong! *That*...is a long time ago! It still doesn't excuse the fact that you never informed anyone else about your treasure."

Soolchakan sighed. "Neenatha…or Holla…ordered me to not consume any more alcoholic beverages and so it became totally unimportant to me…in all ways."

Joogdam had an evil smirk on his face. "Well…since it is so unimportant to you, I will not rescind the order of Neenatha… or Holla. Instead, we're going to have a party. All Owlamites are invited to…attend…however, all members of Team 7016 will not be in the party to have fun. They will be serving. Guess what they will be serving!"

Soolchakan sighed. "Golden Age Liquor?"

Joogdam smiled triumphantly. "Absolutely! All of the rest of us will enjoy it…and you will watch all of us enjoy it…but, you will not be able to enjoy it with us."

Soolchakan had mixed emotions about it. One of the women had banned him from drinking. Joogdam did not change that. Here was this liquor that was 9,000 years old, and yes, it was a memory of one of the things that had been manufactured in the city of Owlam before the firestorm attack. It was booze but it was *his* booze. Joogdam was taking it away. He wondered if Joogdam was going to take anything else away from the Team as a result of finding this booze.

Joogdam called everyone to a large conference room. All of the tables were set up for a party instead of a meeting. He announced that there was going to be a treat that had not been seen by most of the remaining Owlamites for a long time. There were a lot of strange looks from the others as they entered the room. None of them could figure out what this secret was. Joogdam ordered Team 7016 to bring the treat in. When they came in with the bottles on carts there were all kinds of gasps as the others realized what it was.

Joogdam looked around grinning. "Since Team 7016 kept this secret from us, they will not be drinking with us. We will enjoy it. We will enjoy something that most of us have not seen... for nearly nine thousand years."

Number 18, Ampiypiy stood up from her seat. "Sir, I've never really liked alcohol. I'd rather not..."

Joogdam snarled at her. **"I SAID THAT WE ARE ALL DRINKING! All except Team 7016. When I say that we are all drinking, other than 7016, I MEAN IT!"**

Ampiypiy sat down looking rather frightened.

Team 7016 started placing glasses in front of everyone. Soolchakan opened a bottle in order to start pouring. As soon as he opened it a strange smell came out of the bottle that stung his eyes and nose. He stared at the bottle in a strange manner. He wanted to say something about it to Joogdam.

Joogdam saw that Soolchakan was about to speak and he jumped up from his seat. **"SILENCE NUMBER 5! We are not interested in anything that you have to say. All we want from you is to pour the drink and let us enjoy...keeping your opinion to yourself. In other words...with your mouth shut."**

Soolchakan bit his lip and started pouring. He shook his head as he poured. There was something wrong, however, he was ordered to be silent and pour. He obeyed the *Voice of Power*. As always, he and every other Owlamite must obey.

There was some circulation in the room that was taking the smell out of the room away from him. He still could not identify what the problem was, however, he knew that something was just not right. He continued to pour. Once all of the glasses were distributed, the women of 7016 each opened a bottle and started pouring the drinks as well.

Joogdam picked his glass up and swirled the yellow liquid around in it. "Yes, my people, this is going to be an extraordinary pleasure. Something that none of us has tasted since…Neenatha." He looked over at Soolchakan. "Or was it Jahong? Or was it Holla?" He chuckled and shook his head. "No matter! We are here in the now. We are going to enjoy." He stood up. "Remember that the best way to enjoy the Golden Age Liquor is to let it spend as little time in the mouth as is possible. You pour it in your mouth and swallow immediately. You will feel it burn all the way down until it hits your stomach and then…euphoria!"

Team 7016 continued filling glasses until all of the others had something in their glass.

Joogdam looked around smiling. "Does everyone have some…excluding Team 7016? Hold your glasses up!" He smiled triumphantly. "Now, a pleasure that Number 5, Soolchakan has kept from all of us for almost 9,000 years." He held his glass up high. **"Now…throw it down your throat and enjoy…DRINK!"**

Having been an order given using the *Voice*, even Ampiypiy did not hesitate slamming the drink.

Suddenly almost everyone in the room let out a pained squawk. Those who did not react immediately followed suit rather quickly…including Joogdam. The belligerent smile was gone and all that was on his face was shock and pain. Many of them started clutching at their chests and going down to their stomach as the liquid went down the esophagus. Fifty-three Owlamites all started falling to their knees or just prone on the floor with blood coming out of their mouths.

Kiyalee looked in shock at what was happening and started convulsing with a hand over her mouth.

Soolchakan pointed to Kiyalee and hollered at Chyning. "Get her out of here!"

Chyning was not ready to continue watching what was going on so she gladly grabbed Kiyalee and Jumped both of them to a bathroom where Kiyalee could aim her spray at a toilet. Soolchakan and Bonarain continued watching the horror that was unfolding in front of them. Those that were still alive were choking on their own blood as they continued clutching at their stomachs. With the same suddenness in which they had all fallen, most of them started bleeding profusely from their abdomens. All of the crying, choking and squawking finally came to a halt and all that was heard was a strange sizzling as blood still leaked from mouths and abdomens.

Soolchakan swallowed hard. He looked at the bottle that was still in his hand. There was still a little bit of the liquor left in the bottom. He walked to the closest table and carefully poured a small amount of the liquid onto the table. Immediately he heard a sizzling sound and before he could count to five, the liquid had dissolved a hole through the table and was now sizzling and bubbling on the floor.

Bonarain had tears running down her cheeks. "What… happened?"

Soolchakan sighed sadly. "After 9,000 years…this…hard liquor…somehow turned into…some kind of concentrated acid."

Bonarain was shaking a little. "But…why didn't this… acid…eat the bottle?"

He sighed. "If I remember anything from my chemistry classes in school, liquid acids do not eat glass. It will dissolve just about everything else, but not glass."

"But…what…do we do…about them?"

Soolchakan huffed. "What am I supposed to do? THEY'RE ALL DEAD! I'm not a god! I can't bring anyone back to life. The only thing left…is a…funeral pyre…for all of them."

Bonarain sank to her knees looking around with fear in her eyes. "And then…there were four!" She looked up at Soolchakan as if she were pleading for…something.

Now came the horrid task of removing all of the bleeding bodies to the area above the gorge. Now came the task of 53 more funeral pyres.

Kiyalee was tasked to bring wood because she could not go near the bodies without convulsing and spewing again. Once all of the bodies were on the pyres and the fires were going, she was able to come back. Even though the bodies had that stench from burning, she was able to put up with that. She was even able to assist in gathering the ashes to spread them over the original city of Owlam.

"What do we do now," said Chyning sadly?

"We exist…therefore we continue living," said Soolchakan. "What else did you have in mind?"

Chyning stomped a foot angrily. "But there's only four of us! How do we defend this entire planet…with only four of us?"

Bonarain shrugged with her eyes downcast. "Less targets for any enemy," she said sadly. She looked up. "Unless you're suggesting that we just…give up."

Soolchakan looked at one of the bottles of liquor that had somehow been brought up to the top of the cliff. He took a piece of wood that still had a flame on it. He poured the liquid on the ground. It started sizzling as it dissolved soil. He placed the flame in the liquid and it immediately burst into a huge flame that burned the acid so quickly that the fire was out in less than one heartbeat. One huge flame that turned into black acrid ball of smoke as it rose up. "We also have a new weapon," he said flatly.

Bonarain sniffed. "8,993 years after the firestorm and… now there are only four. All we can do is…live…as long as we can."

Kiyalee looked up sadly. "All for the memory of the great city of Owlam?"

Chyning sighed. "As long as we are alive…Owlam will be remembered."

"So what else do we do now," asked Kiyalee?

Soolchakan scoffed. "Whatever we want to do. Who…is going to stop us?"

The women did what they wanted to do. They departed without saying where they were going. Soolchakan was not that worried because he knew that he could always contact them telepathically. He went to the main computer room and kept himself busy with some of the memoirs of others during the boring times of watching the monitors for incoming outworlders.

After a full month had gone by he decided to contact the women and see what it was that they were doing.

"This is Soolchakan calling all three of you…what are you doing…for so long?"

Bonarain answered back. **"Can we get back with you on that? We're rather busy right now**."

He frowned. **"I'm getting very tired of being the only one watching these *chokwad* monitors! One of you is going to come back and watch them for a while. I would like to do something else, myself, for a while**."

Chyning appeared in the room. She sniffed and gave him a rather sullen look. "Can't this wait?"

He snarled out loud. He gave her an angry glare. He leaned back in his chair and folded his arms across his chest. "If you want me to stay here, you'd better give me a good reason as to what is so important for the three of you, where not one of you can come here and relieve me for at least one day."

Chyning looked down at her fingernails. She looked up biting her lip. "We...are almost finished...well...yeah we're finished...for the most part."

"WITH WHAT?"

She jumped back. "We've been in Ciscaumen!"

He looked up contemplating. He cleared his throat. "Which one?"

She clasped her hands behind her back looking a little guilty. "All three of them."

He felt a little confused. "Ciscaumen East, Ciscaumen West and Divider Ciscaumen?"

She nodded.

"Doing what?"

"Freeing a lot of women from slavery."

He was a little taken aback by that. "Were they...*in*...slavery?"

"You could say that, yes."

He was slightly taken aback. "Uh...how?"

She sighed. "In Ciscaumen...none of the women had any rights...at all. They weren't living creatures...to the men, they were property. They weren't even allowed to have names. The men of Ciscaumen...traded, sold and bought women like...livestock...or other property."

He nodded in comprehension. "So...what exactly did you

do?"

"We led a revolt," she said with a jovial smile.

He sat there a little stunned for a moment. He cleared his throat. "Did you…win?"

"You could say that, yes." She contemplated for a moment. "Some of them…were actually a lot better at fighting than what we initially gave them credit for. The women who are still in Ciscaumen now have rights. They have the right to have a name, they have the right to wear clothing, they have the right to say *no* to a lot of things…where they had no rights before."

He nodded in comprehension. "Was that…all that happened?"

She flushed and looked off to the side. "Well…not really."

He closed his eyes and let out a little growl. "What else happened?"

She clicked her tongue. "It seems…that some of them… didn't really like the idea of making…peace with men who had… abused them…so badly…or even staying there…in Ciscaumen… any of them."

"Okay…and?"

"There is a large group of them…who left."

He nodded with a concerned look on his face. "And… went…where?"

"You know that…Bertheel Isle?"

"Yes."

She flushed again and started looking a little guilty. "They...went to Bertheel and it seems...that they...conquered... the inhabitants...of that place."

He raised his eyebrows. "You said...conquered?"

Her face seemed to turn even redder. "They...are establishing...their own government there...the Ciscaumen women that left...that is. They are...making a place where...it is only...women...in charge...of anything...and everything...in Bertheel."

He closed his eyes and sighed. "Are you...assisting with... this?"

She wobbled her head back and forth. "Sort of," she said as she looked up at the ceiling in a guilty manner.

"Two wrongs don't make a right!"

"We...we're trying to...help them...not do...anything... really stupid."

He snarled. "**Bonarain, Kiyalee...get back here...NOW!**"

He had used the *Voice of Power*. They had no way of avoiding obedience. Both women were back in the computer room instantly. Both looking a little concerned.

"We still need to help them," said Bonarain.

He shook his head. "I think you've done enough. You've established...a new government...in this world of ours. If they're going to...continue...I suggest that you let them stand...on their own." He sighed. "I think that we've had quite enough of conquerors and conquering. Let's…just leave it alone for a while and stop…meddling in the affairs of others on this planet…unless they directly affect us."

Kiyalee got a little churlish. "You mean like the Teltermak?"

He harrumphed at that. "There are only four of us left. I don't think they can find us. Even if they do…I think that we can hide from them…somewhere on one of those ships in dimension 45."

Kiyalee squawked. "Do you know what it is going to take…to keep most of them usable? I…won't have much time for anything else!"

He smiled. "I think that…four will do nicely. Four ships, one for each of us, if necessary…plus keep at least one of the planet killers in working condition."

Chyning scoffed. "What do we do tomorrow?"

"Pester a few Teltermaks and continue trying to find out why they wanted everyone else dead, while they wanted to capture us alive." He shook his head looking a little worried. "The three of you…you didn't get involved…in any of the…hand-to-hand combat…in Ciscaumen…did you?"

Bonarain smiled. "Not really."

He scowled at her. "That's not an answer, that's an evasion," he growled.

She huffed. "The stronger men…in the fight, we…might have…held their arm back…as they were trying to swing a sword or…throw a punch…or club one of the women."

Kiyalee perked up. "Oh…did you hear about that big conference going on in Paselter?"

Soolchakan was almost terrified of what he might hear now. "What…conference?"

"Most of the world leaders have representatives at the conference…right now," she said merrily.

He shook his head. "While you were conquering… and despoiling Ciscaumen and Bertheel, you heard of…some conference…in Paselter?"

"Oh yes," said Bonarain! "It seems that they're getting together to make an attempt at getting everyone on the same page… as far as the calendar, measurements and a few other things."

He was now thoroughly confused. "Calendar? Measurements?"

"They're trying to make a calendar…that everyone uses… in the same manner," said Kiyalee. "That way, whenever someone talks about a certain date…say in Tabrow, they'll be talking about the same date in Peegruch or Agrosha or…Ciscaumen. Everyone will be using the same calendar."

He nodded. "Okay. That sounds interesting. Now…what about…measurements?"

"Measurements!" Bonarain looked jovial. "How we measure dry goods, how we measure liquids, how we measure the temperature and how we measure distance. They want to get everybody on the same page there as well."

Kiyalee snickered. "Where have you been lately?"

He glared back at her. "WATCHING THESE *CHOKWAD* MONITORS WHILE THE THREE OF YOU HAVE BEEN GALAVANTING ALL OVER CISCAUMEN, BERTHEEL AND PASELTER!!!"

All three women backed away a little looking rather guilty and a little scared.

He calmed himself a little. "We are now going to take turns...watching these monitors. I know that...it is not going to be that easy a task...seeing as how there are now only four of us. The main goal is...to keep anyone from conquering...this planet and...forcing us to...hide even more than what we've already been doing."

"What about that conference...in Paselter," asked Chyning?

He sighed. "When they reach an agreement...I guess we can adopt the same things that they come up with...in order for us to be able to understand what others are talking about. Otherwise we'd sound very ignorant...in trying to trade with someone else."

Bonarain frowned. "We're not...going to attend?"

"No," he said emphatically! "I think that...you've done enough...interfering with the lives of others...on this planet...at the moment." He sat back down in a chair. "How long is this conference supposed to take?"

Bonarain shrugged. "They said that it will take as long as it does...in order for them to all agree on the same thing."

He closed his eyes and grimaced. "Oh, *h'oolyach*! A bunch of politicians, all sitting in the same room, arguing over a subject...any subject. That could take...decades!"

It did take years.

Seven years after Soolchakan became *Voice of Power* number fifty, was the 9,000th anniversary of the firestorm weapons changing the lives of the people of the city of Owlam and many others. While other races were flourishing, the Owlamites were down to only four members.

Two years later an alarm went off in the gorge. None of the four had ever heard that alarm before and were very puzzled (and terrified) as to why it was blaring. When they called up the information on the computer they were completely shocked at what they saw. The long sewage chute that emptied far away into the ocean was being...invaded (?). Someone was marching their way up the sewage chute. Wading through mountains of old and new sewage and refuse trying to find the other end of the chute.

Bonarain was looking at the monitor looking as if she were about to join Kiyalee bending over a trash can losing her lunch. "Someone is coming up that...through all that horrible mess and...who could possibly be that desperate?"

Chyning was straining her eyes trying to see. "Who is it?"

Bonarain shook her head. "The only lights that I see... they have some kind of light on their hats. That light is messing with our sensors. We can't see who it is through the glare."

Soolchakan snarled in frustration. "There's insufficient light in the chute! We're going to have to…go down there and…take a look…with some light of our own."

Chyning gave him a dirty look. "We? Which…*we*…are we talking about?"

Bonarain smiled as she handed a flashlight to Chyning. "Stay in Observation. That way you won't…smell anything…or come back…tracking…anything."

Chyning took the flashlight and snarled. She vanished. She was near the area where the chute emptied into the ocean. While in Observation she was able to look around in the faces of the intruders. "**I don't believe what I'm seeing! These people have…claws…on their hands**."

Bonarain tried to do some thinking. "**Give me a full description of those…*muck* sloggers**."

Chyning grunted in disgust. "**They have skin that's dark tan. They're about six taja in height. They have retractable claws on their hands and…oh *h'oolyach*! They're barefoot…in that…*stuff* and…they have retractable claws on their feet as well!**"

Soolchakan shook his head. "**Retractable claws on both hands and feet. That sounds like the Perek. That's an Elf race…that lives in the central part of South Chilamte**." He scoffed. "**What are they doing in our sewage chute?**"

Chyning hung her head. "**Do you want me to ask

them?"

Bonarain snickered. **"Read their minds, Dearie**."

Chyning concentrated on the Perek minds. She suddenly perked up. **"They're trying to find a good place…to hide their personal fortunes. This tunnel…looked inviting**."

Soolchakan looked at Bonarain in horror. "A tunnel full of…raw sewage…looks inviting? What kind of people are they?"

"I don't think I wanna know," said Bonarain looking nauseous.

Soolchakan checked the reservoirs. "It looks like all five of the tanks are full." He huffed. "No surprise there, seeing as how there are only four of us using the water. They're filling up faster than we can use the all of that water."

Bonarain nodded. "Right, we've been collecting a lot of the rain water…and with only four of us…we haven't had any reason to do…a major flush."

Soolchakan shuddered in disgust. **"Chyning, how deep in the chute are they**?"

Chyning looked around disgusted. **"As near as I can tell…they're about eight kilotaja deep in the tunnel**."

Soolchakan had a mischievous grin on his face. "We have a good reason to flush now. Hit all five of them…simultaneously."

Bonarain was surprised. "Why all five? Wouldn't one be sufficient?"

He shook his head. "At that distance…by the time the

leading edge gets there it probably won't be a torrent. It'll likely be just be a trickle. If we hit all five…at the same time…that much water…it won't have enough room in the tunnel to slow down. It'll hit them hard and…hopefully change their minds about using our…*dump* chute…for anything."

Bonarain shrugged. She lined up all five of the icons on the monitor. She hit the execution button on all five simultaneously and all five tanks emptied completely into the chute. "It may take a while to get where they are. They're still some distance away."

He sighed. "Let the laws of physics do the job."

Chyning sent back. **"These people are already sensing something wrong already. I can see their hair being blown back a little. That water rushing around up at the top of the chute is already affecting the air down here…and they look worried.**"

Bonarain frowned. **"You say that…the air is already being moved…at that distance? How can that be**?"

Soolchakan huffed. **"It probably has something to do with the fact that, all things taken into account, it is a relatively small tunnel with no side passages. All that water…is pushing the all of the air out rather quickly. Unfortunately, we'd need one of the physicists to explain just how…but none of them are here anymore.**"

Chyning Jumped forward into the tunnel a little way. "These **bimyocks aren't stopping. They're still trying to forge ahead…and find some kind of side path or…area that they can store their goodies.**"

Soolchakan sniffed and looked off to the side. "**Pretty soon...they're going to get a very rude awakening. If it is really a hiding place for their treasures that they're looking for...why don't you do what you do best and... explore the holds of any ships they have there...and... obtain...some of their goodies.**"

Chyning stood there with a naughty (and greedy) smile. "**What makes you think that their goodies are on their ships?**"

Soolchakan grunted. "**They're currently looking for a hiding place. They'd have to have some of the stuff with them, now.**"

Chyning put the flashlight in a pocket and giggled. She Jumped to the opening. She looked around at six somewhat large ships. Their sails were all hanging limp which surprised her. The crews that were still on board the ships were pulling the slack sails up to tie them off. She chose the largest ship, Jumped to it and started her treasure exploration.

Soolchakan had another thought. "**Chyning, do you think that we could send Kiyalee out there with you...to explore any ships that are there?**"

Chyning shrugged. "**Couldn't hurt.**"

"**Good! Come back and get her and take her out there.**"

Chyning giggled. She Jumped back to where she had left Kiyalee. Kiyalee was sitting in a chair with her eyes closed holding her stomach.

Chyning tapped Kiyalee on the shoulder. "Are you ready to go treasure hunting?"

"Are you sure you want me there?"

"It won't be inside the sewage tunnel."

Kiyalee opened her eyes. "That's one *very* good point. Okay, I'll go."

The two women returned to the small group of ships and started exploring cargo holds. There were numerous items in crates. Since they were in Observation, they did not need to worry about any wooden barriers in Home dimension. They simply poked their face through the wood and took a look inside. They started Jumping everything back to the gorge in order to look through the plunder later. None of the crews were noticing any of the pilferage because they were busy with other things. They would not be worrying about their treasures unless the ones exploring the smelly tunnel gave an affirmation of this being a good hiding place.

Soolchakan was getting a little impatient. It seemed to be taking a long time for the flood to get to that end of the chute. He had to remember that it was over 1,000 kilotaja. He licked his lips as he thought. "Bonarain, why don't you get out there and watch the chute while the others explore for goodies."

"Is that the only reason you want me out there?"

"No! I was just thinking. If the Dragon Defense Force has a dragon that is patrolling that area…how come there is no alert by the Dragon Headquarters as to…an intruder near the cliffs?" He shook his head. "There has to be some other reason for them to… climb up that tunnel through…mountains of…refuse."

Bonarain looked a little shocked. "Good point."

"You're better at finding motives of others when you read their minds. Try doing the same here."

"I'll call one of them back to help Jump me to the ships."

"You don't need to interrupt them."

"I don't know what the ships look like. I need them to landmark for me."

"You know the cliff that is just above the chute exit, don't you?"

She contemplated for a moment. "Yes, I do." She stood up, smiled and vanished.

He went back to looking at the dark monitors.

Bonarain called back. "**I don't see any of the dragon patrol anywhere in the area.**" She looked over the cliff. "**Oh, that smell is terrible. I'm going to go to Observation as well. Then I won't have to smell it.**"

He clenched his teeth. 'You should have already been there,' he thought.

Bonarain called back again. "**I've never seen the water in this area this calm. There is absolutely no surf whatsoever. Usually it is pounding against the cliffs. Today…it is just…flat!**"

Soolchakan shrugged. **"It had to happen sooner or later. Those *doovofts* just happened to find the opening…at the right time."**

Bonarain Jumped down to the ship that was closest to the chute. **"I'm on a ship now. I'm standing near someone who looks…rather important."**

Soolchakan grunted. **"What makes him look important?"**

"All kinds of superfluous, colorful and fancy frills on his shirt. Plus he is wearing a rather large and ostentatious hat."

He snickered. **"I'll take your word for it."**

"One thing I have found out…is that it is a pre-invasion set up. This grand *bimyock* is the one in charge and he's hoping that they can find a secret way in to invade and do some conquering of their own… from within."

Soolchakan squawked in disbelief. **"Even, with the Dragon Defense Force out there?"**

"They're hoping to undermine the Dragon Force and take over anything and everything that is left over."

Soolchakan sighed as he pondered what to do next. **"Kiyalee and Chyning, have you finished the task of emptying their cargo holds?"**

"We finished that part some time ago," sent Chyning.

He smiled. "**Would you like to have some fun… sabotaging their ships**?"

Kiyalee came back. "**Whatcha got in mind**?"

"**A ship without an anchor can't sit in one place very long, can it**?"

Bonarain broke in. "**We have a bunch of the ones in the tunnel who are running out and diving in the water. They look…somewhat panicked.**"

Soolchakan suddenly had a frightening thought. "**All three of you…get up to the top of the cliff to observe… NOW! We don't know what's going to happen when all of that muck and water hits those ships.**"

"**Don't panic**," sent Bonarain. "**We're up on top now. We've got an interesting view of…OH *H'OOLYACH*! The mess just got here! There's this…huge torrent of… *brown muck*…just blasting out of that chute!**"

Soolchakan scoffed. 'What color were you expecting,' he thought?

"**Look**," sent Chyning! "**The big ship that was closest…the thing is being pulled under! The anchor isn't letting it float away in the flood and…it just went under!**"

"**That other one just flipped over**," sent Kiyalee.

"**There goes another one**," sent Bonarain. "**It just had a huge slit ripped in the hull…from the anchor chain. It can't stay afloat…with that much damage to…**

yup! The thing is sinking...a lot faster than I thought it would."

Soolchakan calmly listened. He pulled up an icon on the computer and reset the intruder alarm on the exhaust chute. He wondered if he should go and watch the spectacle that was unfolding on the eastern cliff of High Country. He sighed and decided against it. The women might give him a few more graphic descriptions of what was going on and he really did not need to see it.

Suddenly Kiyalee reappeared in the computer room... holding her stomach and looking very queasy. She looked up at Soolchakan. "Don't worry. I don't have anything left in my stomach...to lose."

He frowned. "What made you leave?"

She shook her head. "All those people...swimming in that..." She put a hand on her stomach and the other over her mouth and gagged. "It was just...horrible to watch."

Bonarain called back. "**All six ships have floundered and sunk. I don't think the Perek are going to find out... any time soon what happened to their treasure or the reconnaissance mission.**"

Soolchakan shook his head. "**What a shame**," he sent sarcastically.

6

The haul from the Perek ships was considerable. They had obtained a rather large amount of gold, silver, copper and over 14,000 precious gems. All of the metals had been melted down and were in bars, balls, globs and any other odd shape of whatever the molten metal was poured in to allow it to harden.

They had no concern at all about any of the Perek people finding out what happened to their treasures. All of the Perek Elf people who were in that small task force either drowned in the fecal blast from the chute or died when they attempted to walk south on what little shore there was along the high cliffs. It would take someone at least twenty days of walking to get back to Peegruch and when the surf conditions got heavy at high tide, all survivors were smashed and pounded against the jagged rocks at the base of the cliffs before their bodies were washed out to a watery grave.

Six years after the Perek fiasco, the mixed council in Paselter finally came to some conclusions that all of them agreed upon.

All data prior to the establishment of the worldwide accepted calendar became known as the Unknown Times or UT because there was a considerable amount of information that had been lost in all of those strange legendary explosions from the sky. There was a lot of information that was just tales and possible myths that were told of the past and most of the written transcripts of these events were lost. All data after the establishment of the calendar was called "After the Unknown Times" or ATUT. Most of the people of this day did not know about computers because all of that had been blasted to unrecognizable fragments when any outworlder had attacked. All of that technology was lost – to most peoples and countries. Now they were going to establish libraries in universities in order to have places to store all of the written data about the history of the planet…that they knew about.

Liquids and dry goods were measured as ten spoons to a cup, ten cups to a pitcher, ten pitchers to a bucket and ten buckets to a barrel.

Grains were still measured in bushels while crops of fruits, vegetables and tubers were measured in baskets.

They had a new way to measure the temperature called "Abfar" and the Owlamites were having a terrible time understanding it. All that they could really understand was that the higher the number, the hotter it is. The lower the number the colder it is. Beyond that they could not understand what it was based on.

In the year Two ATUT, there was another invader that came in and started ogling the mineral wealth of Bri. The Owlamites Jumped to Bri with great trepidation on their minds. With only four of them remaining, any loss on their part was totally unacceptable. They found thirty-five unknown vessels orbiting Bri as the invaders were doing what everyone else had done and were scoping all of the mineral wealth of the planet.

All of the ships were long cylinders with a point on one end and rocket exhaust funnels on the other. There was no noticeable difference between any of them.

Bonarain snarled out loud. **"Which one do we go to… to find out who is in charge**?"

Chyning had been looking all of them over as she orbited the planet. **"We got one ship watching all of the others do the work. Usually the one in charge is the lazy *bimyock* who does nothing other than tell everyone else what to do. They sit off to the side while everyone else works. That one might be our flagship."**

"That sounds about right," sent Soolchakan. **"We might as well go there. I can't see anything that leads us in any other direction."**

Kiyalee harrumphed. **"Are we going in there in the normal way**?"

"I can't think of anything that has worked any better than that," sent Soolchakan. **"So, yes, standard operating procedure is the rule of the day."**

Kiyalee stuck her tongue out at him. She knew that he could not see her since she was in her fighter and he in his, however, it still made her feel better to be able to do it without receiving any reprimand. She flew to the rear of the big ship and headed in to where she figured the main engine control room was located. She was a little surprised at what she found. "**Hey, these *doovofts* have a bunch of wasted redundancy here. They got two light speed engines which seems kinda normal. They got *four* different sizes of conventional engines. Apparently they like the idea of having sufficient backups for any contingency.**"

Chyning was doing a very rapid reconnaissance of the middle of the ship. "**This ship is not worth our time…as far as money is concerned. It is totally a military ship. It has, so far, nothing worth stealing…unless you want a lot of conventional military weaponry. I don't see nuthin' else worth taking.**"

Soolchakan and Bonarain were on the Bridge.

Bonarain looked around and shook her head. "**Not much for comfort, are they?**"

He snickered. "**Full utilization of all space in the ship. Don't waste any room on anything superfluous. Utilize all space that you can without any waste.**" He sighed. "**Get their language while I look over their consoles.**" He had done a quick scan and he decided that he was going to look at something else as well. There were several of these…people (who looked very much like normal Heyyah, other than the fact that their skin was pale red)…were walking around using some kind of small hand-held computer. That device piqued his curiosity.

Bonarain was reading the mind of the one that she guessed

was in charge. She found very quickly that she had guessed correctly. She scoffed as the translation started coming through. **"They call themselves the...Chinchisossok! They *are* here to conquer. They're also drooling over the mineral wealth of Bri. They've labeled Bri as Zanzoy-Komok-12. They've also labeled Hardooth as Zanzoy-Komok-4. They only stopped here, on their way to invade us, to gaze in awe at the mineral wealth. As soon as they're finished with the inventory, they're heading on to Hardooth...for a large collection of slaves...to do some mining here on Bri."**

Soolchakan sighed. **"Then we need to change their minds right now. Here and now! Any light show of a ship blowing up here won't be seen from Hardooth and it won't give any superstitious *bimyock* another invented deity to worship."**

Chyning came back. **"Which ones should we start with? Should we make sure that no one on Hardooth can see any of the explosions by hitting the ones on the far side of Bri?"**

He shook his head. **"Start with any one of them that you want! Just wait until I'm finished looking at something on this flagship. It is interesting and...maybe I might purloin one or two."**

Bonarain sniffed in disgust. **"I'm going to stick with this flagship for a little while. I'm rather interested in some of the information that I'm picking up from them... plus I'll need to monitor their reaction when the first one**

of their ships blow up."

"**Good point**," sent Soolchakan. "**Okay, you two…go get rid of some of the other ships**."

Kiyalee and Chyning flew out of the flagship and each picked another one of the ships to go to and start the demolition. It did not take long. The first ship blew up and the reaction on the Bridge of the flagship was immediate. All ships went to red alert and all personnel were ordered to their battle stations. No one knew who or what they were looking for, they were just told to look for anything out of the ordinary.

A second ship blew up. The Commander of the flagship ordered a retreat away from the planet. There was no specific direction, he simply wanted everyone to get away from the planet…just in case there was something there that was causing this catastrophic problem. This could not be coincidence. Two ships do not blow up without some form of attack. Where is or are the attackers?

A third ship blew up. Then a fourth ship blew up. The Commander ordered the task force out of the star system immediately. The order given was for them to get out of the system by the most direct route possible and then all of them were to regroup at coordinates Voy-Kon-Chee (whatever that meant). After observing where they went, it turned out to be approximately 1.4 million kilotaja outside of the orbit of Denhahbon.

Kiyalee and Chyning were still wondering which ship to blow up next. Since the remaining ships had all flown out of there and then regrouped, the two women were not sure which one was the flagship.

"**Soolchakan this is Kiyalee. Which one of those *bimyock* buckets is the one that you're on? They all... well they have different markings on the outside, but until Bonarain teaches us their language...I still don't know which one is which. I don't want to blow up the one that you're investigating.**"

Soolchakan chuckled to himself. "**It seems that they led us all down a strange path when they retreated. I'll get in my fighter and show myself to you...just above the Bridge of this ship**." He climbed in the fighter, closed the canopy and raised the fighter up out of the enemy vessel. "**Can you see me?**"

"**I see you**," sent Chyning.

Kiyalee was a little confused. "**Where? I don't see him at all.**"

"**The one to the far left**," sent Chyning.

"**What...where...oh...I can see you now**," sent Kiyalee.

"**Good**," sent Soolchakan! "**Now...if you're going to blow up any more of them...hit the ones that are furthest from this ship.**"

"**Hold off on blowing any more of them**," sent Bonarain. "**I still need a little more time to get their full language. If you scare them off completely...they may run...even further this time.**"

Kiyalee scoffed. **"So what! It doesn't matter how far they go, we can still Jump back to Hardooth from any distance."**

"I know," sent Bonarain impatiently. **"The problem with this bunch is that they don't think clearly and I can't get them *clearly* when they're in full panic mode. Give them a little time to calm down before we start gleaning the herd again."**

Chyning sighed. **"Say when."**

Soolchakan went back to closely examining the unusual little hand-held device while Bonarain went back to fine tweaking in understanding the language of these people. They were very intelligent people with some very sophisticated (and interesting) technology, however, they did have the bad habit of panicking very easily.

Bonarain was sitting next to the Commander as he was being briefed on (what little) his science experts could figure out regarding the detonation of the four ships. She sat there calmly interpreting the muddle of thoughts that he was going through as he was of a mind to strangle all six of the experts because all they could give him was wild theory and innuendo.

Soolchakan waited until one of the Chinchisossok put his hand-held computer down. As soon as it was placed on a desk, Soolchakan walked up and stared at it as closely as he could. The screen was tiny yet the readout was clear. It had a keypad that was incredibly small, however, they had some pointed stick that went with the machine that was used to hit each key, one at a time, without hitting more than one. He was studying it when the alien reached over and picked it up. This irritated Soolchakan a little because he wanted to be able to study the thing without interruption. He decided that the next one that was placed on a desk would be hopped to Spy dimension with him and then he would be able to perform some uninterrupted scrutiny of this little marvel.

Bonarain looked over at Soolchakan every few moments wondering what he was doing. She shook her head and went back to getting the full depth of the language. It had some strange syntax and some even stranger idioms they liked using persistently.

Soolchakan finally saw one of them put the hand-held down. He got to it as fast as he could. He chuckled to himself as he reached for the miniature apparatus. He did the hop and picked it up…and an intruder alarm went off. He had goofed. In a little mind mix-up, he had not hopped the device into Spy, he had hopped himself into Home dimension. He had been concentrating on the wrong thing when he performed the hop. Now there was a loud klaxon blaring away and everybody on the Bridge was staring at Soolchakan in complete shock (and there were several who were panicking in different ways).

The Commander stood up. "KILL THAT INTRUDING ALIEN!"

Soolchakan and Bonarain both could only think of one… thing at the moment: "Oops!"

Before Soolchakan could think of the imagery to hop himself back to Spy, one of the Security personnel on the ship pulled out a pulse weapon of some type, aimed and fired. Soolchakan did not know where it came from, however, some kind of new imagery filled his head. The beam from the pulse weapon hit him and it felt as if his entire body was covered with some kind of stinging insects and fire. He inadvertently held his hands out as if to make an attempt at blocking the beam. Instead, rays came shooting out of the tips of his fingers and went back at the man shooting at Soolchakan. The torso of the alien became nothing but red mist spraying all over the place. Dismembered arms, legs and head flew off in different directions. The red mist might have splattered on the wall behind the man, however, that part of the wall was equally destroyed. On the other side of the wall was a corridor and the wall on the opposite side of the corridor suffered equal damage.

Bonarain saw Soolchakan pull off some kind of counter-attack with the pulse ray and she ran towards him. Another Security man fired his pulse weapon at Soolchakan and once again the ray was diverted back at the shooter. His body was splattered into a red mist and all of the desks, consoles and personnel behind him suffered equally in being shattered into small pieces of debris. Bonarain reached Soolchakan, grabbed him and hopped him back into Spy.

Soolchakan shrieked in agony as he held his hands up close to his body in a great deal of pain. He could not clench his fists. He simply held limp hands up to his chest as he clenched his teeth and screamed in pain several more times.

Bonarain looked at his gloved hands and noticed that the tips of the fingers of the gloves were burned away and smoldering.

He now attempted to get the gloves off, however, his hands were limp and were not cooperating at all. She pulled the gloves off of his hands and noticed that the tips of his fingers were much darker than what they should have been.

She was pretty much shaken herself. "What did you... how did you...WHAT HAPPENED?!"

He looked down at his hands. "I...don't know. I...got some...strange imagery in my head...and...when he fired...I... don't know what happened! I...somehow...just willed the energy...from the beam to go...back where it came from. I also know that my FINGERS ARE IN AGONY!"

She was taken aback. "Uh...imagery? What imagery? Can you...give it to me?"

He hugged his limp hands up to his chest and closed his eyes. He tried to concentrate on that same imagery...and send it to her. He opened his eyes. "There's too much noise. I can't concentrate."

She huffed. "Let's go to Observation...and try it there."

He nodded and they both hopped to Observation.

In the silence he now was able to send her the imagery. They both had to close their eyes in order to not be distracted by all of the pandemonium being created by the crewmembers running amok, looking for the intruder.

She cleared her throat and looked a little perplexed. "That *is*...different." She closed her eyes and licked her lips as she ran it through her mind several times. She opened her eyes and looked around rather concerned. "Only one way to find out." She hopped to Home dimension.

One of the Security personnel pointed at Bonarain. "There's another one!" He aimed his pulse weapon and fired.

Bonarain absorbed the impact of the ray, held her hands out towards the man who fired and rays shot out of her fingers (blowing the fingertips of her gloves off) and blasting that man into another display of red mist…while demolishing everything behind where he had been standing. She hopped back to Observation and now it was her turn to scream in pain.

Soolchakan had a little feeling back in his hands (other than pain), however, they were not fully functional yet. He had to use a double pawing method to assist her in getting her smoldering gloves off. "Let's get back to Spy dimension…get in our fighters… and get out of here. We need to figure this thing out!"

She looked at him smirking. "Really," she said sarcastically through clenched teeth?

"Do you have an extra set of gloves in your fighter?"

"Yes, we all do…remember…Shaffani ordered us to keep some extra equipment in our fighters…gloves are on that list."

He nodded. "Yes, she did do that. Let's go!"

They climbed in their fighters and had a difficult time donning the extra set of gloves. They watched around them as pandemonium was the rule of the moment. All of the crew of the ship were looking under desks, behind some removable panels and everywhere else, trying to find the two intruders who had blasted holes in the ship with rays from their hands. They finished the arduous task, started their fighters, closed the canopies and took off.

Once outside the ship Soolchakan was not really sure that he wanted Kiyalee and Chyning to go back so soon. **"This is Soolchakan. Kiyalee and Chyning, if you want to blow up a few more ships…go ahead and do it. Bonarain and I have to get back to Hardooth. We have something that we…have to figure out."**

Chyning came back slightly upset. **"How many of these ships should we blast? I mean do you want the whole bunch dead…or what**?"

"Keep blasting them until they turn tail and run at full speed. We've given them something to think about…and tell some pretty tall tales once they get back…home…or wherever they may be going."

Kiyalee sighed. **"If that's the case…we'll take turns. You blast one then I'll blast one…until they blast off out of here."**

Chyning shrugged. **"Sounds good."**

Bonarain interjected. **"Don't blast the flagship! They were the witnesses to what just happened. They're the ones who'll be telling the tall tales. We want *them* to be able to get back and tell what happened."**

Kiyalee huffed. **"So, what happened**?"

Soolchakan responded. **"*That* is what we're going**

back to figure out for ourselves."

Both Kiyalee and Chyning came back with a very loud **"WHAT?"**

Soolchakan sighed. **"We'll tell you all about it…later. For now, go knock a few of them out of the sky**."

Chyning snarled. **"I can hardly wait to hear this one**."

"Me too," sent Kiyalee angrily.

Four more ships were blown up before the remnants of the task force fired up their engines and departed in great haste. With the same amount of haste, Kiyalee and Chyning Jumped back to Hardooth for some kind of explanation to the enigmatic statements made by their colleagues.

Soolchakan and Bonarain were in the main apartment, nursing their scorched fingertips. They were both going over the imagery in their minds. When Kiyalee and Chyning entered, they started doing some mind reading and they were now privy to the imagery that was in question.

After seeing it at least four times in the minds of the others Chyning was getting very impatient (as usual). "So what is this *h'oolyach* that you keep going over? I'm not familiar with it…at all."

Soolchakan sighed. "With this imagery, that I have no idea where it came from, I was shot with a pulse weapon by one of those aliens."

Kiyalee was shocked and thoroughly confused. "And how are you still *alive*?"

He gave her a disgusted look. "Somehow...I absorbed the energy from the beam and..." He held up his hands to show the fingertips. "...fired the energy beam back at them...by sheer will power."

"With devastating results," said Bonarain. "The one who fired the weapon was pulverized and liquefied in less than a heartbeat...along with the wall behind him...and a wall on the other side of a corridor. Another one of them fired another beam at him and...that one was totally dismembered as well...along with several computers, desks and everything...and everyone else that was behind that man."

He looked up from his fingers. "Then...she tried it after I gave her the imagery. She did...pretty much the same thing to one of them. That stopped them from firing at us because they were suffering a far worse situation than what we were."

Chyning blew a raspberry. "*H'oolyach!*"

"I don't believe it either," said Kiyalee.

Soolchakan let out a frustrated growl. "We're going to have to prove it to them."

Bonarain smiled at the other two women. "If I have to burn my fingers again...I guarantee you that the two of you are going to burn your fingers as well...seeing as how you're doubting us."

Soolchakan sighed. "All of us hop to Spy...and Jump to the top of the gorge."

The three women did the hop and Jump and started looking

around for Soolchakan. He came up a few moments later carrying a pulse pistol.

He looked around. "Do you see anyone up here? I'd hate to have an audience while we try this out."

All four of them scanned in all directions. They saw no one.

Bonarain sniffed. "I guess that we can go ahead and hop to Home dimension. We can't hit anything in Home if we're in Spy."

The four of them performed the hop.

He smiled at Bonarain. "Since I did it twice already and you've only done it once, you get to be the one who demonstrates it to the others."

She sniffed. "That's okay, because I wanted to try something anyway."

He frowned. "Like what?"

"We aimed our fingertips at the…enemy. Suppose we do it with the hands open wide. I think that with a larger area throwing the beam back at them…it should hurt us less…at least that's what I'm hoping."

He pondered and nodded. "Sounds good. Let me know when you're ready…and what your target is."

She pointed to a very large boulder. "I'll aim at that. I think that it'll give a good demonstration…of how destructive this reverse beam can be."

He started moving to the other side of the boulder.

Bonarain huffed. "Where are you going?"

"Upwind of the thing! I don't want any of the dust blowing back on me."

She licked a finger and stuck it in the air to test the wind. She shrugged, nodded in approval and followed him.

Kiyalee and Chyning both looked completely disgusted. Neither one believed that they could reverse a pulse beam after being hit with it. They wondered just how far the joke was going to go before admitting that they were fabricating a big one. They followed with very skeptical looks on their faces.

Bonarain took a deep breath. "Now...put that thing on a low setting...in case the pulse beams from this are different from those Chinchisossok."

Soolchakan adjusted the weapon and prepared to shoot her. Even he looked a little uneasy regarding this experiment.

She closed her eyes and did a little more deep breathing. She held her hands out with the palms aimed at the boulder. "Go ahead!"

He fired. Kiyalee and Chyning both gasped. They were stunned. They did not think that he would do it or that she would allow herself to be used that way.

Chyning huffed. "Hold on! That was the lowest setting and..."

At that moment two rays of light came out of Bonarain's palms and hit the boulder. There was no great explosion. There was a slight breeze that blew some dust off of the boulder.

Chyning now looked a little startled. "How…did you do that? Was that some kind of change from that Kalash trick?"

Bonarain ignored the question. "Put the setting up a little higher. Maybe the output is equal to the input."

Soolchakan pondered the thought for a moment. "Very possible." He moved the setting to approximately 30% power. He aimed the weapon. "Ready?"

Bonarain aimed her palms at the boulder again and sighed. "Go ahead."

He pulled the trigger again.

Kiyalee and Chyning were both ready to voice a protest, however, it came too late and now they once again saw the beams coming out of her hands. This time the beams were a little more powerful. There was a place on the boulder where some dirt had settled and a weed was growing out of the dirt. The weed was seared to a crisp and the ashes were blown away.

Bonarain nodded. "It is exactly that. The output is equal to the input. Set it a little higher."

He was still uncomfortable about doing this, however, he did remember how he had blown two of the aliens away along with everything behind them. He turned the setting up to 55%. He cleared his throat. "What about the pain? Are you…having any pains…in your hands from the…exit beams?"

"I barely felt the first one. The second one…was a little warm. It was warm but not uncomfortable."

He looked down at the weapon. "Are you ready?"

She aimed her palms at the boulder again. She took a breath. "Go ahead."

Kiyalee and Chyning were standing there with wide eyes and hanging jaws as he fired again. There was a strange crackling sound coming from the boulder for the briefest moment. There were two cracks in the boulder where the beams had hit. The area around the cracks was a little charred.

Bonarain clicked her tongue. "That tingled a lot more… and felt a lot warmer. Warmer but again…not uncomfortable." She closed her eyes and sighed. "Full power this time." She clenched her teeth and aimed her palms at the boulder again.

He looked down at the weapon and slowly moved the power up to 100%. He was even more nervous now. He aimed the weapon at Bonarain. "Remember that…it is full power. Let me know…when."

She raised her hands and clenched her teeth. "Go!"

He fired. Her entire body started glowing. That was something he did not remember seeing when they were on the ship. Two blinding beams shot out of her palms and the entire top of the boulder disintegrated into dust. The vast majority of the dust was blown away from the foursome by the wind and the force of the blast.

Bonarain was flapping her hands trying to cool them down with a pained look on her face. "Hot! Hot! Hot!"

Kiyalee and Chyning slowly walked over to the remains of the boulder. The top was gone and there were two grooves where her palm beams had directly hit the rock.

Chyning swallowed hard and looked at Kiyalee. "They weren't joking."

Kiyalee just stood there shaking her head. She tried to say something, however, no sound came out of her mouth as her lips moved.

Soolchakan sniffed as he looked at the remnants of the rock. "Did it burn as badly as it did...on the ship?"

Bonarain sucked air in through her clenched teeth then blew on her hands. "It burned...but not as bad!"

He nodded. "So the more of our body we use...to expel the power...the less it burns."

"Seems that way," said Bonarain as she was now looking at her palms for any searing or scarring. She kept blowing on her palms in an attempt at cooling them off.

He sighed. He handed the weapon to Bonarain. "All right...I'll give it a bigger test. Let me see...if I can send the beam out...with more of my body...other than just my hands." He reached down and flipped his red stone behind his back. He held his arms out wide and faced what was left of the boulder. He sniffed. "Anytime you're ready."

Bonarain aimed the weapon and fired.

He clenched his teeth as he tried to hold the power for a few more heartbeats. His body felt as if he were on fire. He finally pushed the power out using his full arms and upper torso as the firing point. A huge beam came out and blasted what was left of the boulder…and the ground where it had been sitting.

The three women walked over to the beginning of the four taja wide trench that had been seared into the earth. The cone shaped trench was over forty taja in length and was much deeper at the far end. They slowly turned back to Soolchakan and noticed that his chest was steaming and his shirt was gone. The front had been burned off. The back simply fell to the ground because there was nothing to hold it in place any more, with the entire front gone.

He turned around and picked the remains of his shirt up off the ground. It was just the back of the shirt as the front was nothing but ashes. "I think…that if we're going to use…full body…in order to expel any power beam like that…we had better take a good look at our wardrobe…and see if we can find something that can take the…*heat*."

Bonarain snickered. She looked at the other two women. "Which one of you wants to try it next?"

Chyning backed away holding her hands up and shaking them. "No, no, no, no, no, no! I'm not…ready for…anything like that."

Kiyalee swallowed hard. "Do…I have to…even think about it?"

Soolchakan sighed. "It is a powerful defense for us that we can turn to something offensive against…anybody. You both are going to learn it. Do I have to use the *Voice* in order to make you comply?"

Kiyalee sighed. Her shoulders sagged. She walked up to Bonarain. "Give me the imagery, again. I suppose…it is a pretty good defense. If we can turn their weapons against them and survive…that's a whole lot better than the *other* option."

While Bonarain gave Kiyalee the imagery, Chyning was still standing off a little to the side, still looking at the other three as if they had lost their minds.

After giving the imagery three times Bonarain huffed in disgust. "The imagery is *not* gonna change! You *will* have to try it…sooner or later. You might as well get it done…now."

Kiyalee had a look of desperation on her face. She walked over to a smaller boulder taking several controlled breaths as she faced the rock. She swallowed nervously. "Okay…I'll try it… BUT ON A LOW SETTING!"

Soolchakan had a slight problem holding back a laugh. He coughed a little to disguise it. "That's…fine. I'll knock it down… to the lowest setting. You can get used to it…easily that way."

Kiyalee aimed her palms at the new rock. She bit her lip as she prepared the imagery in her head. Her voice was shaking as she was talking herself into the procedure. "All…right I'm… ready…to try…it. GO!"

Soolchakan actually had the weapon on 20%. The lowest setting was 4%, however, he did not think that a setting that low would be a proper learning mode. He fired a short burst.

Kiyalee gasped and her body started glowing. Two beams shot out of her palms, hit and shattered the boulder. A few smaller rocks that were on the boulder flew off away from Kiyalee and the big rock. She brought her hands down and her entire body was shuddering as if she were attempting to swipe thousands of insects off of herself. "That…is WEIRD! I don't…know…what to… say…"

Bonarain smiled. "What, you don't know what to say about that unique sensation?"

Kiyalee looked at her wide-eyed. "YEAH! Unique… *sensation*. Good words." She shuddered again.

Soolchakan adjusted the weapon. "Would you like to try a higher setting?"

Kiyalee looked at him fearfully. "I guess…I might as well…get it out of the way."

He adjusted it to 70%. "Whenever you're ready…let me know."

Kiyalee faced the remains of the boulder again. She wrung her hands a little and then held them up. She bit her lower lip. "Wait…wait…wait…NOW!"

He fired. Her body had a brilliant glow around it as she absorbed the energy. The beams then shot out of her palms and the remains of the boulder were turned into a dust storm.

Kiyalee turned to Soolchakan still holding her hands outstretched. "What was that…setting?"

"70%."

She shook her head rapidly. "I tried it…but…I…I…

I'm not ready for 100%...not yet…no, not yet…not now." She continued shaking her head.

Bonarain was ready to admonish her for quitting.

Soolchakan interrupted. "She tried it and now she knows it." He cleared his throat and turned his gaze to Chyning.

The other two women turned to Chyning with patronizing looks.

Chyning had a look on her face like a defiant and disobedient child. She looked around as if she were trying to come up with a good excuse for not attempting this new phenomenon. She scowled as she walked up to Bonarain. "Gimme the *chokwad* imagery," she muttered bitterly.

Once again the imagery was given three times before Chyning was ready to attempt it. She now gave Soolchakan another dirty look. "I'll bet you're really enjoying shooting us, aren't you?"

He sighed. "This is a new defense. It is a very powerful weapon against any enemy as well. Plus, it'll give them one nasty surprise, just like it surprised those *bimyocks* that we already blasted."

Chyning scoffed. "It's a weapon against someone with *power* weapons. What about someone with projectile weapons?"

"We always have Spy dimension…or Ghost," said Soolchakan flatly.

Chyning turned to a very large dead tree that was approximately fifteen taja from where she was. "Give me the full power. I might as well get it out of the way...now."

Soolchakan was not too sure of that idea. He adjusted the weapon to 85%. "Are you ready?"

Chyning aimed her palms at the tree. She took one deep controlled breath. "DO IT!"

He fired.

Her body started glowing and she let out a slight squawk of surprise. She suddenly brought her right hand down and aimed only the fingers of her left hand at the dead tree. The spot where she aimed was hit by the beams from her fingers and was blasted into splinters and sawdust. With that section of the tree blown away, the top of the tree started falling - towards the quartet.

"HOP TO SPY DIMENSION," hollered Soolchakan!

All four of them went to Spy as the big branches crashed around them in Home dimension. Three of them were very glad to be in Spy.

Chyning was holding her left hand up to her chest while she spun around in agony, spewing curses from all of the different languages that she had learned since the firestorm attack.

Soolchakan sighed. "Her education in foreign languages is really paying off," he said sarcastically. "She just let out a whole bunch of cussing in at least forty languages."

Bonarain gave him a disgusted look, closed her eyes and shook her head. "Why is it that everyone wants to learn that stuff first?"

Kiyalee stood there smiling. "You learn that so that you can cuss someone out and they don't know whether they've been cussed or complimented. They don't know how to react, they just stand there confused," she said merrily. "Too confused to admit they're confused."

Chyning vanished.

Bonarain looked around confused. "Where'd she go?"

Kiyalee snickered. "If it burns as badly as you said…she's probably looking for something that'll cool her fingers off."

Soolchakan shrugged. "Either the kitchen sink or the bathroom sink."

Bonarain scoffed. "She only has 6,900 apartments to choose from."

The three of them Jumped to their regular apartment – 12-562. They heard water running in the kitchen, as well as some grunts and squawks of pain. They walked into the kitchen and hopped back to Home dimension.

Bonarain shook her head. "Told yah! The bigger the area that you deploy the energy, the less the pain…and the less the damage to your body."

Chyning pulled her hand out of the flow of cold water. They all saw that the tips of her fingers looked somewhat charred, especially the index finger.

"You might be scarred for life," said Bonarain. "I hope that you learned a valuable lesson from that."

Chyning just sneered and then winced as she put her fingers back in the flow of the cold water.

Her fingers were changed forever. She had no more finger pads on her left hand. The fingernails were somewhat deformed and both were things she had to live with because she did not believe that it could possibly be as painful as the others had described...until she found out for herself.

7

In the Spring of the year 15 ATUT, the four Owlamites were still trying to get used to the new types of measurement that had been decided on by the committee at the great summit in Blasinigan, Capitol of Paselter. Soolchakan was muddling over it while Bonarain sat at another table eating a makka melon and was snickering a little over his tribulations.

"Every one of them agreed to this…fifteen years ago," mumbled Soolchakan. "I wish they had come up with something…a little easier."

"That's why it took so long," said Bonarain cheerfully. "No one could agree on *anything* that anyone came up with in the first ten years."

He shook his head. "I can understand that. I imagine that each one of them…tried to use the measurements *they'd* grown up with…in *their* homeland." He sighed. "Maybe if we'd gone to that convention and did some mind control…some of this would be according to our normal measurements and…we wouldn't have such a problem with any of these measurements…or words."

"They still use bushels to measure grains and baskets to measure fruit, vegetables and tubers." She shrugged. "Is that so hard?"

"No," he grumbled. "The liquid and dry measurements aren't so hard either. Ten spoons to a cup, ten cups to a pitcher, ten pitchers to a bucket and ten buckets to a barrel. That part is easy enough. Temperature! Who decided on...this? Water freezes at 8 degrees Abfar and it boils at 104 degrees Abfar. Why such off beat numbers? WEIRD! Then there is...time. One...*Mith*... equals one heartbeat. 100 Miths is 1 Mithist. 100 Mithist equals 1 Mithpell and...10 Mithpell in one day."

"They all agreed to it," said Bonarain as she stuffed some more melon into her mouth.

'I wish she'd stop saying that,' he thought. "Then this... distance...measurement. One Teck is...what?"

She swallowed and shook her head. "One Teck is equal to one half of a decitaja."

He nodded. "So...it takes two Teck to make one decitaja." Then it takes 100 Teck to make a Teckist and 100 Teckist to a Teckpell and 100 Teckpell to make a Teckfar."

She nodded with a patronizing smile on her face. "That's what they decided on."

"You don't have to be so smug about it," he grumbled. "I've seen you go to that new table...in order to figure it out for yourself."

"I do...yes. I still go to that list...but I don't whine about it."

He tried to change the subject. "This...calendar stuff. That seems a lot easier. Even though they interrupt some of the months…with these other days…they could have numbered just as easily."

She frowned. "What interruptions?"

He huffed. "Look at the first year – the year 1…ATUT. It didn't start on the first day of the month of Statichy…it started on the Fall Equinox. The *next* day was the first day of Statichy. Then there are thirty days in that month. The second month – Whegire is thirty days with no interruptions. The third month – Strebale goes 29 days and then is interrupted by the Winter Solstice. Then after the Solstice, we have day number 30 of Strebale. The next three months – Roistume, Lergan and Marrem are each thirty days uninterrupted. Then comes Zerbolud. Once again, the first day is the Spring Equinox. The second day of Zerbolud is actually Zerbolud the first. Then in the eighth month – Citendali, we have fifteen days. Then an interruption they labeled as the High Holy Day. The day after is the sixteenth and on until we have thirty days. The ninth month – Tulivren is uninterrupted. The tenth month – Thorinale does not start on the first, it starts on the Summer Solstice. The next day is the first. Then comes the eleventh month – Inamyon with no interruptions…just thirty days. Then the twelfth month – Consoray has no interruptions but it has thirty-*one* days. There are actually six months that have thirty-one days, however, only one actually calls it thirty-*one* days. The others have those silly interruptions of the Fall Equinox, the Winter Solstice, Spring Equinox, Summer Solstice and…the High Holy Day! We have five days during the year that are not days, they're events! What is that High Holy Day for?"

She snickered. "That day is the day that everyone in the

world…can practice their religion…without anyone questioning the reason that it is being done on that day. Many of the religions have certain holy days they practice that…gets in the way of commerce and a few other things. By having one day…where everyone in the world can celebrate without anyone questioning it…that was decided by that committee."

He nodded and sighed. "Then the days. Initikoy, Gosskoy, Tadkoy, Hartkoy, Miviskoy, Leegkoy and Astekoy. Why seven days? Weren't there some places where…they went with a ten day week?"

She sighed and shrugged. "The majority voted on a seven day week. It did upset a few nations but remember…they sent those people there to decide on one system. Once that system was agreed on and voted into existence…everyone had to accept it or… they might suffer some kind of nasty chastisement for wanting to be so different, or, they would have to go through all the trouble of conversions. Plus, they'd have to do some quick figuring, if they wanted to get it in line with the others. The easiest way was for everyone to accept the same system."

"It still amazes me…with all of the technology that was destroyed by all of those alien attacks how they could still remember that it takes 366 days for Hardooth to complete one orbit around Holgotho…equaling one year. They didn't have to vote on that."

She chuckled. "They couldn't change the laws of physics… or astrophysics. It is something that has been known for several millennium. All of those enemies may have been able to destroy their computers and all of their other electronic gadgets but they couldn't destroy the common knowledge of how long one year is."

"So you're siding with that committee and not the way that we always practiced it."

"What's wrong with that? At least that way…everybody, including us, we're all on the same page."

He sneered at her. "I just don't like the way that you say it. You seem to be acting prudish." He turned away from her and continued reviewing some of the items on the list of measurements. He sighed. "No matter what, I still have to get used to it…all of it."

She was tired of (what she considered) his complaints. She decided to teach him a nasty lesson. She put another spoonful of the melon in her mouth, stood up and silently walked over to him. She reached to the back of her neck and got some of that bothersome mucus from the scales on her neck. She reached around and smeared the mucus all over his face. She went back to her seat wiping the rest of the mucus on her pants while snickering. She had given him something to really think about. She sat down to finish her melon. She looked back at him smugly and was totally shocked by the look on his face. There was a wild look in his eyes and he was bent over pulling at his crotch. She got back up and started backing away from him fearfully not knowing what might happen or what to expect because of that insane look in his eyes.

"**Get back over here**," he snarled.

He had used the *Voice of Power*. She had no choice but to comply. She started walking back to him. He reached his left hand up behind his neck. She grimaced in horror and closed her eyes because she knew what was going to happen. She had smeared her mucus on his face. Something that had never been done by any Owlamite to another. Now she knew that she was going to get a very unwelcome "facial" with his mucus.

She felt his mucus being rubbed all over her face…and she nearly went into shock. Suddenly her heart began racing. She felt some cramping in her abdomen. Cramping that she had not felt since…her last menstruation period…over 9,000 years ago. There was a burning between her legs as well. She felt as if she would die if she did not have sex right now. She was wondering just where she would find a man to do it with seeing as how he was impotent.

Then she opened her eyes. He had dropped his pants and she could see that he had an erection. She did not know how or why all she knew was that she needed to have sex with him…right now. She could not get her pants off fast enough.

Bonarain woke up feeling incredibly tired…and very hungry. She felt her eyes and nose burning from the stench of raw sewage. She sat up. She looked around trying to assess what was going on with all of the strange manifestations. She had just awakened from sleeping – why was she so tired…and hungry? Before Soolchakan had copulated with her she had just eaten over half of a makka melon, so, why was she so ravenous? Why did her entire bedroom have the unwelcome stench of a very old outhouse?

She was in her bed. She was in her bedroom. She was

in apartment 12-562 in the gorge. Soolchakan was snoozing in the same bed to her right. The mucus that he had spread on her face was dry and caked. The bed was soaked with urine and both she and Soolchakan were laying in their own feces, a lot of feces. More feces than either one of them could conjure up in one day.

She punched Soolchakan to wake him up. He stirred and growled. She was rather irate. "WAKE UP," she croaked! She hit him again harder.

He sat up with a start. "What...what's going on...why are you in bed with...whose bed is this...and what's that smell?" He was looking around rather baffled.

"You're in my bed...in my bedroom...with me...and you left your *h'oolyach* all over my bed." She gave her oration with clenched teeth.

He stared at her still looking very confused. "You... smacked me...in the face with your...mucus. I...almost immediately...got an erection! For the first time in...over 9,000 years...I got an *erection*."

"Then you smeared your...mucus...all over my face."

He frowned. "Then...we both dropped our pants and we..." He looked around the room. "I don't remember coming up here to the bedroom."

"I don't either," she said sadly. "But we did! And now... my bed...is...a sewer."

He shook his head. "I am...*sooo* hungry." He got up off of the bed.

"DON'T WALK AROUND LIKE THAT! All of that… *h'oolyach* is dropping off of you…and you're…tracking it all over the room."

He looked at his feces covered body. "How could we have…done this much…in just one night?" He stepped up on the bed. He hopped to Ghost – minus the fecal matter. The feces fell back onto the bed.

She snarled in anger. "Why are you putting that stuff back on the bed?"

He hopped back to Home dimension and snarled back at her. "One: The bed is already covered with it and you're going to have to replace the mattress anyway! Two: You don't want me walking around here tracking it all over the room. Isolating the stuff in one place is the best way to do it. The bed is already covered and *imbedded* with it." He huffed at her. "Right now, I'm going to wash my hands…and get…SOMETHING…to eat. I'm so hungry, my big guts are eating my little guts!"

She looked away in disgust and scoffed. "How can you think of eating…before cleaning yourself?"

"I'M HUNGRY! I'm very, very hungry!" He headed for the door. "I *am* going to wash my hands, at the very least, I'm going to shove…*something*…down my throat. Then I'm going to that Zhozhick ship that we captured and take a shower in that special decontamination chamber. That'll clean me off a lot faster, and better, than taking a shower here in my bathroom."

She sat there for a moment doing a little considering of what he had just said. Yes, the mattress was absolutely going to be replaced. It was beyond cleaning. Yes, she was extremely hungry as well. That decontamination chamber sounded very good right now. She decided that she was going to get decontaminated first - then eat. She hopped the mattress (with all the mess) to outer space in #45. She hopped to the Zhozhick ship in #45. She set the decontamination chamber for a full body cleansing. She stepped in the chamber and clenched her eyes shut. She knew that it would start at the top and she wanted that caked mucus off of her face... now.

He Jumped to the main room on the first floor of the apartment. The smell in here was just as bad as the smell in her bedroom, however, it was a completely different odor. He saw the melon she had been eating was sitting there rotting. He touched the rotten melon with one finger and hopped the nasty thing into outer space in dimension #2. The smell in the room improved instantly...a little. He went to the kitchen. He washed his hands up to the elbows – three times – before even thinking of opening a refrigerator.

He found two ripe crimson a*ntaya* fruits and gobbled them down, seeds and all. He saw a *denshiga* fruit and it was gone in a very short time as well. With the *denshiga*, he did spit out the seeds because they were rather large and very hard to swallow because they were covered with spikes.

With some of the juices of the fruit dripping down his face his stomach did feel a little better. He hopped to #45 to the ship with the decontamination chamber. He saw that Bonarain was already in there getting cleaned off. He hit the full body cleansing for himself and stepped in another chamber with his eyes clenched shut.

While his face was being sprayed he decided to mentally communicate. "**Bonarain, I'm trying to figure out exactly what happened.**"

She clenched her teeth tighter. "**I** *don't* **want to talk to you right now!**"

"**Well we** *are* **going to talk about it NOW. Whether you want to or not! Any questions?**"

She eased up on her aching jaw. "**Okay, what did you want to talk about?**" She did not really want to even think about it, however, she knew that he could use the *Power* and make her do it anyway. She figured that she might as well get it out of the way, now.

"**As soon as you...vandalized my face with your mucus...I got an erection. For the first time in over 9,000 years I got an erection! What happened to you...when I avenged myself for the...facial...mucking?**"

She sighed. "**It felt...as if...for the first time in over 9,000 years...that...I menstruated...or ovulated. I had those nasty cramps that always went with it and then... for some reason...I felt as if I were going to die if I didn't have...intercourse...right then!**"

He shook his head sadly. "**It sounds as if...that has been the secret all along. We were always capable of... procreation...but...we were always too polite to...hit someone else...with that nasty neck muck.**"

She groaned. **"That means…that any and all of us… could have had children…9,000 years ago."**

"And every year since."

"With a three to one ratio of women to men, there would have been a lot of very lonely women."

He chuckled. **"What if one of the *Voice of Power* had authorized, seeing as how it was a three to one ratio, polygamy?"**

She shrugged. **"Then polygamy would have been accepted and legal…if one of them had authorized or ordered it."**

"And we would have been forced to make a much larger apartment area in the gorge…a very long time ago."

"Yup! The problem now…only one man and only three women. Who would Kiyalee and Chyning mate with? There are only four of us. That makes for an incredibly small and unacceptable gene pool."

"Yes it does. So now we have a new problem. We can…have sex…but…what happens to the love life of any children?"

"If I have a son…he could…wed either Kiyalee or Chyning but…there is still the problem that…your genes will be…in all offspring…no matter what."

He stood there laughing as he was being sprayed down. It was difficult keeping his mouth shut while the full body spraying was going on. "**Do you think that either Kiyalee or Chyning would want to wed a man who is NINE THOUSAND YEARS younger than they?**"

She chuckled. "**Not a chance. I wouldn't.**"

"**Another thing that's bothering me...why did we wake up...so tired and wallowing in our own excretions?**"

She scoffed. "**If that is what sex is for us...I really don't want to do it again, ever. That was just...too nasty.**"

He sighed. "**I think that it had something to do with how long we were asleep. We didn't just go to sleep after copulating and then...awaken the next morning. I think we were out a little longer than that.**"

She shook her head in disbelief. "**That's ridiculous!**"

"**Weren't you eating a *makka* melon, just before you did that nasty assault...on my face?**"

She mentally rolled her eyes. "**Yes, I was eating a *makka* melon! What does that have to do with anything?**"

"**How long does it take for a *makka* melon to... rot...after cutting it, but not eating it?**"

Seeing as how the decontamination was finished with the upper part of her body and was now spraying everything below the ribcage, she opened her eyes and looked over at him as if he had lost his mind. She still had to keep her arms up or the machine would admonish her for dropping them and blocking the decontamination process. She could not figure out why, all of a sudden, he was so interested in that silly melon. **"WHO CARES ABOUT THAT MELON?"**

He was a little displeased with her evasion. He decided to ask…using the *Power*. **"What is the method in which a *makka* melon rots? How fast does it rot and when does it turn those nasty colors and start stinking?"**

She was taken by surprise by his use of the *Power*, however, she still had to comply. **"A *makka* melon starts going through the rotting stages almost immediately. That's why you have to eat the thing just after cutting it. The first stage is a bitter taste…after about half a day it is really bitter. The second stage is that the flesh turns from orange to blue…and is somewhat translucent. That is after a full day. By the end of the second day, the flesh has turned brown and starts to stink. At the end of the third day, it is turning black and will stink up the entire house. If you don't get rid of it, then it will start to grow black hairs that are full of some very nasty bacterium, according to what Doctor Shurmook told us, initially about the melon."**

He nodded his head. **"Thank you. That really didn't hurt a bit to tell me that, did it? When I went downstairs, to get something to eat…that melon was black and had a really foul smell…that stunk up the entire room and it had some hair like things all over. That means that we were unconscious for a full three full days…after copulation."**

She stood there in shock. Her arms involuntarily dropped

and the machine instantly started talking in that electronic voice, telling her to get her arms back up. She raised her arms with a grunt of exasperation. **"But…how…I don't understand if we were…HOW?"**

He pondered for a moment. **"If you could come up with a complete sentence, I might be able to respond… with a complete sentence."**

"You said that the melon was growing black hairs and…very smelly. Yes, because of that, I have to admit that…we were unconscious for three days. I just don't understand…how we could have possibly…been that tired…after one…episode…with sex."

He was finally able to open his eyes as his decontamination continued down his body. He sighed. **"How long…were we… in the…act of sex? I remember starting…the deed. I just don't remember finishing. I remember that I was extremely tired…after a while but…I just couldn't stop… doing…*it*."**

She looked back at him rather ill at ease. **"I…remember that you were going at it for a really long time…and…I… didn't want you…to stop. I…don't remember…when you finished…doing…*it*…either."**

He shook his head. **"How do you remember it…from before the firestorm attack?"**

She clenched her teeth. **"If we were asleep…for three days…then that means that today is the twelfth day of the month of Citendali in year of 15 ATUT. You…attacked** me...on the ninth day of Citendali. Up until the ninth day of Citendali...I was a virgin. I never...," she sucked her lips in. "You know what I mean."

He closed his eyes, shook his head and let out a slight growl of frustration. "So you have nothing to fall back on as far as what it might have been like...9,000 years ago?"

She gave him a patronizing look. "That's what I just said."

"I don't remember ever having any...three day...sexual epic event." He shook his head. "I don't remember ever thinking that something like that was even possible. I remember a few *bimyocks* who, in a drunken stupor, made up some kind of tall braggadocio tale, but, I never really believed it possible."

She chuckled. "I don't think that it was, or still is, possible for any Heyyah. As Owlamites, we just experienced it...and...it seems that it is possible...for an Owlamite...because you...uh...we just did it."

He nodded. "So, on the ninth day of Citendali in the year 15 ATUT, we just had sex...for the first time...by any Owlamite...and I'm wondering if that is what would or could have happened...all along."

She nodded back. "That's what happened. Whether we like it or not...that IS what just happened."

"What do we tell...Kiyalee and Chyning about this...epic tryst?"

"**We tell them the truth. It's not like…we intended to deceive or…hurt either one of them. Not one of us…ever smacked each other in the face with…our… neck mucus. In 9,000 years we were all so polite about keeping our nasty mucus…off of others. Now…we find out that…the nasty mucus…is part of the secret of…our species.**"

He lowered his head and growled. "**I guess that you can learn new things, no matter how old you get. And you decided to be the first to be so impolite as to purposefully get your *h'oolyach* on someone else.**"

"**Yup!**" She flushed and shook her head sadly.

He gave her a side glance. "**You said…that you did… all of a sudden have…a period…for the first time since the firestorm. Is it a possibility that…you're…with child?**"

She stood there in shock. She could not think or talk. The thought of getting pregnant that quickly was not really within the realms of reality…for any Heyyah. She was no longer Heyyah, she was Owlam. Seeing as how this was the first time any Owlamites had copulated, she could not give any form of an educated guess. A completely wild asinine guess was in the realm of possibility. "**I don't know. Since…this is the first time…that any Owlamites have…copulated…I absolutely don't know.**"

"**Okay, give it a few months…and then…you should know for sure.**"

She swallowed hard. "**A…few months…yes…I**

should know…then." The decontamination was finished. Now she was covered with the slick dripping goo, whatever that gooey stuff was, when the decontamination was done. Now she headed for the shower to clean the goo off. She stepped in the shower and started cleaning herself off. "**Please don't tell either Kiyalee or Chyning…until I'm certain**."

He shrugged and sighed. "**I'll keep quiet. I'll let you be the one who gives them the information…one way or another, what the outcome of this *event* turns out to be**."

"**Thank you**."

His decontamination was finished. He moved to a shower stall and they both finished all of the cleansing without another word of communication. After the shower was over they both went back to her room and got rid of any other mess still remaining in the room. After the room was aired out they both went to their computers to add some thoughts to their memoirs.

Memoir additions: Citendali 12, 15 ATUT. It was discovered that the mucus leaking out of the back of my neck is what makes the opposite sex of my race able to have sexual relations. We had sex that was so passionate and exhausting that we were asleep for three days. On Citendali 12, 15 ATUT we awoke and went over the event. Possibility of a pregnancy is…. He shook his head in aggravation. The first Owlam pregnancy in history. It is too bad that we did not know this information nine millennium ago. We might not be just four Owlamites. We could be millions…or possibly billions. Now it might be dangerous, because of such a tiny gene pool for us to perform any more procreation - if a child is the result of this odd union. So how do we use this new information for the benefit of our race?

Bonarain spent the next few days looking up anything and everything that she could find on pregnancy. She did not have any of the medical staff to assist her so she had to find out, on her own, all information regarding her possible condition.

Several times during those days she used her mind to perform a complete tour of her body. She mentally looked at every one of her internal organs, paying special attention to her uterus. She had done these body searches before, however, she had ignored her reproductive organs because it had seemed a waste of time because they were not doing anything. They were just there, taking up space in the lower part of her torso. Now, she wished she had paid more attention because at this time she did not know if there had been any changes. If she was pregnant then the changes would be obvious…if she had something to fall back on…from before the sexual episode.

The High Holy Day took place during the month of Citendali. That special event day always took place between the 15th and 16th of Citendali. The four Owlamites did celebrate the day with their normal religious rituals regarding the Great Maker. Kiyalee and Chyning did notice an unusual and different attitude in Bonarain, however, they did not make a big fuss because everyone gets moody every now and then.

Seven days after waking up from the epic escapade, Bonarain was mentally looking inside her womb. She suddenly found the tiniest little speck. It had been rather undetectable before this time…either that or she had just missed it because it was so small. It was there and…it was alive. She focused on the speck for quite a while before deciding to wait a little longer before any announcement was made. She was pretty certain that it was a zygote, however, she still wanted to wait until it grew a little more and started "taking shape" before absolutely declaring a positive on her pregnancy.

She went back to all of the medical information on gestation.

Nearly six weeks after the "event" the four Owlamites were sitting in the main room of their apartment having a meal together. After finishing what they were eating, Kiyalee and Chyning both sat there staring, rather perplexed, at Bonarain. Soolchakan tried to keep from staring because he was rather certain what had happened. He had promised that he would keep quiet and was doing just that. He was still burning with curiosity.

Bonarain finally noticed her audience. She glanced back and forth between Kiyalee and Chyning. "What?"

Chyning shook her head. "What is *wrong* with you?"

Bonarain frowned at her. "What *are* you talking about?"

"Your appetite," said Kiyalee. "You just finished a… *dinsamp* melon. A big one…all by yourself. I couldn't eat an entire one of those things…by myself…even on a dare. HOW?"

Bonarain tried to laugh it off. "I was…hungry."

Soolchakan leaned back in his chair. "Today is the twelfth day of Tulivren in the 15th year of ATUT. Maybe today…you should make a…*special*…announcement."

Kiyalee looked at Soolchakan. "Huh?"

Chyning snarled suspiciously. "Something is going on here. I wanna know *what*!"

Bonarain sighed. "Yes. It has been…six weeks…since…" She trailed off and cleared her throat.

Kiyalee was getting even more aggravated. "Since… WHAT?"

Bonarain huffed. "Back on the 9th of Citendali…we… Soolchakan and I…accidentally discovered…that the mucus coming out of our necks…has been the secret of…procreation… all along for…Owlamites."

Chyning looked very skeptical. "*H'oolyach*! What's really going on?"

Bonarain huffed again. "I'm pregnant!"

Kiyalee looked at Soolchakan. "But…you're impotent." She looked at Bonarain. "Who is the father? How could you possibly be pregnant…when you haven't had a menstrual period… since the firestorm?"

Soolchakan cleared his throat. "I am the father. The other day…or six weeks ago, she decided to get rudely facetious and she slapped me in the face with a handful of her neck mucus. I instantly achieved an erection. I slapped her in the face…with my neck mucus and neither one of us could…resist…having sex…

right then and there."

Kiyalee reached to the back of her neck and rubbed some of the mucus off. She held her hand out displaying the mucus on her middle finger. "Are you telling me that this...goo...is what would make me...have a period?"

He shook his head. "No. Your...*goo*...would make me have an erection. *My* goo...is what would make you...or any other female Owlamite...have a period." He licked his lips. "That is what happened. She, is now pregnant...as a result of that... event."

Chyning flopped back in her chair and folded her arms. "I don't believe it!"

Bonarain sighed. "You can say that now. In...about... seven...and a half months...I think...you'll change your mind."

"Probably sooner than that," said Soolchakan. "You'll probably start...*showing* in less time than that. From what I've read about...pregnancy...most women start showing about the fourth or fifth month. Definitely in the sixth month." He sniffed. "The only problem here is, we have no idea how long an Owlamite woman will...gestate. This is the very first Owlamite pregnancy and...there is just...so much...that we don't know."

Chyning belched. "I still don't believe it. If it is true... well...as you said...we'll see in a few months...whether you're... *showing*...or not." She huffed and shook her head.

Bonarain sighed. Her shoulders sagged as she nodded her head. "Yup!"

Bonarain continued looking into every medical journal that she could find. She had to give up on certain ones that gave specific information about alien species that had enormously different characteristics unique to their species. She did place a lot of her dependence on the ancient medical journals from Owlam that were all written prior to the firestorm attack. These gave all kinds of information on how long it took for the zygote to change to a fetus and the forming of all of the appendages and internal organs. After reading these items, for the fiftieth time, she started taking an even closer look at the child growing in her womb.

She found that the left leg was developing slower than the right. She used every bit of her will power to alter that mutation. One kidney was not developing properly. She changed that. The genitals were not – oh…I have a boy – she had to correct the way that the different parts were developing. She found a problem with the brainstem. She found a problem with the spleen. She found a problem with several other organs that she exhausted herself doing everything with her willpower to correct the anomalies.

She had to think of a lot of things regarding her unborn son. The only thing that she could think of was that somehow, he was developing abnormally because of some lingering effect from the firestorm weapons. The doctors had been worried about that residual energy. The energy had killed other mammals, birds, plants and insects long after the attack. The doctors could not see any disturbing results on the Owlamites. They had stated that the Owlamites were apparently immune to the dreadful things that were happening to other creatures. It still, somehow, was causing difficulty in the formation of a fetus…even after 9,000 years.

Day after day she would look over her son. If she found anything that was inconsistent with normal development (according to all of the recorded information) she did everything she could to use her willpower to correct the problem.

The 22nd day of Inamyon, 15 ATUT, and Kiyalee was staring at the lower abdomen area on Bonarain as she was preparing a meal for herself.

Bonarain noticed that stare because it had become habitual. "What's your problem?"

Kiyalee looked up. "What's *my* problem? No, what is *your* problem? Yes, I see your gut getting bigger, but, I think that's because of how much you're eating. Soolchakan killed one of those humpback bovines…and that gave us enough meat to last for at least three weeks…if all of us were eating normally. You… you ate practically an entire flank by yourself…over about five days. Then there was that thing with the *ninsaka* juice. I made a pitcher of it and Chyning made a pitcher. You guzzled both of them down in just one lousy day."

Bonarain flushed. "Yes, I drank both pitchers." She sniffed. "I…was thirsty and…the juice is delicious. Yes, I ate…a lot of the meat from that bovine. Remember…I am eating for two."

Kiyalee blew a raspberry. "*H'oolyach*! You're just getting fat from gluttony."

Bonarain stormed across the room with her teeth clenched and her arms held tightly at her sides. Kiyalee looked up in a condescending manner, ready to start some punches flying if Bonarain really wanted a physical confrontation.

Bonarain stopped about five paces from punching range and started sending some images. The images were of the fetus in her womb. Kiyalee was now in shock as she was actually seeing the partially developed fetus. The head, the body, the arms, the hands, the legs and feet...and the fact that it is definitely a boy. Kiyalee stood up with her jaw hanging and her eyes wide in wonder. Bonarain grabbed Kiyalee and their foreheads softly met. Now Kiyalee was getting images that were even clearer as to the developing child.

The images stopped and Bonarain backed away panting and perspiring heavily. "Now do you believe me?"

Kiyalee cleared her throat and chuckled nervously through her panting. "That...is...*real*? There is really...a little boy... growing...inside of you?"

Bonarain sat down, still panting. She wiped the perspiration from her forehead. "He's real! He is there...or here...in my womb. Now, do you believe me?"

Kiyalee flopped back down in her chair. "Uh...I...can't argue..." She looked down at the slight paunch in the lower abdomen area on Bonarain. "That really *is* a baby that's developing in you. YOU *ARE* PREGNANT!"

Bonarain sniffed. "I know. That's what I've been telling you all this time. I'm sixteen weeks along and...I still don't have a clue as to what the gestation period is for an Owlamite."

Kiyalee wrung her hands showing some uneasiness. "Why don't you...do what you just did...with Chyning? You convinced me...now that I've seen it...uh...*him*." She frowned. "What... are you going to name...him?"

Bonarain smiled. "I'm going to name him Shalam (*in Owlamite it means "Beginning"*)."

Kiyalee chuckled. "I still think...that you should have... done...what you just did to...both Chyning...and myself...a long time ago. Maybe then...we wouldn't be giving you such a hard time."

Bonarain looked at Kiyalee thoughtfully. "Could you call her? I'm still a little tired from the tour that I just gave you."

Kiyalee smiled. She closed her eyes and sent a mental message to Chyning. Chyning showed up a few moments later.

Chyning looked a little angry. "Are you really going to tell me that she convinced you about this mythical baby?"

Bonarain started sending the images of the baby.

Chyning just stood there in astonishment as she received the visions. After receiving all of the images she turned pale and looked for a place to sit. Seeing as how there were numerous chairs in the room it was not hard to find one and plop down on it. "You...weren't joking! You...you are...*pregnant*! All this time..." She reached to the back of her neck and got a finger full of the mucus. "...this stuff...is...an Owlamite aphrodisiac?"

Bonarain nodded. "Yes it is. All the time that we were

being so polite…by not getting any…drainage…on someone else. It is the only way we can procreate."

Chyning scoffed. "What's the point now? With a gene pool as small as ours…it just…ain't feasible or practical."

"I don't know," said Bonarain. "I've been…performing some repairs…to my child. Somehow, in the womb…I can manufacture these repairs…and so far…they are staying stable. He did have a few problems before, but, I have been able to correct them."

Chyning raised her eyebrows. "He?"

Bonarain smiled. "Yes, it is a boy and I've named him Shalam."

Chyning looked askance. "Really? Beginning? Beginning of…what?"

"Maybe an entire race of Owlamites who can maintain a population…without getting killed by aliens," said Bonarain.

Kiyalee scoffed. "Inbreeding through incest causes all kinds of mutated problems."

"I'm aware of that," said Bonarain flatly. "However, considering the fact that I can perform repairs on my child… at least while in the womb…we could probably teach all of our offspring…to do the same."

Kiyalee looked even more skeptical. "You aren't talking about…Chyning…or me…actually becoming the wife…of your son…are you?"

Bonarain pursed her lips than clicked her tongue. "I haven't taken anything off of the table...yet." She looked off to the side and flushed.

Chyning hung her head. "Oh, this is *not* happening." She looked up. "You couldn't possibly believe that...I would wed... your son." She suddenly looked worried. "You...don't...do you?" Now she looked really worried.

8

Bonarain kept on researching all of the medical journals she could find. The difference now, though, was the fact that Kiyalee and Chyning were studying them as well. Bonarain did not know if they were looking through them to prepare themselves for a pregnancy or if they were just curious because of the fact that the first Owlamite baby was soon to be born.

The new year arrived with the Fall Equinox. Now it was the year 16 ATUT. In the northern hemisphere it was getting cold. In the equatorial area where High Country was located, it was still warm and humid with the normal high precipitation. The month of Statichy went by followed by Whegire and Strebale and the Winter Solstice.

Bonarain was getting bigger and was becoming more ravenous each day. Kiyalee and Chyning had to make several trips to Fortress Island to obtain a number of *fresh* fruits and *fresh* vegetables for their pregnant comrade. They did not seem to mind the chore because they were just as eager to see the child born as was Bonarain.

Soolchakan was taking most of the duties of watching the monitors for any invading aliens. The main reason he was watching the monitors was to keep from hearing the three women constantly babbling about the baby and how it might be affecting the entire body of Bonarain, not to mention the lives of all four adults.

The month of Roistume began. On the second day of the month Bonarain marked down that it had now been thirty-four weeks since joining with Soolchakan. She checked the charts from many centuries ago in regards to the development of Heyyah babies. The development was directly in line with that one. Each week she would check again. Each week it was still in line. The weeks went by…35, 36, 37, 38 and then the month of Lergan. The seventh day of Lergan was 39 weeks and Bonarain was more than ready to get the little wiggling monster out of her. He seemed to relish the pleasure of using her bladder as a punching bag and she could not count the number of times she had to go relieve herself.

Bonarain checked the calendar with her two female comrades. "Today…is Lergan the 28th. Today makes exactly forty-two weeks since…" She cleared her throat. "Since I smacked him in the face with my neck mucus…and he hit me back and…" She suddenly let out a cry of surprise.

Kiyalee backed away a little startled.

Chyning scoffed. "So it's 42 weeks. It ain't that momentous."

Bonarain looked at Chyning. "No! My…I…I think… my…water just broke!" She looked down at her body somewhat horrified. "My pants…just filled up…and…it ain't urine…or the…*other*!"

Kiyalee turned a little pale. **"Hey Soolchakan! I think you'd better get in here! Bonarain thinks…she's about**

to pop! You're about to meet your son."

The mental reply came back sounding a little disgusted. "**Get in where? I don't know exactly where the three of you are.**"

Now Kiyalee flushed. "**We're in the main room downstairs in the apartment. Bonarain said that she thinks her water broke.**"

Soolchakan quickly checked the monitors for any movement of any kind. He snarled in frustration. The last thing that any of them needed was for some invader to show up now. He looked carefully at the ones on Bri. He saw nothing out of the ordinary. He Jumped to the main room where Bonarain was waddling in a very unusual fashion.

"Let's get her up to her bed," said Soolchakan.

Bonarain gave him an angry look. "I already had to replace one mattress because of…!" She clenched her eyes and mouth shut. "I don't want any of this…muck…on that new one."

He snarled to himself. "Get her up on the counter. We'll work from there."

The three of them helped her get up on the counter. Chyning started assisting in undressing Bonarain. So far there had been no contractions, however, when the pants were pulled down it was obvious that is was amniotic fluids that had saturated the pants. Kiyalee saw the mess and started turning a little green.

Soolchakan saw Kiyalee put her hand over her mouth. "We don't need any of that right now! If you're going to puke…get out of here. Why don't you go watch the monitors for a while?"

Kiyalee looked back at him sniveling a little. "I just got out of there less than one mithpell ago."

He smiled sweetly at her. "Then help with the birth."

Kiyalee slapped both hands over her mouth and gagged. **"I'll go watch the monitors during this…."** She vanished.

Chyning chuckled. "That was a slick way of getting her in the monitor room."

"It was necessary," said Bonarain in an agitated manner. "Last thing I need is her puking all over me…or the baby, right now."

Chyning shrugged. "Good point. She might have blown her chow on the baby." She looked at the mess on her hands. "Got any suggestions as to what we do next?"

Bonarain laid her head back on the counter. "Get me a pillow…and assist in any way that you can."

Chyning nodded her head, vanished and reappeared a moment later with a large pillow. "Is this one okay?"

Bonarain closed her eyes and shook her head as she hugged herself. "It's a pillow! It's fine! Put it under my head."

Soolchakan turned on the computer in order to try finding some guidance from any medical journal that he could find. He had another thought as the computer was warming up. **"Kiyalee… are you all right in there**?"

"As long as I don't have to watch…what is

happening…I can function…without losing my lunch."

"Good! Watch the monitors. We'll let you know when it happens."

Kiyalee looked up at the bank of monitors still feeling a little queasy. 'I'm sure you will,' she thought.

Bonarain had her first contraction. She let out a loud moan and had a look of total surprise on her face. "Oh that was… primitive…and totally…painful," she gasped.

Chyning looked baffled. "Primitive? Painful? You couldn't think of any more appropriate words?"

Bonarain glared at her. "Shut up! It HURT!" She laid her head back waiting for the next one with worried anticipation. "Read…something about…how long it'll…or should take. I don't like these pains and…I don't want to spend a whole day dwelling on these…pains."

Chyning started running through the information on the computer. "Hey…this information is…up to date. Who…who fed all of this information in…and when?"

Bonarain growled. "I did it! When I was getting information from all of those sources I fed it in as I got it. I didn't really pay attention to what I was typing in…I just did it. Maybe if I had paid more attention…I wouldn't need you to check…but…" She moaned in agony as another contraction hit.

Chyning scoffed and looked back at the screen. "According to this…the contractions can last…" She pulled back from the screen looking a little disgusted. "They can last…for several mithpell."

"Like how many," asked Soolchakan?

"It's not unusual for…labor to last…fifteen to twenty-five mithpell."

Now Soolchakan was the one who was horrified. "One and a half to two and a half *days*? That's…ridiculous! There's got to be a better way."

Chyning shook her head. "According to this she won't be able to deliver until…huh?" She got closer to the screen. "Until her...birth canal...has expanded…to…" She looked up at Soolchakan rather worried. "We have to stick a finger in her vagina to see how wide it is. She can't deliver…until she's… expanded."

Bonarain looked at Chyning in dismay. "Stick your finger…WHERE?"

Chyning pointed at the screen. "That's what it says!" She looked back at the screen. "It also says that we're supposed to be timing the contractions."

Bonarain frowned. "For what?"

"That's another sign," said Chyning nonchalantly.

Soolchakan shook his head. "Maybe you should have paid more attention to what you were typing. There's got to be a better way."

Chyning gave him a big smile. "Surgery!"

Soolchakan groaned in disgust. "Do you know any

surgeons that we can trust?"

Bonarain sighed. "So you have to look at the clock after each contraction. I don't understand how that helps."

Soolchakan grunted. "This is ridiculous." He walked over to Bonarain looking at her abdomen. "I've got a better way."

Bonarain looked at him terrified. "Don't you start any experiments on me!"

He hopped his arms into Ghost. He reached for her stomach. She pulled away. He shook his head in frustration. **"HOLD STILL!"** He had used the *Voice* and she froze. He reached his hands inside her. He closed his eyes as he moved his arms around a little. He licked his lips.

He nodded. "Okay, I've got it," he said. He pulled his arms away from Bonarain and hopped his arms back into Home. In his hands there was a very small new-born infant – complete with the afterbirth.

Bonarain was staring at him in total amazement. She did not know whether to laugh or scream at him. She just gasped as she looked at her son in the hands of Soolchakan. The baby had been taken out painlessly (for the most part).

He took the baby Shalam to one of the tables and laid the child down on some towels that had been placed there earlier. He started cleaning all of the afterbirth and the amniotic fluids off, starting with the face. He had a suction device to clear out the fluids from the nasal and oral areas of the child. After clearing the air passages he clamped the umbilical cord. He cut the cord on the outside of the clamp. He looked back at Bonarain. **"You can move now."**

Bonarain came out of the trance. She tried to get up and moaned in pain as she settled back down on the counter. She closed her eyes. "Not yet," she croaked.

Soolchakan suddenly jumped back from the baby as he heard the child crying. "Oh! What is this?"

Chyning sat there giggling. "You definitely are a father now. Your son just peed on you." She shook her head while mocking him. "Look at that arc!"

Bonarain was laughing as well, however, she still could not get up.

Chyning sniffed. "If he's finished with his toileting, why don't you take him over and introduce him to his mother." She turned away and went into another laughing fit.

Soolchakan growled as he pulled his *soiled* shirt off. He cleaned the urine off of the child, wrapped him in a towel and took him over to be held by his mother…for the first time, in a place, other than the womb.

Bonarain gratefully accepted her son and started laughing and crying as she saw the face of Shalam, out of the womb, for the first time. He looked exactly like his father. He had those big blue eyes, forehead and chin. He had no hair at all on his body. She had to hold him with one arm and wipe tears out of her eyes in order to get a good look at him. "I'm a mother!" She sniffed several times. "I *AM* a mother!"

Soolchakan sighed. "9,024 years after the firestorm attack...the first Owlamite baby is born." He sighed again. "In all that time...the secret of procreation...was in that nasty goo that drains out of the scales on the back of our necks." He shook his head. "All that time wasted...and the doctors didn't even know it...or figure it out."

Chyning shook her head. "Who said sex was fun. With that goo...it sounds like it is just downright...nasty!"

Bonarain sniffed several times. "But the result...a baby... this beautiful...it is definitely worth it." She held her head back. "I need something to blow my nose!"

Soolchakan grunted. "You wanna use my red shirt? It's already soiled...with something else. A little snot won't hurt it," he said sarcastically.

Chyning was laughing uncontrollably as she brought a clean towel to Bonarain. She handed the towel to Bonarain and walked away still laughing.

Soolchakan took Shalam. "I'm going to hold my son for a while. Chyning...go get a...blanket or something. She's still laying here on the counter...naked from the waist down."

Chyning vanished and reappeared very quickly with a very large bath towel. She covered Bonarain with it. "Here, Sweetie. As soon as you get a little strength back, we'll get you upstairs and...bathed."

Bonarain nodded and smiled. "Thank you."

Soolchakan looked up looking a little startled. "Oops!"

He chuckled timidly. **"Kiyalee, Shalam is born! We now have a new Owlamite!"**

Kiyalee looked away from the monitors and smiled. **"Thank you for telling me. When do I get to see him?"**

"Check all the monitors real quick like. If nothing is moving, come on down and have a look."

She swallowed hard. **"Is...all of the mess...cleaned up?"**

Soolchakan and Bonarain both sighed. Chyning giggled.

He looked at the table where the afterbirth was sitting on a towel. "Chyning, get rid of that...mess. Then we can have Kiyalee get her look-see without up-chuck."

Chyning went into another giggling fit as she hopped the afterbirth into dimension #45. She could not think of a better place to get rid of the thing at this time.

Kiyalee showed up in the main room and got to hold Shalam and do her oohs and ahs over the child.

Bonarain was still laying flat on her back on the counter. She watched as each one of her comrades carefully held the little boy. "I'd get up but...I don't seem to have any energy. That really took something out of me. Even though I didn't have to go through a long process...it is still..." She shook her head. "I'm weary."

Chyning went into another round of gales of laughter.

Kiyalee backed away from Chyning. "What's the matter

with you?"

Chyning wiped tears from her eyes. "Yeah, she's right! Soolchakan really did take something out of her."

Bonarain snarled at Chyning. "That is absolutely NOT funny."

The comment sent Chyning into a new round of laughter.

Soolchakan took his son. "Kiyalee, would you be so kind as to assist Bonarain up to her bedroom? I think that...well take her to the bathroom first so that she can get cleaned up. Even though I delivered Shalam in a...totally unconventional way... the...event has drained her energy."

Chyning was just chuckling now. "I can help her as well."

"You can go watch the monitors," snarled Bonarain. "I don't need to be laughed at anymore, especially when you're taking it completely out of context."

Chyning chuckled a little harder. She held her hands up as in surrender. "Okay, okay...I'll go to the monitors." She took one more look at Shalam and grinned. "He is a cute little thing isn't he?" She vanished.

Soolchakan was slowly rocking the baby. "Have we got some of those bottles ready for him yet?"

"Yeah," said Kiyalee. "Remember...according to the instructions you have to heat it..."

"I KNOW," barked Soolchakan. "I'll get the thing ready so I don't freeze his little mouth or stomach. Now get her up to the bathroom…to bathe."

Kiyalee took hold of Bonarain and the two of them vanished.

Soolchakan looked down at his son and sighed. "What have we done?" He continued rocking the boy. "I'm surprised that you're not squalling already." He looked toward the kitchen doors. "Let's go find something for you to dine on…before you start bellyaching." He walked to the kitchen thinking in a few philosophical terms. "Who'd have thought…I'd be…9,060 years old…before my first child was born. Amazing!" He smiled as he looked at his son. "I once had small round-top ears like you. One day, I guess, you'll have points on those ears and then…they'll start to become the tall ostentatious things that your parents have growing out of the sides of their heads. Ours have been growing for over 9,000 years. Yours are just…fresh out of the womb."

It did not take very long before the two main things that controlled the lives of the four Owlamites were the monitors and a newborn baby. For most parents, sleep deprivation was the main problem with a baby. Owlamites were different, however, because they required very little sleep. They could go for months at a time without sleep because they did not really exert themselves so far that they required that much rest.

Chyning was the most restless as far as the baby was concerned and she grew bored with taking care of him faster than any of the others. Kiyalee was next to become tired of changing diapers and bottle feeding. Soolchakan and Bonarain could not weary of the task because they were the parents.

Days turned into weeks and weeks turned into months. The child was developing slowly, however, he did develop like any child. He started sitting upon his own, he started crawling on his own, he started walking on his own (albeit a little unsteady at first) and like every child – whatever he was supposed to keep away from - because it was dangerous – that is what he always headed for. Like any child he was always seeking the swiftest, and most gruesome, form of death. Whatever could hurt them the most was always their first and most important objective because it was so fascinating, to a toddler…and they would scream like crazy when they were removed from the item they were attempting to get hold of or beat on it.

Months turned into one year. Then two years…and Bonarain was getting very worried.

"Look at him," said Bonarain. "He…just isn't growing. He hasn't gained very much weight…he hasn't grown more than four tecks since he was born."

"He is healthy," said Soolchakan.

"Yes, but…he's just not growing!"

"What are you basing your concerns on?"

Bonarain pulled up some information on the computer. "According to this, he should be a lot taller, maybe put on some more weight and…I don't know, he just seems to be…too small."

Soolchakan looked at the information and scoffed. "That stuff is all in regards to a child that is born of two Heyyah.

Remember that Shalam is the first Owlamite baby. We have no guidelines for his...physical development. He has all of the mental faculties of a child that is just over two years old. Haven't you been reading his mind to see what is going on inside that skull?"

"Yes, and that's how I know when to chase him down and get him away from the oven. He always wants to climb up there and see what is up there...boiling away."

Soolchakan shook his head. "Precisely why we don't teach him anything about dimension hopping or Jumping...for at least another fifteen to twenty years. Who knows where he'll end up?"

"Especially if he's hopping and Jumping on his own... with the curiosity of a child." Bonarain hung her head. "I hate to think of it."

Soolchakan smiled. "Well at least, through sending mental images to him, it didn't take very long to potty train him. Aren't you glad that you don't have to change anymore diapers?"

She sighed. "That *is* a blessing." She snickered. "And he is getting better aim with a fork and a spoon."

"Plus he's becoming more capable of dressing himself."

Bonarain smiled as she thought of the accomplishments.

Two years old...three years old...four years old. He continued developing mentally. His physical body did not seem to be developing at all. Soolchakan had to keep reminding Bonarain that he was the first Owlamite child and this was the prototype guideline they were going to have to watch for any other Owlamite children that…might just happen to come along.

Shalam turned five years old on Lergan 28, 21 ATUT. He was given a party to celebrate being five years old. He was still not much larger, physically, than a toddler, however, his mental faculties continued to improve.

He was frustrated though. He still did not understand that oven thing where all of the food came from. Every time he tried to go near it to explore the thing, one of the adults was always there to stop him from climbing up on the stove. He would see Mommy and Daddy both working on something on that strange computer thing. He would sneak behind the furniture and slowly creep toward the kitchen. Somehow…when he finally got to the kitchen…Mommy or Daddy…or Auntie Kiyalee or Auntie Chyning always got there first and…always kept him away from the oven. He was determined that one day he would get there first. He did not know how yet, but the goal was in reach…maybe. It almost seemed as if they could read his mind…but, of course, that was impossible…right?

Lergan 28, 26 ATUT, Shalam turned ten years old. He had physically grown slightly. His ears had the tiniest little point on the tops. He was learning all kinds of new things on the computer about the surrounding areas and why, as a child, he needed to stay in the gorge until he was ready to go out there and see the world as an adult.

Bonarain shook her head as she continued checking things on the computer. Any Heyyah child would be much taller and more physically developed. His development was still in the area of a three-year-old Heyyah. His mental abilities were above that of a ten-year-old Heyyah, mainly because he had four adult Owlamites who were constantly feeding him information mentally and thus increasing his knowledge in a much greater fashion than any Heyyah.

Soolchakan laughed a little. "Have you ever considered another child? Maybe with two…or three…we might see… something that becomes more of a pattern."

She gave him a dirty look. "The thought of…waking up… three days later…and I was laying there…wallowing in my own excrement. I don't want to think about that. We'd have to have Kiyalee or Chyning come in there and…clean us up…while we're sleeping. It is just too *revolting* to think about." She looked up at him suspiciously. "You could…use the *Power* and…order me to do it."

He nodded. "I could. I won't. Or at least I don't want to. Considering all of the stuff you went through while you were pregnant. I don't think that I could force you to go through that again. If you want another child that's one thing. For me to *make* you do it…no…I'll leave the decision up to you."

She bit her lip as she stood there worrying about it. He was saying that he did not want to force the issue, however, he could change his mind at any time and make her think that it was her idea. She wished that she, and all other Owlamites, could understand this strange *Power* and why it was what it was and how it could move from one to another at the instant moment of the death of the one who had it before. It was very irritating and confusing.

Shalam felt frustrated in many ways. He did not like being confined to the apartment area in the gorge. True there was plenty of space in the area and he could go to just about any apartment he desired…as long as he stayed away from the fascinating oven. He had made several attempts at climbing the thing. Then one day, Daddy had walked up to him and, in a very strange voice, commanded him to not go near an oven, especially when food was being prepared. Since then, he had obeyed and stayed away. He could not understand why he was so compelled to obey Daddy, when he constantly made every attempt at *not* obeying Mommy… or either Auntie. It was so strange. Then there was also those two infuriating statements they all made: You'll understand better when you are older. And: We'll explain it to you when you are old enough to understand. Just exactly when was that momentous day supposed to arrive in the saga of growing up?

Shalam turned 15 years old on Lergan 28, 31 ATUT. Suddenly the four big people started explaining all kinds of things to him. Once again he was informed that he was still too small to go out there on his own. While these people, called the Heyyah, grew faster, they also aged faster. Any Heyyah that was his age was much taller. He looked like a Heyyah child that was only about 5 years old.

His age was fifteen while all four of them were over 9,000 years old. He had no concept of what they were talking about in regards to being that old. He had a full grasp of mathematics and counting, however, the thought that the big people were 600 times older than he was…it was just too hard to grasp…at this time.

The big people talked about horrible wars they had been through and that at one time, most of these apartments had been inhabited by other big people like themselves. Only those people did not survive all of those wars. At first he thought that fighting in a war would be something exciting. Then Daddy, very firmly, explained that there was nothing fun about war. People die in war. They die in horrible ways in war. The people who *cause* wars are the only ones who should die so that they cannot cause others to sacrifice themselves for a greedy leader. They only start wars because of something called over-zealous ambition. They want to rule others in cruel and vicious ways. They kill those who do not obey them completely.

He was introduced to new things in those funny computers that the big people were constantly playing with. The games that they played were boring because all of it was information and not some game where you move pieces on a board and win or lose. You just…learn something. How dull.

He found out that there were other people out there who were not anything like…us. There were all kinds of people of different races, some of whom had wings, some had green skin, some had blue skin, some had purple skin, some had nasty looking sharp teeth, some had faces that looked more like animals and some had a vast variety of different colors of hair. Others had differences that he could not believe…at first. He was informed that he could meet some of these people someday…once he was bigger. Once again, he could hardly wait for that day.

This gorge was located in a place called High Country. They were defended by some Dragon Force. He saw the huge flying lizards going overhead on many occasions. He so wanted to be able to ride on one of them because it looked as if it would be so much fun. He was informed that one day he would be able to do things much more exciting than riding on a big flying lizard. What he would be able to do, they did not explain, they just told him that some day in the future, *when he was bigger*, he would do wondrous things.

Daddy drew a line on the wall and informed Shalam that when he was as tall as where that line was…without standing on his tippy-toes or on a box, then they would explain a lot of the wondrous things they were keeping from him. He stared at that line in frustration and anticipation many times, attempting to will himself to be taller.

One day, after turning sixteen years old, Shalam overheard a strange conversation about…sex. It was then explained to him where he had come from. He found that there were some tremendous differences between the bodies of men and women. Their bodies had some drastically different things in regards to plumbing and reproductive organs. He did not believe it at first. Then he was allowed to see things on the computer that gave some very informative details about the differences between men and women and what their bodies actually did do. Daddy had to sit him down and explain a few other things about the nasty goo that started draining out of the back of his neck. That was a very enlightening and shocking piece of information.

When Shalam turned twenty years old, the four older Owlamites realized they had to stop treating him like an infant. He was now *twenty years old.* Even though he still looked as if he were only about five or six years old, mentally he was a twenty year old and they now saw that they would have to treat him that way if he was ever to develop into an adult. If you continually treat someone like a child, they will continually act like a child. If you want someone to act as an adult, treat them as an adult. They had to accept the fact, from observing him, the Owlamite child ages a lot slower physically…or at least that was what they were hoping was the case.

Time marches on. When the four elders started treating him as a mature adult he started acting in a more mature manner. He realized that he was not an adult physically, however, his mental faculties were definitely that of an adult. When he got a firm grip on the fact that the four elders actually were over 9,000 years old, he accepted that he had a good long life ahead of him and if he had to, very slowly, mature physically – so be it.

In the year 76 ATUT, when Shalam turned sixty years old, he had finally grown considerably and the points on his ears were becoming more pronounced. Bonarain realized that something else was changing in him. She tried talking to him about it. He refused to communicate. She gave up and intruded on his thoughts.

She went to Soolchakan. "Since you are a man…I think that you need to talk to your son."

Soolchakan looked up from a mug of hot kwatha. "About…

what?"

She sighed. "I know the body of a woman. I know what happens there. I don't fully understand some of the things about the body of a man."

"And?"

"I think that our son has finally gone into puberty."

Soolchakan put the mug down. He turned to her and raised his eyebrows. "Indeed?"

"Yes." She took a deep breath. "I...kinda...intruded on his thoughts and...he is looking at his...chin. He noticed a couple of hairs...growing out of his chin." She flushed. "He...also... has noticed...some..." She closed her eyes and her face got even redder. She cleared her throat nervously. "...pubic hairs."

"We never did discuss the changes in the body with him... did we?"

"No, we didn't. If he were a girl...I'd talk to *her*. He's a boy..."

Soolchakan got a wide-eyes look of awe on his face. "Really," he said with wide-eyed sarcasm? "I hadn't noticed."

She snarled at him. "You need to discuss some things with *your son!*"

"I will," he said calmly. "As soon as I'm finished with this kwatha."

Another area was opened up to Shalam in the computer. He read it with his mouth hanging open. "You…knew that this… was going to happen to me?"

"Yes, we did, son," said Soolchakan quietly. "Seeing as how you're an Owlamite and…the first ever Owlamite offspring… we had no idea when it would start. This is all a part of growing up."

"I don't understand why you keep all of these things from me!"

"Son, I know that you're tired of hearing this, but…again, you are the first ever Owlamite offspring. We didn't know what to expect. We did tell you that you do have a tremendously long life expectancy and…now we find out that because of this long life… it also takes quite some time for an Owlam child to physically mature. Right now, your mental knowledge is that of any Heyyah that is sixty years old…without being senile. Your body though… is that of a very young adolescent. We don't yet know how long it'll be before you are a totally physically mature adult.

Shalam sighed. "Are there very many more surprises?"

"Probably." Soolchakan shrugged. "Absolutely. We are still learning some new things…because of you." He looked off to the side. "The only way that we can…confirm…that what you have experienced is normal…is for us to have…another child."

Shalam cleared his throat nervously. "One thing…I was thinking about…is that…I don't want to be like you…in a certain way."

Soolchakan frowned. "And what way is that?"

"I don't want to hurt your feelings, but...the...hair...on your face. I...don't want to have...a beard. I'd...like to get that hair off of my face."

Soolchakan thought about it and it had been...how long since he had shaved all of his beard off? He had trimmed the hair thousands of times, he had not shaved. He had to think back on it in order to teach his son how to shave without ripping his face to shreds.

Once Shalam had learned about a razor and how to use it, he shaved daily for three weeks...and then decided that it would be easier to just let the beard grow and he would have a lot less burning irritation on his face.

There were several other changes that occurred, mostly the fact that he was growing in height faster than he had before. It was not really that noticeable if he were measured every day. Once every two weeks gave them the results that he was growing much faster.

His voice was changing. His voice was now lower than the high alto of either Kiyalee or Chyning. It was now lowering below the contralto of his mother. He wondered if his voice would sound anything like the low baritone of his father. Time would tell.

Soolchakan went to Bonarain thinking about a few things. One thing was his 83 year old son. The other thing was...the episode where Shalam had been conceived. "You remember how... you hit me in the face...with your mucus and what happened?"

She gave him a discourteous stare and folded her arms. "I have a son! How could I forget what happened...every time I look at *my son*?"

He smiled. "It's not the fact that you did it...I was thinking of...how you painted my entire face with it." He shrugged. "Then, I returned the favor."

She huffed and closed her eyes. "Your point?"

"I was thinking...what if...it had just been...a...dab? If it had been just a very small amount of mucus...would it still have the results of...both of us being...sexually overly aggressive...but not to the point where we can't stop...until we were so physically exhausted that...we end up sleeping for three days?"

She now looked a little worried. "Are you suggesting that...we do it again...but only...hit each other with...a finger full of mucus?"

He shook his head. "No, not a finger full...just...a dab... on the end of the finger."

She shook her head. "I'm not ready to...go through that again...just for an experiment. I don't like the idea of waking up three days later in a bed full of... If you wanna try something like that...do it to Kiyalee or Chyning."

"It wouldn't be the same," he said flatly. "They are not you. It would have to be you...in order to get...a true comparison. We need your reactions."

She clenched her teeth. "Are you going to order me to do it...or...just...*dab* me in the face?"

He chuckled. "I don't really want to order you to do it. I don't think it'd be fair. It still makes me wonder."

She closed her eyes trying to think of some argument against what he was saying. She suddenly felt his finger slide across her forehead and instantly she had a menstrual cramp in her abdomen...and a burning between her legs. She glared at his smiling face.

"You're the one who initiated it last time...I thought I'd do it this time." He chuckled. "Remember...**just a dab**."

He had used the *Voice*. She wanted to slap his face off, however, she obeyed. She shakily reached for the back of her neck and got a small amount of the mucus on her finger. She rubbed the *dab* across his forehead.

He gasped and stood up. That was when she noticed that he was not wearing any pants. He was wearing a robe. He had been planning on starting his experiment all along.

He leaned over and grunted. "Your bed or mine?"

"Yours," she snarled! "You...*reptile*! I already had to replace a mattress because of that mess. This time it'll be yours that needs replacing."

They both Jumped to his bedroom. He dropped the robe. She got her pants off as quickly as she could and joined him on the bed.

Before he started the "joining" he smiled at her again.

"Take a quick look at the chronometer. Notice the date and time."

She did.

"Now, you'll be able determine exactly how long we are out...with just a dab."

Bonarain woke up with a start. She looked around his bedroom. She saw Soolchakan snoozing on the bed next to her. She remembered what he said and looked over at the chronometer. They had been asleep for only six mithpell. She huffed. "He was right!" Then she noticed that she still had her shirt on. She had removed only her pants and boots. Her shirt reeked of perspiration. 'Probably both his and my sweat,' she thought. She got up stripped the shirt off and headed to the bathroom to bathe. When she finished her bath, she checked the bed and he was gone.

She sat down on the bed and sighed. She started that inventory of her body again, paying special attention to the interior of the womb. She looked back at the chronometer. He had taken her on Marrem the fourteenth, 101 ATUT. She counted the weeks ahead in order to determine when any offspring from this joining would occur. She came up with late in the month of Strebale, 102 ATUT. She did not notice any zygote...yet. It was five days before she was able to find that familiar speck that would grow into another Owlamite offspring. She found Soolchakan. "You reptile," she muttered. "I have another one growing inside me."

He came back in the room and gave her an equally dirty look. "When it was your idea it was okay. When it was my idea... all of a sudden it becomes wrong. My, how hypocritical of you."

She did not argue because she knew that she could not win an argument with the *Voice of Power*. "How many more children are you planning on making me manufacture in order to satisfy your experimental desires?"

He scratched his chin. "The point behind that was to determine if we would still end up...copulating for such an extended amount of time that we ended up sleeping for three days. The amount of mucus is what determines how long we end up... performing the act. I'm not going to try to tell you to have any more or make you have any more children. I...or should I say... we needed to know. If it is just a dab, then we don't have to worry about waking up in our own filth, three days later."

She stuck her tongue out at him. "I'm still mad at you."

"That's part of life," he said calmly. He walked away. 'When hasn't she had some complaint about me,' he thought? He shook his head. 'Women!'

9

Bonarain was discovering that the second pregnancy was very much like the first one. All of the problems she had during the first one were coming back in the same nasty format – none better but none worse. She was also going through the same things with going over the developing fetus, finding and repairing anything that seemed untoward.

As soon as the fetus started taking shape and developing, she started the ritual of organizing her thoughts and changing what needed to be changed. Even though it had been 86 years since she had done the same repairs on Shalam, it seemed rather familiar and she was ready to do it again in order to come up with another perfect child.

Rather quickly, she realized that this was another boy. She decided on the name Monaha (*in Owlamite it means: "Restore"*). This was the beginning of a new chapter in the Owlamite race. Restoration of a population (depending on what Kiyalee and Chyning were planning on doing). She was not sure how far it would go, however, she had repaired one child, she was in the process of repairing another and she was more than ready to assist any other Owlamite female in the repairing of their child…or children.

Kiyalee and Chyning were both very skeptical as to whether or not the intention was for them to wed the two sons of Bonarain. They were both aware of the fact that the only male genes that were in any of the new Owlamites all belonged to Soolchakan and that still made for a dangerously tiny gene pool. The final results of that thought were not positive.

Soolchakan and Bonarain were not very sure about attempting to talk the other two women into wedding the two boys. They also realized that this gene pool was too tiny. The Owlamite race was in deep trouble as far as procreation. There was a rather large conundrum about this as well as any moral situation concerning incest.

All of the bad thoughts did not deter Bonarain from continuing in the process of making sure that Monaha came out just as perfect as Shalam. She went through the daily ritual of mentally going over the developing body of Monaha and changing anything that seemed unusual or contrary – as far as all of the guidelines in the medical journals were concerned, and what she had learned from her first pregnancy.

Bonarain also considered the possibility of Soolchakan wedding and mating with both Kiyalee and Chyning. If she could talk them into it and the result was any female offspring, then there would be at least one mate for each one of her sons. One problem was…how do you talk the two of them into a polygamous relationship with Soolchakan? The other problem, of course, was…do you really want these children mating and procreating a race of mutated, inbred idiots?

The more Bonarain talked about it with the other two

women, the more Kiyalee became cautiously interested and the more Chyning wanted to avoid the subject altogether - if not flee in mortal terror.

She continued with her regular practice of going over the body of Monaha. She knew that once he was out of the womb, she felt that she had no way of improving or repairing anything.

Strebale 26, 102 ATUT, her water broke. This time, before any of those painful and irritating contractions occurred, *she* hopped her arms into Ghost, reached in her womb and pulled the newborn out...afterbirth as well.

She did all of the cleaning and cutting of the umbilical cord...and ended up being the one getting a golden baptism from the bladder of her newborn son. She shook her head and wiped the urine off of her face. "Shalam did it to Soolchakan...now... Monaha did it to me." She sighed. "Is this face full of urine...a major part of being a...parent...I wonder?" She looked down at the wet stains on her shirt. "Okay, baby boy! We're gonna take a shower together. That way I get all of the amniotic stuff off of you and...I get your...*wet*...off of me."

Bonarain now went around showing her new baby to all of the Owlamites (what few there were).

Soolchakan looked deep into the face of his new son. "Now...we're going to find out if Monaha...is anything like Shalam. If he is...we've got a long road ahead of us...in raising him. Shalam is 85 years old and...he's still in the later stages of adolescence." He nodded. "This one is just...in the starting point of his life."

Kiyalee snickered. "It's just too bad that you didn't have your two babies closer together. Shalam could've had a playmate while he was growing up." She smiled. "Now…we're going to have to go through the same things with this one that we did with Shalam. Another child who seems to go out of his way looking for anything and everything that is too dangerous to play with…and wanting to play with only those things."

Chyning was holding the baby with a rather disconcerted look. "Are you trying to make me want one of my own?"

"No," said Bonarain flatly. "I'm just showing off my new baby boy."

Chyning rolled her eyes and huffed. "Why do I find it impossible to believe you? I guess I have to give you the benefit of the doubt…but…I still think that there's some kind of coercion here."

Bonarain took the baby back, looking a little disgusted. She went to show him to his older brother.

Shalam looked at his brother with trepidation. "Did I… look…like that?"

"Yes," said Bonarain sweetly. "You were once a baby as well and we have those pictures of you. All those years ago, we all held you in our arms like this. You weren't much bigger than he is now. But…like you…he'll grow up. It'll take some time but, he will grow."

Shalam nodded. "Finally…another one of my generation."

Soolchakan was not sure how to take that observation, however, it was totally correct and accepted.

Monaha was soon crawling then waddling then walking. Again, like every small child, he did everything he could to search out and find death. Anything that his parents tried to keep him away from, that particular item, or room, was where he wanted to go to the most. He ended up being slightly more hard-headed than Shalam. This did indicate that each one had their own different personality.

The thing that somewhat startled the adults was that he was almost the same in the physical realm. He grew at the same rate Shalam had grown. Even though he was mentally maturing past his physical appearance, he was developing, physically, very slowly, just like his brother.

When Shalam turned 90 years old, the four adults took a good close look at him and decided that everything about him showed that he had finished growing. He was now fully physically mature. Sixty years from birth to adolescence. Ninety years from birth to full grown adult. He had basically been completely mentally mature by the age of 35. They wondered what the Heyyah would think of this. The normal Heyyah was old at 75. A new Owlamite was not even fully grown. The average lifespan of the normal Heyyah was 110. Four Owlamites were over 9,100 years old and showing no signs of old age.

Now Shalam was introduced to the world of mental

communication as well as dimension hopping. He was also introduced to all of the different type of one-seat fighters and large attack ships that the Owlamites had at their disposal.

His response to all of this new education: "You *were* reading my mind, all the time," he muttered bitterly. "Now, I know why I couldn't get away with anything. That was low."

Bonarain shrugged. "We had to keep you safe and alive. It was necessary."

He simply snarled.

"Watch Monaha," said Bonarain angrily. "You'll see why we didn't let you know until now."

It was the beginning of a new year. The Fall Equinox was the day that began the year. Soolchakan still did not like the idea that the calendar had 361 days and 5 events. They had Tadkoy, the 31st day of Consoray in the year 110 ATUT. The next day was not the 1st of Statichy, 111 ATUT, it was Hartkoy the Fall Equinox, 111 ATUT. The *next* day was Miviskoy, 1 Statichy, 111 ATUT.

The day was Leegkoy, 2 Statichy, 111 ATUT, when Kiyalee started making all kinds of inquiries to Bonarain about motherhood, pregnancy, nursing and anything else she could think of regarding what the mind and body had gone through while carrying Shalam and Monaha.

Bonarain saw how Kiyalee was talking around the subject, however, she felt that Kiyalee was seriously thinking about motherhood for herself. What Bonarain could not ascertain from the conversation was whether Kiyalee wanted to have a joining with Soolchakan or Shalam...so she asked.

Kiyalee looked somewhat angered and shocked. "I have absolutely no plans of being hitched with a...child...who is...over 9,000 years younger than I! I am currently 9,139 years old. In 861 years, my age will be a five digit number...if we actually do live that long. His will still be a three digit number...for a very long time."

Bonarain looked off to the side grimacing. "Don't remind me about age. I'm four years older than you are."

"Right! Would you want to have a child husband?"

Bonarain sighed. "I don't think so. But...why would you want to have a polygamous relationship...with Soolchakan?"

Kiyalee licked her lips and looked around nervously. "We...are...the four of us are...the first generation of Owlamites. Shalam and Monaha...are the start of the second generation." She sniffed and bit her lip. "You said...that you...repaired...both of your sons...while they were in the womb. If I have a...girl... and...she...joins...with one of your sons...do you think that we could show her...how to repair her baby...in case of some nasty... mutation from...the joining of possible...recessive genes?"

Bonarain was a little shocked. "I think that we could. If you have a girl, I certainly hope that we can. Otherwise...the prospects are...rather grim."

Kiyalee flushed. "So...what do you think...are the prospects? Do you think that maybe...Soolchakan...would go along with it?"

Bonarain exhaled in a loud manner and shook her head. "You'll have to ask him. I can't speak for him."

Kiyalee backed up a little. "You want *me*...to ask *him*?" She looked very worried.

Bonarain smiled. "Why not you? You're the one who brought this subject up."

Kiyalee snarled back. She sat down and pouted for a few moments. "I guess you're right. If I want this...I'd have to...talk to him...myself." She sighed. "Do you know where he is...right now?"

"You can always call him mentally," said Bonarain with a big grin.

She closed her eyes. "**Soolchakan, this is Kiyalee, I need to talk to you.**"

The response came back. "***You* need to...talk...to *me*?**"

"**Yes, I do. Where are you?**"

"**Watching the monitors, because you women are always so flaming busy...with *one* baby. Any more stupid questions?**"

Kiyalee grinned. "**Bonarain can watch the monitors for a few Mithpell.**"

Bonarain opened her mouth to protest, however, she was abruptly cut off.

"You wanted me to talk to him. If he consents…he and I will be a little busy." She grinned at Bonarain again.

Bonarain snarled. "Let's Jump to the monitor room…but first…" She closed her eyes. **"Shalam, I need you to watch Monaha for a while**."

Shalam came back. **"Is it important**?"

"YES IT IS IMPORTANT! Now…get to the main room in 562 and watch your little brother for a while…or go watch the outer space monitors."

There was a very short pause. **"I'll watch the monitors**!"

Kiyalee giggled. "You gave him a choice."

Bonarain stuck her tongue out at Kiyalee, then started giggling.

Kiyalee Jumped to the monitor room. Shalam was already there doing a quick scan of monitors to see if there was anything new on them. She put her hand on Shalam's shoulder. "You may be here for a while."

He shrugged. "I'd rather be here than watching Monaha," he said dryly.

Soolchakan sat there with his arms folded across his chest. "Now, what is so important?"

Kiyalee swallowed. "Let's…go to…the second floor of our apartment…please."

Soolchakan sighed in frustration and then vanished. Kiyalee followed him.

Soolchakan was looking around the main room of the second floor. "I don't see anything here that's new. What's going on?"

She cleared her throat. "I…I'm not sure…how to…say this."

He grunted in frustration. "You open your mouth and use words for communication. Or…like any intelligent Owlamite, you use mental communication. Now…WHAT DO YOU WANT?"

She pointed to her door. "In my bedroom." She slowly walked to her room.

He followed shaking his head. He was getting a little upset over her taking the *very long way* around the barn, however, he was, at least, a little curious.

Once in her bedroom, she turned around while getting a dab of her mucus on her finger. Before he realized what she was doing she ran a stripe of her mucus across his forehead.

He immediately bent over, pulling at the crotch of his pants. "What…are you doing?"

She started unbuckling her belt. "I want a baby. I want a baby by you. I don't want to have a baby by…someone who is several *millennium* younger than I am." She kicked her boots off. She unbuckled the magic knife from her leg. She pulled her pants off and kicked them off to the side. "What do we do now?"

He glared at her. "What does Bonarain have to say about this?"

"She told me to talk to you."

"That *wasn't* talk!" He was still staring angrily at her while panting heavily. He reached up behind his neck and got a dab of his mucus.

She closed her eyes and grimaced in anticipation of what was going to happen. She felt a little nauseous. She felt his finger run across her forehead. Almost instantly the nausea was gone and there was a burning desire in her mind and a very strange feeling in her abdomen and crotch. She opened her eyes and mouth in shock and gasped.

"You asked for this," he growled!

"I know," she whined as she grabbed her crotch!

He pushed her backwards on the bed. He disrobed from the waist down and crawled on top of her.

Kiyalee was being rather rudely jostled. She opened her tired eyes and looked up at Bonarain.

"You've slept half the day away," said Bonarain merrily. "Are you happy with what happened?"

Kiyalee sighed. She sat up, yawned and stretched. "I... guess so."

Bonarain scoffed. "I see that he approved."

Kiyalee chuckled nervously. "I...didn't give him...much of a choice."

Bonarain was now confused. "What?"

"I...hit him...in the head...with my...mucus...before he knew what was going on."

Bonarain brought her hands up as if she were going to choke Kiyalee. "You didn't ask...first?"

Kiyalee smiled. "I...couldn't voice it. I just...striped his forehead...and...I guess he figured it out...because he...put some of his...on my face." She sighed. "Now...I'm going to need your help...in...how that...repair process works...just in case I need it for my...baby...if I have one." She sighed again.

Bonarain closed her eyes and shook her head. She opened her eyes and sniffed. "You won't even know for at least five days. The zygote, right now, if there is one is just too small to see." She turned and headed for the door.

Kiyalee felt a little desperate. "Aren't you going to wake him up?"

Bonarain stopped and looked back indignantly. "Right now, that's your job."

"But...I don't want to...touch him. He's all...sweaty and...smelly."

Bonarain smiled. She crossed her arms. "And who is at fault for that?"

Kiyalee stammered a little.

"If you didn't want his sweat on your bed...you should've done *it* on his bed." She grinned, turned and departed the room.

Kiyalee snarled at herself. She looked away as she pushed

against his side several times. She pulled her hands away and looked at her palms as if she was expecting to see something nasty on them. She wanted to go bathe, however, not while he was in the room.

He looked up at her and snarled. "Are you happy now?" He grunted as he got up off of the bed. "I should slap you."

"Please don't," she said quietly.

He picked up his pants, boots and magic sword...and vanished.

"Happy? I suppose so," she said quietly. "I suppose I am happy." She sniffed, got up off the bed and headed for the bathroom. "To the tub."

Five days later, in the main room of the apartment, Bonarain and Kiyalee were sitting facing each other with their eyes closed and foreheads pressed together.

"There it is," said Bonarain. "Do you see that little dark speck?"

Kiyalee giggled. "Yes...I see it. Is that the beginning of my baby?"

Bonarain leaned back. "Yes it is. Why couldn't you go for Shalam?"

"Again, I didn't want someone who was 9,000 years junior to me." She looked at Soolchakan. "I wanted someone...of my generation. Besides, if we had known, from the beginning, that this...nasty goo...was the secret of having babies, we would've been practicing polygamy from the start. Three times as many women as men...monogamy would have left a lot of lonely women out there. And I imagine that...someone...among the other forty-nine, who were the *Voice of Power*, would've ordered polygamy to be legal. I can't see any of the others saying no to the act."

Soolchakan had been stirring his spoon through some kwatha. He had been watching the two women while they were looking for the zygote. He turned his gaze to Chyning.

Chyning saw his look. She raised her hands up and waved them back and forth. "Don't look at me! I didn't have anything to do with this."

"No," he said grimly. "I was just wondering if you were gonna pull a stunt like that as well."

"No, no, no, no, no, no, no." She guffawed while shaking both hands back and forth. "I don't have any desire to be a mommy."

"Not yet," said Kiyalee grinning.

Chyning pulled her fist back as if she wanted to go over to Kiyalee and punch her. She snarled with her teeth bared. She turned away shaking her head and put her full attention on the bowl of diced fruit in front of her. She shoved a large piece in her mouth and started chewing while purposefully looking away from Kiyalee.

Kiyalee did not have any of the morning sickness problems

that Bonarain had suffered through. Instead, she went through a long phase of uncontrolled flatulence along with a few bouts of dizziness. They switched her diet to more protein than vegetables and the excessive gas slowed considerably.

Bonarain and Kiyalee had numerous bouts with looking over the fetus (which, they discovered, was definitely female). There were many repairs that had to be accomplished on her body as she developed.

Chyning eavesdropped on one of the repair sessions. She sat quietly watching while Bonarain and Kiyalee were leaning forward touching foreheads, with their eyes closed, focusing on the task at hand. They finished and leaned back in their chairs. They both let out a sigh of relief.

Chyning could not hold back. "You didn't notice that did you?"

Bonarain was slightly startled by the interruption. "What? Notice…what?"

Kiyalee frowned with suspicion.

"Your…stones…they…merged and glowed," said Chyning haltingly. "The blue and yellow…merged and…became green…and…glowed. They glowed the whole time you two were…doing…whatever you were doing."

Both women looked closely at their stones.

Bonarain smirked. "Are you sure?"

Chyning scoffed back. "If you don't believe me, then why don't you ask Soolchakan to sit in on the next session? Better yet…have both Shalam and Monaha sit in on the session." She scratched her chin. "By the way, are you sure that this one…is a girl?"

Kiyalee smiled. "Absolutely! My little girl is coming along nicely."

Chyning nodded. "Uh…what…is her name?"

Kiyalee's smile got even bigger. "I've decided to name her Aya *(in Owlamite it means: "Blessing")*.

Chyning looked off and clicked her tongue. "Really? Aya? Okay, this is your child. I guess…" She frowned. "Did you talk to Soolchakan about…the name?"

Bonarain snickered. "He said that since we had to go through all of the aggravation and irritation of gestation, we could decide. He will let us know…if he doesn't like it."

Kiyalee giggled. "When are you going to want one?"

Chyning gave her a nasty glare. "I told you that I'm not interested in being a mommy. I *mean* it! I meant it when I said it before, I still mean it now." She huffed angrily.

Bonarain shook her head. "Are you really going to tell me that you have never wondered what it would be like to raise a child of your own?"

Chyning snarled. "I've watched how you raised Shalam. I'm watching you with Monaha. I'm seeing Kiyalee pregnant. I'm even surer now than I was before."

Bonarain looked at Kiyalee and chuckled. "Okay. We'll

see."

"We'll see nothing," growled Chyning. She huffed as she stomped away.

The days went by. Monaha had a birthday celebration and then later Shalam had a birthday celebration. Monaha was 9 and Shalam was 95.

Monaha looked at his mother. "When is your birthday?"

Bonarain grimaced. "Uhm...unfortunately...we don't know. We were born...in a day when the calendar was a rather fluid thing and very different. It changed...when a new leader came to power. There were a few leaders...before the firestorm attack and...Soolchakan is leader number fifty...since the attack. We never knew...a regular calendar...until this one was approved of, just over a century ago."

He looked a little surprised. "So...how do you count your age?"

Soolchakan smiled. "We just add another year to our age on Statichy the first." He chuckled. "We can't be more than 183 days off...one way or the other."

The Summer Solstice arrived. Kiyalee was feeling rather miserable. "How much longer? I want her...*out of me!*"

Bonarain chuckled. "You're right around 39 weeks. Remember that I delivered both of my boys at almost exactly 42 weeks."

Kiyalee put her hands on her stomach. "You hear that you little monster? Three more weeks and you don't get to use my guts as punching bags...ever again."

Chyning scoffed. "Still want to know why I don't want to be a mommy?"

Bonarain shook her head. "Once the child is out of you... you don't have to worry about that at all."

"No, you have to keep the hard-headed little beast away from anything that can kill it. They always seem to want to find the most dangerous things and have an insatiable desire to play with them. They also look for things that are extremely fragile and just...beat on them with both hands." Chyning scoffed again. "Hey...where's Soolchakan and Shalam?"

Kiyalee looked up. "Soolchakan is teaching Shalam a few things about hopping to the other dimensions and Jumping as well."

Chyning jumped up from her seat. "Who...is watching the monitors?"

Bonarain looked horrified. "Oh...*h'oolyach*! One of us had better get in there."

All three Jumped into the monitor room. They all three noticed that there was some movement around Bri. Bonarain was the first to get to the controls and magnify the ship orbiting the mineral planet. They all gave out a loud sigh of relief when they recognized the space shuttle craft. Soolchakan was piloting it and

Shalam was looking out with wide-eyed wonder and a massive grin.

Chyning chuckled. "Right now, if anyone else was orbiting Bri, I think that Soolchakan would have informed us."

Kiyalee growled. "I don't need a scare like that right now." She looked down at her stomach. "I couldn't fit into my spacesuit right now." She placed her hands against her back and stretched a little. "Come on Thorinale the 22nd. That day is exactly 42 weeks and, that day, I can get this child *out* of me...I hope."

As the due date approached, Bonarain and Kiyalee kept on looking the child over for any more possible mutations or damage in a more urgent manner. Kiyalee had gone over the entire body of Aya over a thousand times, however, she was still not fully satisfied that the child had been fully repaired. Bonarain remembered that she had been the same way when she was carrying Shalam and Monaha so she was very patient with all of the concerns running through the head of Kiyalee.

Kiyalee sighed after another marathon session. "One more time tomorrow on the twenty-first of Thorinale. Then...on the twenty-second...it should be time to give birth."

On Thorinale the 21st, her water broke.

Chyning once again was looking at the humor of the situation. "Do you wanna go over your little girl again...before or between contractions?" She turned away giggling.

Kiyalee wanted to do some major damage to Chyning, however, there was something a little more important going on that had to precede any revenge. She turned to Bonarain. "How soon should we pull her out?"

Bonarain shrugged. "When Soolchakan did it to me the first time, I had only had two…or three contractions…" She looked up in thought. "…I think." She shook her head. "It doesn't matter! The way he did it…it can be done at any time." She chuckled. "And from what I hear about other races of women when they give birth, they'd love this system that he invented."

At that moment Kiyalee experienced her first contraction. She almost screamed in pain when it hit. She was sitting on a chair when her water broke and now she was leaning over (as far as she could) in pain with her teeth clenched. The pain subsided and she sat up with a look of wide-eyed horror on her face. "Get this baby out of me…NOW!"

Bonarain and Chyning helped Kiyalee get to her bed and got her laid out flat.

Bonarain smiled. "It won't take long." She hopped her arms into Ghost. She reached into the womb area, hopped the fingertips into Home dimension, found the baby, hopped the baby into Ghost and pulled the child out…afterbirth and all.

Kiyalee looked in horror at the mess in Bonarain's hands. "What…is THAT? I thought we repaired her!"

Bonarain smiled. "Don't worry, my new mommy. That's just the afterbirth…still wrapped around her. Once I get rid of that mass, you'll see your little girl. Now, you just relax."

Kiyalee laid back, however, she was still very concerned

about Aya – as any new mother would be about her first child. She was a little surprised that, right now, she did not feel nauseous in any way at all.

Bonarain removed the afterbirth from the baby, cut the umbilical and tied it off. She looked up at Chyning. "Get rid of that mess, will you?"

Chyning looked at the afterbirth and nearly gagged. She touched it with just the tip of one finger and hopped the nasty thing into dimension #45. She then went to the sink and thoroughly cleaned both hands. Then she thought about it for a moment. She nearly gagged but Kiyalee did *not*...why?

Bonarain finished cleaning the new child. She waited until after Aya did her initial urination. She chuckled when she thought about how it was easier to control where a girl peed than a boy because of the difference in plumbing. She cleaned Aya again, wrapped the baby in a blanket and took her to her very anxious mother.

Kiyalee took Aya passionately and stared deep into the big blue eyes of her daughter. "Hello, my little precious one. Now you're going to have to punch something else other than my bladder."

"Yeah," said Bonarain. "Right now, we need to clean you out."

Kiyalee looked up rather surprised. "What...are you talking about? I don't remember you being...cleaned out."

"I know. And I suffered a little bit because of it. I've been reading up on the subject and I found out that once the womb has been evacuated by the baby…there are other concerns." She smiled. "Just be glad that since Soolchakan invented the method by which we give birth…your vagina is not as torn and ragged as the women of other races when the baby comes out."

As Kiyalee lovingly stroked the top of Aya's head she chuckled. "It seems ironic that it was a man who came up with that method…when he can't ever experience any of the things that we go through during the pregnancy…" She turned to the side with a disgusted look on her face. "…or contractions."

Bonarain snickered. "I'm not complaining. I didn't go through any contractions with Monaha. The ones that I went through with Shalam, they were painful enough."

Kiyalee nodded. "One was bad enough for me."

Both women looked at Chyning.

Chyning backed away. "DON'T LOOK AT ME! I don't want one of those things! I'm having too much fun to get distracted by some squalling little monster who has to be fed and…" She looked away in revulsion. "…cleaned…*constantly*." She looked sideways back at the other two. "I'm going downstairs to get me something to eat. I'm the *only* person that I plan on feeding." She vanished.

Bonarain sighed. "Somehow…we're going to have to talk her into it."

Kiyalee went back to staring at her newborn. "I agree. But how?"

Bonarain had an evil grin. "By foul treachery…if we have to."

Kiyalee looked concerned. "Are you sure you wanna do that?"

"Yes…maybe…I don't know." Her shoulders sagged. "We have to get her involved."

"Think long and hard on it before you do anything rash."

Bonarain just snarled.

In the beginning of the year 116, Shalam was 99 years old. Monaha was 13 and Aya was 4. Bonarain and Kiyalee had been thinking for quite some time about how to get Chyning involved. Chyning would not listen to them at all and they knew that hatching a plan with Soolchakan might not be the best thing to do. He had openly stated, numerous times, that he did not want to influence any of the three women regarding procreation, other than the shenanigan he had pulled to create Monaha. He was still very unsure and uneasy about the horror of inbreeding.

Kiyalee walked into the monitor room. Soolchakan was focusing on something that was moving somewhere near the planet Afkoth. It turned out to be a very large meteorite that slammed into the planet creating an explosion of frozen methane and ammonia that went high into the upper atmosphere of the planet.

He hung his head. "Thank the Great Maker. That was nothing harmful to us."

While his head was down, Kiyalee took a swab and quickly

obtained a sample of his neck mucus. She hastily hid the swab behind her back. He looked up in surprise.

He looked her up and down. "What was that?"

She did her best to act innocent. "What was…what?"

"You…touched…the back of my neck."

She mockingly scoffed. "If I had touched those slimy scales of yours…I'd be burning for sex right now. Do I look like I want you to jump me?"

He now looked confused and cleared his throat. "I… thought…something touched me. Right in the spot…where…" He looked back at the monitors and cleared his throat again. "Nothing! You're right. If it had been you that touched me… there…you'd be dropping your pants and…begging for sex."

"Maybe…it was your imagination." She smiled. "Have you seen anything other than that meteorite?"

He huffed. "No! Sometimes I wish I did see something but…then I know…that…it could be disastrous to us if I did." He nodded. "It's best that…all we see on these monitors is…nothing unusual…or alien."

"I agree," she said merrily. "Who is supposed to relieve you?"

He looked up at the clock. "Shalam is supposed to be here…in about one Mithpell." He sighed. "I can hardly wait."

She chuckled. "That is definitely one good thing about the children growing up. They can help taking turns in here."

He nodded. "Yeah…but it's going to be another 65 years before we can trust Monaha in here. Even longer for Aya."

"True," she said. "But they *will* grow up." She was holding the wet end of the swab away from her. She had to get out of there before she accidentally brushed against it. "Bonarain was wondering what you wanted to eat when you finish your shift."

He sniffed. "I'd like a big slab of that bovine meat. I'd also like a big hot baked tuber…you know…that very yellow thing."

"Sounds good. I'll tell her." She vanished.

He looked around suspiciously. He felt the back of his neck. He shook his head as he picked up a towel and wiped the mucus off of his hand. He went back to looking for any movement on any of the monitors. He then silently chuckled to himself. He remembered how she could not stand the thought of watching a birth. Then when she gave birth she had no problems. He had used the *Voice of Power* on her. He had ordered her to have a stronger stomach when it came to blood and gore. He did not like the idea of controlling others in this manner with the *Power*, however, he was tired of watching her *blowing chunks* every time something messy happened.

Kiyalee held the swab up. "Okay sister-woman, I got it. Now what?"

"For pity sake, don't touch that wet end."

She snarled back at Bonarain. "I'm not stupid." She looked at the business end. "He's going to be in there for another full Mithpell."

Bonarain sighed and shook her head. "Let's hope that it doesn't lose any potency during that time."

"Where's Chyning right now?"

"She had something to eat and said that she might take a bath afterward."

"She's gonna clean her neck."

"Don't worry about that."

Kiyalee shrugged. "Why, we need her mucus to…"

"We need female mucus," said Bonarain with an evil grin! She wiggled her eyebrows.

Kiyalee just cleared her throat and looked away. "Oh." She nodded her head as she carefully held the swab away from herself. "Yes, any female mucus will do the job on *him*."

When Soolchakan came back to the apartment, Bonarain called him to follow her. When they entered the bedroom belonging to Chyning he was very confused.

"Why're we in her bedroom? Is there something wrong with her?"

Bonarain smiled. "Not really. We just need to teach her a little lesson in cooperation."

He narrowed his eyes. "Cooperate…with…what?"

At that moment, Chyning walked in the room, dripping wet, with a towel wrapped around her. "What's going on!? Why are *you* in *my* bedroom?"

Bonarain smiled. "We need you to cooperate with us."

Chyning looked more angry than confused. "Cooperate? How?"

"**Now**," sent Bonarain!

Kiyalee appeared in the room, quickly ran to Chyning and rubbed the swab across the forehead of the unsuspecting victim.

Chyning let out a long loud moan and dropped to her knees. She grabbed her crotch and let out another angry moan. "What did you...what is this...why am I...WHAT'S GOING ON?" She doubled over on the floor in the fetal position while groaning.

Bonarain spoke to her in a patronizing manner. "You need to get involved in the procreation as well. The gene pool is small enough...even *with* you."

Chyning looked up angrily at Bonarain. "I just finished cleaning my neck. I don't have any mucus to smear on him." She groaned. "You parasite!"

Soolchakan scoffed. "Didn't think about that one when you cooked up this stupid plot, did you?"

Bonarain smiled. She reached behind her neck, obtained a dab and smeared her mucus on his cheek.

Now he let out a moan as he doubled over.

Bonarain had an even bigger triumphant smile. "We'll

leave you two to take care of…what needs to be done." She vanished.

"See you later," said Kiyalee merrily. She vanished.

Chyning glared at him. "Why did you go along with this?"

"I didn't know anything about it," he growled. He started undoing his belt. "I swear by all that is holy, I didn't know a thing! If I had…I would've used the *Power* to stop them from…" He leaned over holding his groin and moaned.

She was still folded up on the floor panting. "Can't we just…masturbate and…not do anything…or touch each other?"

He was panting as well. "You know…that they'll just try it again."

"You can stop them…using the *Power*! You could probably stop our reaction…right now…using it."

He closed his eyes and hung his head. "Right now…I can't even think straight. All I can do…is think of…mounting you."

She rubbed her crotch for a few moments. "This isn't helping." She moaned again. "All right…we'll do it…and…kick the *h'oolyach* out of both of em…later."

He was on all fours. "We'll probably be more comfortable… on the bed."

She snarled. "Unfortunately…I think you're right." She looked at the bed. "Let's get over there and…" She crawled to the bed leaving her left hand in her crotch. "One way or another…I'll get them back for this!"

"Get in line," he growled as he crawled to the bed as well.

Chyning woke up. She looked around trying to figure out what all had happened. She was laying on top of him with her left arm trapped beneath him. She pushed herself up and yanked her arm out from under him. Her left arm was a little numb from the circulation being cut off, so she sat up and rubbed her arm to get some feeling back.

He woke up. He shook his head. "I repeat...I had no part in this plot," he croaked. "They took me by surprise as well."

She bared her teeth at him. "You *better* be tellin' me the truth."

"I am!" He stretched a little. "You wanna get off of me?"

She flopped back down. "It is kinda comfortable. You... you're warm."

"Get up, go take a bath, get dressed...and then together we'll go slap the *h'oolyach* out of those two belligerent...*things*."

She rolled off of him and was laying on her back. "I don't remember it...being anything like that. I...just couldn't think... of anything except...spreading my legs and...I didn't want you to stop."

"That...wretched mucus...is really something. I wish the doctors were still here so they could analyze it."

She sighed. "Think that'd change the results any?"

"No, it..." He huffed. "I'm just curious."

She groaned a little as she sat up. "Take that pillow with you. It still has some of your neck *h'oolyach* on it. I'd hate to lay my head down and get…turned on for nothing."

He sat up took hold of the pillow. He yawned and vanished.

She sniffed and sighed. "Where and how hard do I kick them?" She shook her head, got up and headed for the bathroom. She stepped into the bathtub and turned the water on. "That was *rape*," she said angrily. "That was…totally uncalled for. I can't blame *him*…even though I want to. *They*…slimed *him*…and made him do it as well." She took a deep breath and sighed. She sat down in the tub and started scrubbing her crotch. "Oh, I wanna hurt them so badly."

After the bath Chyning went downstairs to get something to eat. She found Soolchakan was there already eating some meat.

"What did you get for breakfast?"

He looked up. "They had some odocoil meat ready for us. I guess they got it ready…in order to...make an attempt at an apology."

She looked at the meat. "Is it antlered or horned odocoil?"

He looked down as he cut another piece of meat. "It tastes like antlered."

"Is it just meat?"

"No, there's some toyskot beans that've been warmed up as well. They're in a pot on the stove."

Chyning looked around a little. "Where are…*they*?"

He shrugged and sighed. "I don't know right now."

She walked over to him and leaned down close to his ear. "You have the capability of making them come back…right now."

He was chewing on some meat so he used telepathy. "**I don't want to see either one of them right now**."

"I do want to see them…right now," she said through clenched teeth.

He swallowed the meat and sighed. He looked in her eyes and saw…something. "**Bonarain! Kiyalee! Get back here to the main room of our apartment…RIGHT NOW!**"

Bonarain and Kiyalee both appeared. Monaha and Aya were with them.

Monaha looked around the room. "I can hardly wait until I learn how to do that," he said gleefully."

Aya just stared in wonder.

Soolchakan glared at the two women. "Who is watching the monitors right now?"

"Shalam," said Bonarain flatly.

Soolchakan pushed back from the table. "You know why you're here now, don't you?"

Kiyalee flushed and looked off to the side.

"We did what we had to do," said Bonarain with no emotions. "We had to get Chyning involved in this."

His face flushed in anger. He did some quick deep breathing

in order to calm himself down. "Even though it involved a form of sexual assault…against *both of us*?"

"The end justifies the means," said Bonarain.

"I don't agree," he muttered.

Kiyalee scoffed. "Well…you weren't going to do anything about it!"

He stood up with his eyes wide with anger. "Because I wanted to give you three the choice as to whether or not you wanted to…procreate!" He pointed at Chyning. "You two took her choice away from her...and me."

Bonarain shook her head. "Our gene pool is small enough. We all have to get involved. I have figured out a way to repair any…mutations…that might occur because of the small choices that we have. I did it for Shalam, I did it for Monaha, I did it with Kiyalee for Aya…I can do it with Chyning. It *is* her duty to go along with it."

He walked towards Bonarain with a sinister look in his eyes. "Only if it is voluntary on her part," he growled through his teeth. He walked up and got right in her face. "Voluntary on her part…AND MINE!" He backed away a little. "It was bad enough when Kiyalee tricked me. Then you and Kiyalee had to trick both Chyning…and me."

Bonarain folded her arms across her chest. "You tricked me! Otherwise Monaha might not be here."

He shook his head. "Is this what we've become? We just sit here playing dirty tricks on each other? **NO MORE TRICKS!**"

He looked at all three women. **"No more dirty tricks…especially when it comes to procreation."** He cleared his throat. "If you want some kind of…special act…done by someone else…you get their permission. Any questions?"

Bonarain and Kiyalee both had a guilty look on their face.

Chyning was still angry. "I'd still like to use both of them as punching dummies."

Soolchakan sighed. "We don't need to go back to those silly fights that Nagasoom came up with. We need to get along and trust each other."

Chyning huffed. "It may be a long time before I can do that."

"You do need to trust me," said Bonarain. "My intentions are the best for all of us and for our future. I will help you make sure that your child is…as perfect as possible."

Chyning simply glared at Bonarain.

Bonarain took a long controlled breath. "Even though you didn't want a child…I can assume that you'll want this child to be…healthy and perfect."

Chyning still just glared.

Bonarain was persistent. "You do want the child to be healthy…and perfect…don't you?"

Chyning just shook her head and sat down. She picked up a fork and started eating.

10

Chyning was very hesitant in allowing anyone to mentally take a look at the interior of her uterus. She knew that she would eventually have to get with Bonarain and take a look at what was growing in there because of experience. Bonarain had taken care of her two children and had aided in repairing Aya. From what she had heard, there had been a considerable amount of repairs to the three children. Now another child was being formed and it would be silly to not have Bonarain take a look, even though Chyning did not trust her comrade very much, any more…at all.

Bonarain tried to sweet talk Chyning as much as possible and did apologize on many, many occasions. She still received nothing but a nasty glare in return. Bonarain was realizing that no matter how much your good intentions were, when you broke the trust of someone, it was very hard, if not impossible, to get it back.

Kiyalee made several attempts at apologizing by fixing all kinds of different fruit plates for Chyning. Everyone knew that Chyning loved eating fruit above and beyond anything meat, grain or vegetable…especially now that she was going to be having some strong cravings. She also realized that it was going to take something quite extraordinary in order to regain trust from Chyning.

Bonarain sat looking at a calendar. "I think that your baby

is going to be born…either late in the month of Inamyon or early Consoray." She received silence from Chyning. "Sooner or later, we need to take a look at the child. Shalam, Monaha and Aya all needed quite a bit of repair. If you don't let me look at your child…I…don't want to think of what may happen…when the child is born."

Chyning finally gave in and allowed the search. Bonarain placed her forehead against Chyning's. She started mentally going through the uterus (through a lot of bitter thoughts from the mind).

"There it is," sent Bonarain. **"Right now, it is nothing more than a speck. As soon as it starts growing, we'll be able to see if there is anything wrong with your baby**."

Chyning was still very blunt. **"And you'll fix it**?"

Bonarain sighed. **"We…will fix the baby**."

Chyning, at first, wanted to snub both Bonarain and Kiyalee for all of the food that they were preparing. Then Chyning became even more ravenous and seemed to have no control over herself. Yes, she would gobble down the fruit plates without a thank you. Yes, she gobbled down the salad plates without a thank you. Yes, she gobbled down the meats, breads and tubers. She did not even realize how much she was eating until *she* devoured an entire dinsamp melon by herself and did not feel stuffed. Those melons were huge…almost as large as a red juice melon. For any one person to eat an entire dinsamp – you were usually being gluttonous…or ravenous…or pregnant.

When Bonarain came to Chyning and wanted to take a look at how the child was developing, Chyning did everything she could to be totally distant and discourteous. She did, however, listen and watch what Bonarain was doing as certain small changes were done to the fetus in order to repair damages that Chyning could not even see...yet.

After fifteen weeks, Chyning went off to her room and decided to do a little exploration of her own on this new life in her womb. She laid back on her bed, closed her eyes and focused on the fetus. She started with the feet. She willed the feet to grow and was amazed at how they did stretch a little. The legs were stretched, the arms were stretched and then she made the buttocks a lot larger. She snickered as she went through the process.

She decided to heavily endow the child sexually. She found a small spot in the front and stretched it out considerably. She looked for the testicles to make them larger and then...what is that...a...labia (?). This is a *girl*! What did she stretch out? She went back and realized that she had stretched a portion of the left labia into a tentacle.

She opened her eyes, jumped up and looked at herself in the mirror. "WHAT ARE YOU DOING YOU STUPID *BIMYOCK*? THIS IS YOUR...*CHILD*!" She stood there staring in shock at her reflection. "It was Bonarain and Kiyalee that...messed with you! This baby didn't do anything wrong! This baby is innocent!" She suddenly realized that she really did care about this child... this new...Owlamite *girl*.

She laid back down on the bed, closed her eyes and went back to the child's body and now she was trying to repair the damage that she had just done. First of all - get rid of that silly tentacle. Then go back and reduce the hips, shorten the arms and legs and reduce the size of the feet. She could not remember what they looked like before she had started so she did her best to make them look normal for the size of the fetus...maybe...hopefully.

By the time she was finished with getting things back to, hopefully, what they were supposed to be, she was exhausted. Both mentally and physically. She was also extremely hungry.

She went back to the kitchen and found that Kiyalee had made a nice big batch of kwatha. She accepted a big mug of the kwatha without any of the caustic attitude that she usually displayed. She was immediately spooning for the biggest lumps that she could find in the thick broth.

Kiyalee was a little suspicious of this new attitude because she had not been chewed out in any way at all. Chyning had accepted the kwatha in, what seemed to be, a grateful manner. Kiyalee just kept it to herself - for now. She gave a friendly smile and then ladled a mug for herself. She allowed herself a few clandestine glances at Chyning to see if she was going to get any more of the scornful remarks. There were none. Chyning was too busy gorging herself with big kwatha lumps and broth.

Chyning finally could not find any more lumps and she put the mug to her mouth and drank all of the broth. She put the mug down and cut loose with a very loud belch. She licked some of the broth off of her lips, wiped her mouth with her arm and looked at the pot on the stove.

"There's more if you want it," said Kiyalee cautiously.

Chyning got up and nearly ran to the stove. She took the big ladle and filled her mug again. She went back to her seat and once again went through the ritual of finding all of the big tasty lumps first.

Kiyalee was feeling a little better about herself, hoping that there was finally some kind of forgiveness in Chyning's heart. She quietly went through her kwatha as Chyning gulped down the second mug and cut loose with another loud belch.

It was time for Bonarain to take another look at the fetus. She set the two chairs close together in the normal face-to-face manner. She sat down on one and Chyning sat down on the other. Bonarain noticed that Chyning did not look as spiteful as she normally did. She was looking worried. At first Bonarain did not think much of it.

The two women put their foreheads together and started the session. Mentally, Bonarain felt that Chyning was still a little distant, however, it was not in the irritated way she had been before, now she seemed worried. There was no point dwelling on that. The task at hand was the unborn child. Bonarain started looking at the exterior of the child and was a little surprised. The feet, the hands, the arms, the legs, the buttock and…what is that…wart (?)…on the front of the left labia. She opened her eyes and noticed that Chyning was perspiring…more than usual.

Bonarain broke the connection and pulled away. "Were you trying…to do some repairs…on your own?"

Chyning opened her eyes. "You did it yourself…from the start. Why? What's wrong?" She looked very worried.

"What I did was…look at things that were in there and… find something that was out of place. I then studied some of the information on it and found what was supposed to be normal. I then repaired it according to what I found in the medical journals."

Chyning got a little defensive. "I thought…that…some of the…limbs…should be larger." She shook her head. "…er… longer." She flushed.

Bonarain shook her head. "Not at this time. Not until the baby is born and starts normal growth outside of the womb." She shook her head and sniffed. "We need to get back in there and get things back to normal. Don't concern yourself with the size of the feet or hands…unless they're not the same identical size."

The two women met foreheads again and now Bonarain was repairing the damage that had been done. After that she seemed to place a great deal of attention on the lungs of the child. Chyning could not understand what was so special about the lungs until Bonarain started making them grow fully in the small chest cavity.

Chyning frowned as she thought about what was going on. **"What happened with the lungs? Why did you do that**?"

"They were entirely too small…even for a fetus. All three, Shalam, Monaha and Aya…their lungs were much more developed at this stage. We'll keep an eye on them as your little girl grows."

After they finished the session, both Bonarain and Chyning were left mentally tired.

Bonarain grunted as she got up. She decided that some small talk might help repair some of the relationship. "Have you...thought of a name for your little girl yet?"

Chyning gave Bonarain the evil eye. "I've been thinking along the lines of what you did...in coming up with a proper name for how I got dumped into this situation."

Bonarain shook her finger at Chyning. "No! I know that... what Kiyalee and I did was...not exactly polite but...*please*...do *not* take it out on your daughter. She is innocent. She didn't have anything to do with...what we did. She is a result of it but...I beg of you...don't take it out on her. If you do then...someday she may find out and start thinking that she was totally unwanted. Then she'll develop all kinds of mental problems."

Soolchakan was in the room now. "I agree." He shook his head. "What Bonarain and Kiyalee did was deplorable. It is not the fault of your daughter."

Chyning looked off to the side and sulked a little. "Okay, you're right. My little girl...is not the one who..." She looked at Bonarain and grunted in disgust. She thought for a few moments. "Her name will be...Zina (*in Owlamite it means: "Surprise"*).

Soolchakan groaned. "Are you serious?"

Chyning stood up akimbo. "Absolutely! It doesn't sound insulting...the way I think of..." She gave Bonarain a dirty side glance. "...what they did. I'll just tell her that I wasn't expecting to be a...mother...but...*surprise*...here you are!" She folded her arms across her chest and wobbled her head haughtily at Bonarain. "If you don't like it...I don't care!"

Bonarain shrugged with a nauseous look on her face. "Zina it is. I guess you could say that we were all surprised by the revelation of how…that nasty muck…coming out of the back of our necks…for *9,000 YEARS*…was the secret to procreation…all along."

Soolchakan sighed. "Remember that she is going to have to live with it."

Chyning smiled at Bonarain. "And so will you. Only you know the *real* reason why. So does Kiyalee and so do I."

Soolchakan grunted in disgust. "Bonarain played a trick on me that resulted in Shalam being born. I played a trick on Bonarain that resulted in Monaha being born. Kiyalee played a trick on me that resulted in Aya being born. Bonarain and Kiyalee played a trick on…" He looked up at the ceiling in thought. "…*both* myself and Chyning and that resulted in Zina." He looked angrily at the three women. "*Enough*…with all of the dirty tricks. If any of you wants to have another child…you come to me…without any form of a clandestine operation. No secrets! No riddles! No subterfuge! Straight forward process of open communication as to what you want and why. Any questions?"

All three women nodded in agreement.

He sighed in contentment. "Good! Now…let's cut open and dig into one of those red juice melons."

The months passed by and Bonarain had many more sessions with Chyning on properly repairing anything wrong with

Zina. She was finally satisfied with the repairs on the lungs and then she did several things to the cardiovascular and digestive systems.

Chyning was totally shocked when one of the last sessions before Zina was born, Bonarain made Chyning actually get in mental contact with the unborn baby. There was nothing there but confused simplistic thoughts, however, the brain functions were working.

Chyning swallowed hard. "Was that necessary?"

Bonarain smiled at Chyning. "Yes, because now you've established a link with your little girl. It'll be a bond between you and...nothing else will ever make you closer."

Chyning sighed. "I don't know if I like that. I think...I should've waited until she was born. Then...at least she has something to look at and experience...outside of the womb."

"That is a definite and good thought," said Bonarain. "Maybe I should have waited for Shalam and Monaha to be born before I did any...established mind link. I'll remember that in the future."

The first day of Inamyon came. Chyning was getting very impatient. She did not like the backaches. She did not like having to spend so much time sitting on the toilet. She did not like the way she walked...or waddled. She did not like the way her ankles felt. "When did you say that I was due?"

Bonarain looked off to the side snickering. "I said late

Inamyon or early Consoray. You just ended week number 38 of your pregnancy. My two times…lasted exactly 42 weeks. Kiyalee gave birth one day before the end of week number 42."

Chyning blew a raspberry. She did some quick counting and groaned in misery. "Four more weeks of Zina bouncing on my bladder. Four more weeks of her…pushing her butt up inside my ribcage so I can't sit properly." She leaned her head back and sighed. "How is this worth it?"

Kiyalee shook her head. "I hope that you'll come to a full realization when you are looking down in the face of Zina."

Chyning bared her teeth and snarled.

Bonarain and Kiyalee both giggled. Soolchakan just went back to what he was doing.

Shalam had turned 100 years old. Monaha was 14 and Aya was 5. Shalam had seen the other two born and was not surprised at what was going on. Monaha had not really understood when Aya was born. Now he was a little older and could understand. Aya was still too young to grasp the full situation of what was going on. All she knew was that soon there would be another little girl and she would have a playmate…in a few years.

Chyning was counting the days. She could not wait until she could walk normally again. She could not wait until she was not hungry all the time. She could not wait until she had no more backaches.

Inamyon twenty-fifth, twenty-sixth, twenty-seventh,

twenty-eighth and the day was nearly there. All she had to do was wait two more days…hopefully. Early in the morning of the twenty-ninth day of Inamyon, her water broke.

Chyning stood there totally in shock. Her pants were suddenly soaking wet with…something. **"SOMETHING IS HAPPENING! I THINK ZINA WANTS OUT! NOW!"**

Bonarain was watching the monitors at the time. **"Shalam! Get in here to the monitor room. I need you to take over while I take care of Chyning."**

Shalam growled to himself. **"I was just in there. Can't someone else do it?"**

Soolchakan growled as well. **"Shalam! Do as your mother told you! Unless you want to be the one to assist with the birth."**

"I'm on my way to the monitor room," sent Shalam begrudgingly.

Bonarain Jumped to the main room of the apartment. **"Chyning…where are you?"**

Chyning grunted in exasperation. **"Oh! You want me to go there? Okay, I'll be right there."** She Jumped to the main room.

Kiyalee was a little confused. "Where were you?"

Chyning shrugged. "I was watching some gourd eaters… eating gourds."

Soolchakan shook his head. "Shouldn't we be doing this

in her bedroom?"

Bonarain gave him a patronizing look. "The mess that's in her pants right now...I don't think she wants that in her bed. It'll be bad enough that we have to clean up the counter. Cleaning up a bed is much harder."

Soolchakan shrugged. "Whatever!"

The two women assisted Chyning up on the counter. At that moment, she had her first contraction. She screamed in agony and then glared at Bonarain.

"Yes, I knew that was gonna happen," said Bonarain. "I just wanted you to know what you're being saved from with that method..." She looked at Soolchakan. "...that he invented...just for us Owlamite women."

Bonarain and Kiyalee hopped their arms into Ghost. They reached into the womb and got hold of the infant.

Bonarain smiled at Kiyalee. "Would you like to do the honors?"

Kiyalee smiled back. She looked down at the abdomen as she pulled the baby (along with the afterbirth) out of Chyning. "One baby...delivered." She grinned at Chyning. "Now, you're officially a mommy."

Chyning stuck her tongue out at Kiyalee. She then laid her head back and let out a contented breath of air.

Bonarain helped clean the baby. "Inamyon the twenty-ninth in the year 116 ATUT, the baby girl Zina is welcomed to the world outside of the womb."

Soolchakan placed several pillows under the head and back of Chyning so she could sit up a little and watch while her child was being cleaned up.

After clamping and cutting the umbilical cord, they wrapped Zina in a clean, warm towel and Bonarain took her to her mother.

"Your child…mother," said Bonarain with a big smile.

At first Chyning looked a little disgusted. She took the baby in her arms while still giving Bonarain a dirty look. Then she looked down in the face of Zina and her demeanor changed considerably. She stared in wonder for a few moments. Then tears started running down her cheeks. "She…she's beautiful!" She could not stop herself from sniffling. "She is my…baby…my child…my beautiful little…Zina."

Zina opened her big blue eyes and mouth and made a bit of a squawking sound.

Chyning started laughing while she was still crying. "Yes, Zina…I'm here. I'm gonna keep you safe…as long as I'm alive." She could not take her eyes off of the face of this new little treasure.

Soolchakan sent a private message to the other two women. "**I think that you may just, somehow, have been forgiven…maybe. But in the future, don't press your luck with another stupid stunt like that**!"

Both women let out a little sigh of relief. They then started the process of removing the pants and cleaning up the nasty mess that always comes along with the joy of a new child being brought into the world.

For the next twelve days, Chyning did not let anybody touch her precious little Zina. She had her child with her when she took her turns in the monitor room. She had her child with her when she was preparing a meal. She did a few hops to other dimensions and had the baby with her then as well.

Bonarain sat at dinner nodding. "It is nice that she is caring for her baby…but…she has neglected…just about everything and everybody else in the process."

Kiyalee looked a little frustrated. "Aya wants to see her half-sister, but…Chyning won't let anyone near her." She turned to Soolchakan. "Could you…ask her?"

He had a fork full of meat near his mouth. "Ask…what?"

Kiyalee huffed. "Ask her to…at least let Aya see the baby."

He groaned. "Why don't you ask her?"

"Because she's still mad at me…and Bonarain…even though she's *totally* taken with that little girl."

He stuffed the meat in his mouth and shook his head while chewing. "She has accepted the fact that she is a mother. How she became a mother…she's still upset with the two of you."

Bonarain huffed. "But you told her to get over it."

He got very indignant. "No, I did *not*! I told all three of you that there would be no more *tricks*. Any kind of future procreation will not have any trickery. No one will play any dirty tricks on anybody else. *That*...is what I said. I never told her to get over...IT. If you want her to get over IT...you two will have to be the ones who do the apologizing. I'm not going to make the case for you."

Kiyalee sat there tight-lipped. "But isn't that what you meant...for her to get over it?"

He closed his eyes and growled through clenched teeth. "Do *not* put words in my mouth. If you try to put words in my mouth, I will *un-put* them immediately. I said what I said and I meant what I meant. I said NO MORE TRICKERY! I did NOT tell...or HINT...that she should get over IT!"

Bonarain now looked indignant. "Are you sure that's not what you meant?"

He hung his head and snarled. He vanished.

Bonarain smiled. "We told him, didn't we? Now maybe he'll do something about this situation."

At that moment, both Bonarain and Kiyalee picked up their plates full of food and smacked themselves in the face with the food. They put the plates back down and stared at each other in surprise and bewilderment as the food dripped down off their faces onto their clothing and laps.

"I think *he* just sent us a different message," said Kiyalee.

Monaha was sitting there at the table confused by what he was seeing. "What message was that? And why did you hit yourselves with your food?"

Bonarain turned to Monaha and smiled weakly. "Don't

worry, my dear."

Several days later Bonarain walked into her bedroom. She stopped in surprise and sniffed. She wondered if the toilet had backed up on her. She looked around the room and closed her eyes, totally repulsed by what she had seen. **"Kiyalee, have you been in your bedroom lately?"**

Kiyalee was a little surprised at the question. **"No, I haven't needed any sleep lately. Why?"**

"I still don't think that Chyning has fully forgiven us."

Kiyalee was now almost in panic. **"What happened now?"**

"I just walked into my bedroom...I haven't needed any sleep for quite a few days now and...I think I may have found...half of the dirty diapers...from Zina."

Kiyalee bit her lip. She closed her eyes and shook her head in disbelief. **"I'll go check my room...now."** She Jumped to her bedroom. She hung her head and groaned.

Bonarain waited for quite a while for a response. She did not receive one so she decided to break in on Kiyalee's thoughts. **"What did you find?"**

Kiyalee grunted at the question. **"It smells like an old outhouse in here. I guess you could say that I just found the other half of the dirty diapers...compliments of Zina."**

Bonarain sighed. **"It may take several days to air this room out.**"

Kiyalee felt a little nauseous. **"Both rooms!"**

"I thought that Soolchakan said no more trickery!"

Kiyalee sighed. **"This isn't about procreation. This is about...a person cleaning up after themselves. I doubt that he'll allow us to split hairs in regards to... foul smelling laundry. We can't compare dirty diapers to copulation. Plus, I don't want to wear another face full of food...especially in front of any of the children.**"

Bonarain clenched her eyes and teeth in realization. She had no desire of wearing another plate of food either.

Monaha started his adolescence at about the same age that Shalam had gone into that stage – age 60. Aya, however, started into puberty at about 52 years old. When the bodily changes started on Zina, she was 53.

The elder Owlamites watched the three children closely. Monaha was going through the same things that Shalam had blundered through in adolescence. Aya and Zina were both going through that awkward stage, however, they started earlier and ended earlier. Monaha finished the development at 90. Aya was done when she was 86. Zina was finished growing and developing at 85.

In the year 200 ATUT, the four elder Owlamites celebrated their birthday on the first day of the year – the Fall Equinox which fell on the first day of Astekoy. Soolchakan was 9,244. Bonarain was 9,230. Kiyalee was 9,228. Chyning was 9,226. They all wondered if they should keep on counting, at first. Their children were very interested in the exact ages, so they decided to keep on counting…just to keep the children happy.

Also in the year 200, Shalam turned 184, Monaha turned 98, Aya turned 89 and Zina turned 84. The four of them were all talking about dating and marriage and other things they had never experienced. They had read several accounts in the fiction section of the computer and were rather curious about all of the things in the stories.

The elders felt that the inevitable was going to happen and they now were getting even more worried about the horrors of inbreeding. Bonarain was hoping that she could repair any damage to the grandchildren the way she had performed repairs on the children. The elders awaited the day when Shalam picked a mate.

Shalam was making noises about becoming a husband. He was constantly seen making eyes at Aya and she was enjoying being spied upon by him. Monaha was making almost the same kind of ogling and advancements to Zina. The parents were pleased that the two boys were not fighting over the same girl. That could cause all kinds of unwanted problems.

One day, Bonarain decided to break in on their thoughts. Shalam definitely had the hots for Aya, however, he was not sure what to do. Even if he did woo her he was not sure what the next step was or why – even after the information from the books. She realized that by shielding their children from the outside world, the four children were incredibly naïve. She called a meeting for all members of "Generation One".

They sent the four children on different errands in different dimensions (not to mention the fact that someone had to watch the monitors).

"Our children don't have a clue," said Bonarain sadly. "They know virtually nothing about the other sex and…what to do if…they did get married."

Kiyalee snickered. "Should we show them some films?"

"We need to educate them in some form or fashion," said Bonarain. She turned to Soolchakan and smiled. "The boys… they don't know what their genitals are for…or how to use them. They know how to pee and…" She closed her eyes in disgust. "…scratch." She cleared her throat, opened her eyes and smiled. "Since you know what it feels like from the standpoint of a man… you have to educate the boys. We will educate the girls."

Kiyalee got a little indignant. "*I*…will educate *my* daughter."

Chyning looked angrier. "I will take care of *my* daughter."

Bonarain glanced back and forth between the two women with a little consternation. "Yes!" She chuckled helplessly. "They are your daughters so…I won't argue with your wants for your children. I'm only…saying that all four of them need some… guidelines. If, as you say, they need to see a film…that might be a good idea. Our main problem is that we overprotected them."

Soolchakan grunted. "Not really. We are Owlamites.

We are different. The reason that the boys don't know anything about an erection is because...they've never experienced one. The reason the girls know nothing about...menstruation...or ovulation...is because they've never experienced it." He sighed. "Because of the way our racial tendencies have changed...the only way for them to experience these..." He looked around trying to find the correct term. "...*sensations*...is to get smeared with the mucus...of the opposite sex. Once they've been smeared...they will now end up copulating and...procreating. "*That*...is our life and legacy...from now on."

Kiyalee shook her head. "Great! The only way that Aya can menstruate is...to end up pregnant...and a mommy."

Bonarain shrugged. "The only way the boys can get an erection...they will end up as fathers."

Chyning chuckled. "So, do we put some kind of limitations on them? What do we tell them after we show them films of... copulation...by other species?"

"We make sure that they understand that the final result of copulation is definitely going to be an offspring," said Soolchakan bluntly. "A new child that brings on all kinds of new responsibilities. I've had sex four times in the last 9,000 years. All four times...we have a new child."

Shalam had decided that he wanted to live in apartment 1-562. He had decided that he was now a man and should not be in the same apartment, or level, as his parents...if he wanted to learn everything about life. Bonarain and Soolchakan still kept an eye on him – discretely of course. They did not want to interfere in his maturing.

On 23 Marrem, 213, the parents of Shalam paid him a visit. There were some things going on in his mind that, well, something was happening. They found Shalam and Aya in his apartment…in bed…asleep…naked.

"I think we're going to be grandparents," said Bonarain rather stunned.

Soolchakan shrugged. "Should we tell Kiyalee that she's on that same list?"

Bonarain nodded. "That'd be advisable. I don't think she wants to be left out of the loop."

Soolchakan clicked his tongue. "They are officially wed… in the newly formed traditional way…of the Owlamites."

Ten days later Bonarain and Kiyalee sat down with Aya to discuss repairing the child in the womb. She was informed of how Shalam, Monaha, Zina and she had received all kinds of attention and that was why she had no physical maladies. At first Aya was very worried, however, Bonarain was able to convince her that all would turn out for the better by mending any problems now.

They started the mental process of searching the womb for the little speck. They had told her that nothing could be seen until at least the fifth day. Aya decided to wait until the tenth day for her own satisfaction. Finding the speck did seem much easier on the tenth day. Bonarain felt that from now on, waiting until the tenth day could save a few headaches.

While Bonarain and Kiyalee were looking at the speck, Aya was speculating.

Aya saw the speck. **"Is it a boy or a girl**?"

Both elder women sat there snickering.

"It is much too early to even guess," sent Kiyalee. **"We won't have a clue until the baby starts developing the arms and legs as well**."

Aya seemed a little disheartened.

Bonarain did not want to seem like she was laughing at Aya. **"What did you want? Did you want a boy or girl**?"

Aya sighed. **"I...don't know. I...want a healthy child. I really don't care...boy or girl...well maybe...a girl**."

"We'll see in a couple of months," sent Kiyalee.

Bonarain sat there with a mysterious smile on her face.

They all three got used to the exact location of the speck and then ended the session.

Bonarain was walking away when she noticed a strange look on the face of Kiyalee. **"What's wrong? You seem a little sad. Are you afraid that your little girl has grown up**?"

Kiyalee scoffed. **"All the wars we've been through. All of the dimensions we've explored. All of the horrid** enemies that we've blasted into extinction. When I think about how long it has been since...the firestorm...I didn't really feel old. I'm now 9,242 years old and I really didn't feel old...until I realized that my daughter is about to make me a...grandmother."

Bonarain could not stop laughing at the thought. "**My son is doing the same thing to me. I don't really feel any older...and I *am* older than you.**"

Kiyalee rolled her eyes. "**By a couple of lousy years. What's that after more than nine millennium?**"

At three months they told her that Aya was carrying a baby girl. They were having one of their sessions and Aya was waiting for the two elder women to start performing some kind of healing or renovation on her daughter. She opened her eyes and saw that both elder women were frowning.

Aya was near panic. "**What's the matter? Is there something that dreadfully wrong with my baby?**"

Bonarain shook her head. "**No...there is...absolutely nothing wrong with your baby girl. I don't get it. When we were pregnant...we were making all kinds of repairs...to the bodies of our children. I can't find... anything wrong...with yours. All of the internal organs and external limbs...are all progressing...totally... *normal*!**"

"**It does seem rather strange,**" sent Kiyalee.

They broke the session.

Bonarain shrugged. "It's a good thing! Your baby is developing...perfectly."

Aya still seemed very concerned. "You...you're sure?"

Kiyalee hugged her daughter. "I'm very sure. I wouldn't lead you down the wrong path."

Bonarain was getting rather curious. "I wonder...what name have you decided on for your little one?"

Kiyalee chuckled. "Your miraculously perfect little one."

Aya smiled. "That sounds good...Jada (*in Owlamite it means: Miracle*). You say that everything is so perfect? That is a miracle...so that is her name."

Bonarain smiled. "We're still gonna keep track of her development...but so far...I can't see anything wrong."

Aya just smiled apprehensively.

The pregnancy went on for the full term with no sign that there was ever any problem developing in the fetus. Every system, every organ, every limb and every bone was developing in a flawless manner.

Roistume 10, 214, Aya shrieked as her pants filled up with a strange liquid. "I think that...my water broke," she wailed! "Is it...time?"

Bonarain giggled. "Yes, my dear, it is. When your water breaks…that baby is coming out…and nothing will stop it."

Kiyalee sent a private message to Bonarain. "**Should we wait until she has at least one contraction…before pulling Jada out**?"

Bonarain shrugged. "**I hate to think it…but yes! She should know…like we do, that our method is saving her from a great deal of grief and pain.**"

They helped her get to a table where they stripped her saturated pants off. They were drying her off when the contraction hit.

Aya sat up and screamed with a look of anguish and horror on her face. The scream changed to a moan. She looked around horrified. She started gasping. "Is this…normal?"

"Unfortunately, yes," said Kiyalee. "But because of a bit of quick thinking by your father…that is the last bit of pain that you'll feel."

Aya looked at her mother as if she were insane. Then she watched as Bonarain and Kiyalee hopped their arms into Ghost and carefully pulled the baby Jada out of the womb. She still looked very worried. "What is that…mess?"

Bonarain smiled. "That…*mess*…is the afterbirth. It has to come out as well. If it doesn't come out, there could be some very nasty problems."

"Severe problems," said Kiyalee. "We take it out as well and get rid of it. We save the baby and get rid of what we don't need."

Kiyalee took Jada off to the side to get her cleaned up while Bonarain placed a blanket over the half-naked Aya. After cleaning the baby and wrapping her in a towel Kiyalee brought her back to her anxious mother.

Soolchakan was standing there watching the proceedings. "The first member of the *third* generation. We welcome…Jada… to the world outside of the womb."

Monaha and Zina were standing off to the side watching what was going on with a great deal of wonder in their eyes. This was a first for Zina. The last time that Monaha had experienced observing any childbirth, he himself had been less than twenty years old.

Now they had another child to observe as she grew up. The boys had matured at a later age than the girls. The physical maturity took a little longer for the boys. The more children they were able to see, the more they would be able to see what differences would be manifested in sex and individuality.

One thing they did notice with this new birth, that they seemed to have neglected with all of the others, was to get a diaper on the newborn as quickly as possible. Jada was in the blanket, in the arms of her mother…and she urinated.

Hartkoy, Statichy 15, 219, it was discovered that Monaha and Zina had become married - in the new Owlamite fashion. Monaha was 117 years old, wanted to move out from the parents apartment and had decided to take up residence in apartment 1-1. Zina joined him – in more ways than one.

The parents of these four members of the second generation were getting a little upset over the fact that they were never informed about any marriage until after the consummation of said coupling. They wondered if this was going to become habitual as well. With only four in the second generation, it was difficult to call it habitual – at this time.

Bonarain and Chyning started the ritual of looking over the fetus as it grew. Just like Jada, they could find nothing wrong with this new life that was forming in Zina. The bewilderment on the faces of Bonarain and Chyning did make Zina very anxious about her baby. Bonarain, Chyning and Kiyalee all did everything that they could to quell any concerns that Zina had gone through. Aya had given birth to a perfect child, why was it impossible for Zina to give birth to perfection as well?

They still kept a close watch on the development of this new baby. When they discovered that it was a boy, Zina decided that since she was starting a new journey as a mother, the child should be named Peldom (*in Owlamite it means: Journey*).

They also discovered with certain fainting spells that Zina was going through that each woman was different in how she progressed through her pregnancy, sometimes radical differences. Zina had none of the morning sickness or uncontrolled flatulence. She also did not get dizzy, she just fainted. Every new pregnancy, and the way the mother reacted, was becoming a full learning process for all Owlamites that now existed.

On Tadkoy, Inamyon 4, 219, Zina felt her water break. They went through the same rituals of pulling the child out. This time, however, they got a diaper on the new boy, Peldom, as quickly as possible…and he wasted no time in wetting the diaper, thus requiring a new diaper.

Now the first generation had a third boy they could watch growing up. They still had the mystery of how the children of Bonarain, Kiyalee and Chyning had been such a mess in the womb and how the children of Aya and Zina were so perfect.

Shortly after Peldom was born, they found out that Aya was pregnant again. A few months later Zina was having her fainting spells again. Both women were pregnant and had the pleasure of trying to take care of very young infants while blossoming out again. It was especially hard for Zina, breastfeeding while she worried as to whether she was going to faint in the middle of the feeding. Chyning and Aya kept a close watch during those feedings.

Bonarain, Kiyalee and Chyning all went through the rituals of looking for anything wrong with the babies and once again found nothing that needed any repairs.

On Citendali 29, 220, a boy named Baktim (*in Owlamite it means: Watcher*) was born to Shalam and Aya.

On Consoray 7, 220, a girl named Zoya (*in Owlamite it means: Nice*) was born to Monaha and Zina. Soolchakan had a little moisture come from his eyes as one of the girls was named after his own Heyyah mother.

Now the Owlamite clan was getting larger and four of them were very young children. Soolchakan looked at each one of his wives, wondering if they wanted to have any more children at this time. They all stated that assisting in keeping an eye on four infants at the same time was a rather large chore at this time and that no more children, especially that young were needed at this time. He did not push the issue because he was one of the ones who had to assist in taking care of four growing children and for the next ten years that was a big enough headache for all of them.

11

The klaxon went off Tadkoy, Tulivren 10, 222 ATUT. In the monitor room, Monaha saw some strange vessels orbiting the planet Bri. He sent out the mental call to all Owlamites (over the age of 10).

Aya and Zina went to the monitor room, with all four of their small children. The first generation along with Shalam and Monaha went to the fighters to find out the intentions of this new intruder.

While the first generation Owlamites were worrying about what might occur, the two men of the second generation had adrenaline pumping through their veins and they were totally inexperienced. Soolchakan read their minds and had to use the *Power* in order to keep them in line and not to do anything rash even before the Jump to Bri.

They found fifteen ships orbiting Bri. They were doing the normal analysis that everyone else before them had done. They had to guess which one was the flagship in this armada. They checked all fifteen before they realized that the one in command had not yet entered the star system. This was a reconnaissance mission of fifteen ships that were to perform some initial exploration before the main invading force came in. They were supposed to be looking for any form of a guardian sensor, however, when they discovered the mineral wealth of Bri, they became sidetracked. The flagship authorized this quick check of the planet because so far no one had sensed any form of sophisticated technology.

From reading their minds and obtaining some valuable intelligence, Bonarain found that the flagship, along with 952 other invader ships, were parked outside the system, somewhere beyond the orbit of the furthest planet Denhahbon.

Soolchakan gritted his teeth as he heard this realization. This was an invasion force that was here to give no warning, just invade and conquer, in the shortest time possible. **"Bonarain, find the flagship! The rest of us…start destroying these ships that are here.**"

Kiyalee came back. **"How many do you want destroyed**?"

"We destroy two each. Then, once Bonarain has discovered the location of the rest of the fleet…we ruin the lives of several of them."

Chyning sent a message back. **"Have you noticed how much these people look like the Mustooza**?"

Soolchakan was not ready to carry on any long conversation about who they were fighting. **"Yes, I have. Have you noticed that they don't have eyes all the way around their heads…and that they do have arms**?"

Chyning grunted to herself. **"Yes, I noticed it.**"

"Good! Let's start blowing up a few ships and scare the h'oolyach out of the ones that survive."

Shalam and Monaha were the first to blow up their ships. Chyning got the next two. Soolchakan and Kiyalee had waited until the others had done their damage in order to make sure that there were not two people hitting the same ship. Kiyalee took out two and then Soolchakan did his damage.

Shalam sent out a message that sounded like he was really enjoying himself. "**You know, that it is amazing. Amazing how much damage you can cause just by introducing some foreign object inside that big cylinder that they use as their light speed engine? I love it**!"

Monaha answered him. "**Totally amazing! We have them right where we want them and they can't do a thing about it**!"

Now Soolchakan really had his jaws clenched. "**Enough chatter! Bonarain, have you found the location of the flagship and the rest of the fleet**?"

Bonarain answered. "**Make a Jump to Denhahbon. Then head straight out from the system. Most of the fleet is here and...they are hearing all kinds of discouraging things about the ships that are inside the system. They've ordered the five surviving ships out of the system if you want to follow those five**."

Soolchakan thought for a few moments. "**Shalam... Monaha...each of you take out another one of the fleeing ships. Kiyalee and Chyning...we head for the fleet**." He growled in disgust. "**Bonarain, do you have their language yet**?"

"Of course I do...why do you ask?"

"Relay a message for me."

"What's the message?"

"This is Soolchakan! I am the Drey Sssorg of the Owlam people. You are invading my star system. If you do not turn around and go...NOW...we will be forced to destroy your entire fleet. There is no compromise! There is no negotiating! You go now...or die in outer space where you are!"

Bonarain came back. "Do you want their response?"

He sighed. "Of course."

"We don't listen to lower life forms. We're here to bring this star system under the rule of the Voonshost Empire. You can either surrender or be destroyed. It is of no significance to me, we will take this star system no matter what. Now we are cutting off all communications with those who will soon be slaves or dead. The next communication you hear from us will be the commands that we give to all slaves...uh...he just cut off the receiver."

He growled. "Looks like we're going to have to bring out the Multifastidigeous Thonlock Communicator... again...and use it to our advantage."

"No problem," sent Bonarain merrily. "What's the message?"

"Are you ready?"

"**Absolutely!**"

"**Do not think that you can cut us off by turning your unsophisticated communication system off. We are on a much higher plane of existence than that. It is we who have to lower ourselves to communicating with parasitic life forms such as yourself. NOW, get you trash away from our star system! I will not tell you again...I will just start destroying your ships...at my whim.**"

Bonarain snickered. "**He's about to blow a blood vessel in his head.**" She watched what was happening. "**He just told his communication officer to cut off all of our transmissions or he'd have the disobedient *foowothip* executed.**"

Chyning frowned. "**What is a...*foowothip*?**"

"**I think it's a dirty word,**" sent Kiyalee.

"**I think you're right,**" sent Soolchakan. "**Okay, we've done our Jump to Denhahbon. Now, where are you and which one of these things is the flagship?**"

"**I'll get up out of the ship and turn on my revolving beacon,**" sent Bonarain. "**The yellow beacon.**"

Soolchakan looked at the mass of ships that were just sitting idle. They were waiting for the order to attack. They had to be stopped out here or...he did not want to think of what might happen with this many ships. "**Kiyalee...you first. Get in there and...take out at least three ships.**"

Shalam broke in. "**Why can't we all go in and start**

blasting them?"

"Because I don't want any one of us hitting the same ship at the same time. It could be catastrophic for us. If only one of us is doing some damage...then that one doesn't have to worry about blowing up one of us."

Shalam was sulking a little. "Will I get my turn?"

Soolchakan growled at himself. His son was just a little too eager to kill. "You'll get your turn...unless they get the message and leave."

Kiyalee picked an area where the ships were very close together. When she upset the balance in the light speed engine and it blew up, the explosion caused some massive debris damage to four other ships that were close by. She Jumped to a place that was not too far from where she had destroyed the first one and performed the same stunt. Once again, one ship gone and four others damaged. She pulled the same thing in another area. "Okay, I've made a mess."

Soolchakan watched for any reaction. "Bonarain, have they changed their minds about leaving?"

"No. As a matter of fact, he is getting ready to give the order that all ships will attack."

Soolchakan cursed. "Take out the flagship before he gives that order!"

About five heartbeats later, the flagship blew up. Six ships that were close by were damaged by flying shrapnel.

Bonarain looked around at the rest of the fleet. "Who is

next?"

Soolchakan shook his head. "**Pick one and let them have it.**"

Bonarain came back. "**Maybe I should pick one and listen to see if they've already chosen a new leader.**"

Soolchakan did not have to think long on that one. "**Good idea. Do it.**"

They all waited anxiously for a while. Bonarain had chosen one at random and was listening to the chatter that it was receiving.

Bonarain scoffed in disgust. "**They've got the second in command out here...and he's getting ready to give the order. He's already commanded that the damaged ships are the only ones that are to stay behind.**"

Soolchakan growled. "**Destroy the one that you're on and go get another one.**"

Another ship blew up and damaged a few around it.

Soolchakan was getting really frustrated at the hard-headed attitude of these people. "**Bonarain, what is the frequency that they're transmitting on. Maybe we should all be listening in on their chatter.**"

"**You can't understand them yet. I'll listen and see...what they're planning on doing.**" She picked another ship and listened in on the "classified" frequency. "**They're getting ready to do an all-out attack.**"

Soolchakan just shook his head. **"Chyning, you go to the far right of the formation. Start blowing up ships and head in towards the center continuing to create havoc. Monaha, go about half-way to the right. Hit one and then head in to the center, blasting as you go. Kiyalee, you go to the far left, blow one and start heading in to the center. Shalam, go half-way to the left and blast coming to the center. Bonarain, blast the one you're in and start heading to your right. I'm going to blast one near the one that Bonarain blows up and head to my right. Any questions**?" He heard none. **"Go!"** He watched for any ship in the center blowing up. When it did, he headed for a ship to the left of that one. He did not like what was about to happen, however, these people would not listen to reason. They had lost several ships, without knowing how, and were still planning to attack.

The six Owlamites that were flying around in the attack fleet were destroying one ship after another. All they had to do was a trick that had worked for several millennium. Throw the mixtures out of balance and the results were an immediate nuclear blast that destroyed the ship. Of course as soon as the item was placed inside the cylinder, they would hop to dimension #2 before the explosion occurred. That way they did not have to worry about any catastrophe happening to them. After counting to five, while flying a short distance from where the blast had occurred, they would hop back to Home (in Spy) dimension and look for another target. Each Owlamite had to blow up at least forty ships before the invaders got the message that they were completely outclassed and had better run before they were killed as well.

Shalam called out. **"There's about ten ships that**

have turned around. Should we go get them?"

"**No**," sent Soolchakan angrily. "**Concentrate on any of the ships that are still headed for Hardooth. If one or two are running, they've received the message and we don't have to worry about them. The only reason that we destroy the ones going away is if they're going to a specific spot to regroup and start another attack run.**"

The numbers got up to seventy ships destroyed by the Owlamites.

Chyning called in. "**I'm running out of trash that I can toss into their light speed core.**"

"**So am I**," sent Bonarain.

Soolchakan shook his head. "**If you have to...Jump back to Hardooth and...get some fresh trash...anything you can get your hands on.**"

"**They're all starting to turn back**," sent Kiyalee. "**I only see three that are...wait one of them turned back. Only two that are still charging forward.**"

"**I see them**," sent Shalam. "**I can get one of them real quick!**"

"**I'll get the one on the left**," sent Monaha. "**You get the one on the right.**"

"**Got it**," sent Shalam.

The two idiotically courageous ships blew up almost simultaneously. Soolchakan got into their minds and could hear

Shalam and Monaha laughing hysterically after the blasts. He was rather disgusted at the attitude of his sons.

He turned his ship and looked at the fleeing leftovers. "**All Owlamites, call in! I want to make sure that everyone is okay**."

Bonarain, Kiyalee, Chyning, Shalam and Monaha all called in.

He looked at the enemy ships as the glow got smaller and smaller.

"**Let's go home**," he sent calmly.

Shalam sounded disappointed. "**Aren't we going to chase them down and destroy the rest of them**?"

Soolchakan sighed. "**No. They have a place to go… and a tale to tell. A tale of how they were being destroyed by an enemy that they couldn't even see. They didn't know the numbers, but they lost over half of their attack force to this…unseen adversary…and were never able to fire a shot back because they couldn't find this unseen foe. Now, we're going back home. Everybody Jump back to Hardooth…now**."

They parked all of their fighters in one area of the gorge. Shalam and Monaha got out of their fighters still pumped up on adrenaline. They could not stop whooping and shaking with joy and exuberance regarding the totally one-sided fight that had just been waged. Soolchakan was thoroughly disgusted with what he saw. He walked over and smacked both of them so hard that he knocked them down.

Now Soolchakan stared at his two very surprised sons. "Get up! I've got something to show you. I want you to remember it! Never forget it!" He turned to the Owlamite women. "Everybody hop to Spy and Jump to the monitor room…**NOW!**"

Five bewildered Owlamites followed Soolchakan to the monitor room. They were still in Spy dimension when they walked in the room. There they found Aya still looking at the monitors wondering what was going on out there beyond Denhahbon. Zina was cowering in a corner with the four young children of the third generation, trying to comfort them while she herself was terrorized.

"**THAT is what war is,**" snarled Soolchakan. "**It is not some…happy-go-lucky game that you play for fun. There is a woman, looking at that monitor, who is praying that her husband comes back from the battle. In the corner is another woman trying to keep from panicking while she also tries to comfort four terrified children.**" He calmed down and cleared his throat. "Go back to Home dimension."

Aya and Zina now had the realization that the battle was over and the other Owlamites had returned safe and unharmed. Aya ran to Shalam along with their two children Jada and Baktim. Zina ran to Monaha along with Peldom and Zoya. The women embraced their husbands with tears in their eyes. The children were wrapped around the legs of their fathers and were crying as well.

Soolchakan did some deep breathing to help calm himself

some more. "Any time you go into battle…it is NOT some thrilling event. It is *horrible!*" He turned to Bonarain. "How many personnel do you think were on board each one of those ships?"

She shrugged. "I can only…estimate…that there were about 800 on each one."

He turned back to Shalam and Monaha. "800 on each one. We completely destroyed some…420 ships. We damaged…I don't know how many others. It is safe to say that we killed over 340,000 of their people. Each one of those people had parents who cared for them. How many of them had a family - spouse and children? I don't know. The thing that I do know is that over 340,000 of them will never return to their homes. There'll be all kinds of grief over their passing, because we took them by such surprise that they have no clue as to how many of us there were or how we were attacking them. They only know that they have lost a considerable amount of personnel to battle fatalities and could not fire one single shot back at us." He huffed. "War is NOT some childishly fun event. It is an unholy horror of death, dismemberment, maiming injuries and mourning over those that are *dead*. You never go into battle…until all other avenues are exhausted. You kill only if it is absolutely necessary."

Shalam looked confused. "But, you ordered us to kill them."

"Only because things got so out of hand so quickly because they were so stubborn and bigoted they wouldn't listen. That kind only understands one thing and that is force. You have to *make* them listen. They refused to listen until they had lost…probably over half of their fleet. Then they listened because they could not even figure out who was doing it or how they were being attacked and they were still millions of teckfar from any inhabited planet. They realized they were outclassed. They retreated. Hopefully they learned the valuable lesson that - you don't come back here. If they didn't…then, and only then, do we go back to killing them. Until then…we try to negotiate with them."

Monaha shook his head. "But…you've told us…of some of the genocidal conquests that you were part of…in the past… before we were born," he said sheepishly.

Soolchakan nodded. "Yes, we did tell you of those things. Remember though, at that time, I was not in charge. Someone else was. We had to go by their orders. We had no choice. I am in charge now and we go with what I say. I don't like haphazard killing because it really accomplishes nothing positive…unless it ends a war with someone who is stubborn and stupidly bigoted to the point where they believe that all other sentient races should bow to them." He sniffed. "Remember that your wives and children were terrified over the fact that you might not return. Now that you have, they are relieved…but still worried that something like this could happen in the future…and you might not return then."

"You always did," said Monaha shyly.

Soolchakan closed his eyes and growled in disgust. He opened his eyes. "Yes…we were lucky enough to return. Let me remind you that after the firestorm weapon went off, we had just over 28,000 of the first generation. How many do you see before you now? Only four of us survived *all* of those battles. Over 28,000 DID NOT! Remember that whenever you want to glorify battles and wars. Think of the dead. They can't celebrate with you. Their relatives can't celebrate with you. The dead are dead and the living relatives can only feel sorrow, wondering why it was their relatives who died while the relatives of someone else is still alive." He walked away still huffing and growling in disgust.

Shalam looked at Aya. "Aren't you glad for us?"

Aya gave him a nasty look. "I'm glad that you're back. I'm glad that you weren't hurt. I…can't say that I'm glad about your attitude. Like he said…somewhere around 340,000 of those others were killed. Slaughter of…anyone…isn't a reason to celebrate."

Zina sniffed as she gave Monaha an equally dirty look. "I didn't like the thought of having to raise these two children… without you. I didn't…join with you to watch you die…before your children can read and write their own names."

Monaha turned to Bonarain. "When you're out there… attacking them…doesn't it get your blood boiling…in…some kind of elation?"

Bonarain sighed and shook her head. "Elation? No. FEAR! Yes. Fear that I might be the next one blown away."

Shalam frowned. "But…we can absorb energy…and… blast it back at the enemy. How could they possibly…kill us?"

"You have to be ready to absorb that energy," scolded Kiyalee. "If you're not ready…the results could be…fatal."

Shalam and Monaha turned to Chyning for some kind of backing from her.

Chyning rolled her eyes. "Whadaya want from me? It is *not* fun to kill. You kill only when and if necessary. They started with almost 1,000 attack ships. We had to cause them no end of grief to make them turn back. That was *not* fun. It was necessary." She huffed. "If…they hadn't turned back…then it would've been necessary to kill all of them."

Shalam narrowed his eyes. "Didn't you do something like that in the past…several times?"

Chyning hung her head. She talked through her teeth. "We were ordered to do so…by whoever was the current *Voice of Power* at that time." She unclenched her jaws and looked up. "Soolchakan is now the current *Voice*. We go with what he says because we have no choice in the matter. We only go with genocide of an enemy…*if* that is the only course that is left to us… by them."

Kiyalee looked up at the monitors. "Shalam…Monaha… go spend some time with your wives and children. Contemplate what they might be feeling…if…you had died. Hold them in your arms while you think about this. See how much your blood is boiling then. I'll watch the monitors for the next shift."

Chyning cleared her throat. "Also, remember, when your children are old enough to take care of themselves…Aya and Zina will each be in a fighter…out there as well. Think about that… before your blood boils again."

Kiyalee looked at Chyning in shock. 'That came out of Chyning? Maybe that woman is finally starting to mature mentally,' she thought.

Bonarain was staring at Chyning, equally surprised.

Shalam still looked somewhat angered. "If you don't like war so much, why fight them at all?"

Soolchakan glared at him. "Because submitting to be a slave to some…over ambitious, self-serving conqueror is even more distasteful. Slavery is even worse than war, especially when you have the means to fight back and prevent the slavery."

12

79 years later in the year 301, the Voonshost returned. Jada was a mature woman now. Peldom, Baktim and Zoya were late in adolescence. According to a decree from Soolchakan, only mature adults could head out to battle. Nine Owlamites were heading out to the fight.

This time the Voonshost were willing to do some talking before they attacked (so they said). Bonarain found the flagship and was listening to what they said and reading the minds to find out what they actually meant.

Because of the number of ships the Voonshost had brought the last time, the defense was not done in the small single seat fighters. They had almost run out of debris to throw into the light speed cylinders. Now, flying there in small ten seat shuttlecraft, they each had plenty of room for all kinds of junk they could use to disrupt the mixture in the engines. The fighters did not leave very much room to carry excess junk.

Bonarain was quietly sitting in the Bridge area of the flagship. She called back to Soolchakan. **"Should we use the mulitfastidigeous thonlock communicator again**?"

He snickered. **"What makes you think that we would use anything else**?" He thought for a moment. **"I'm** going in there. I don't see any reason for you to relay the conversation. You taught me their language so I'm going to use it."

Bonarain leaned back in her seat. "**That sounds fair to me**." She chuckled. 'Less work for me,' she thought.

Soolchakan entered the Bridge. He saw where Bonarain was positioned on the starboard side. He parked his craft on the opposite side of the room. "**Have they made any...attempts at communicating...with anyone outside of their... fleet**?"

"**Nope!**"

He sighed. "**I guess then, that it is up to me to start the dialogue**."

She grinned. "**Yup!**"

He turned the speaker in his ship on. "I am Soolchakan! Drey Sssorg of the Owlam people. Why have you come back to our star system? Didn't you get the message the first time you came here? You are *not* welcome here?"

The enemy Commander looked up startled. He turned to his communications officer. "Prevsovon! I thought I told you to turn off all transceivers until I gave the word."

A man raised up and saluted. "They *are* off, Fenbondon! I...don't know where that...communication is coming from. We were told in the briefing...that these people have some kind of...strange device that...can be heard even when our system is completely shut down. I think...that is what we are hearing."

The Commander looked around rather aggravated. "All right...what did you call yourself?"

Soolchakan groaned. "I am Soolchakan. I am the Drey Sssorg of the Owlam people."

The Commander narrowed his eyes. "Which is your name and...what is your rank?"

Soolchakan looked at Bonarain. "**Is he joking or... what**?"

Bonarain sniffed. "**He's stalling in order for them to triangulate and try to find you...so that they can blast you out of existence**."

Soolchakan huffed. "**How quaint! How childishly predictable**!" He took a breath. "My name is Soolchakan. My rank is Drey Sssorg." He watched as several personnel were quickly tapping on their keypads and looking intently at their monitors. "Now...*bimyock*...what is your name and rank?"

The Commander grinned in an evil manner. "I will be the one to ask the questions."

Soolchakan groaned. 'One of those,' he thought. "Not until you tell me your name and rank. I wonder just what kind of petty underling I'm dealing with."

The Commander looked as if he had been slapped. His body quivered in a strange fashion. "My name is Jeehezhik! My rank is Fenbondon! Are you happy now?"

Soolchakan looked at Bonarain. "**What in the flames is a...Fenbondon**?"

"**He is equivalent to a Senior Officer**."

"**What do they call the Supreme Officer**?"

"**Noonbondon**."

Soolchakan grunted. "***H'oolyach***!" He cleared his throat. "I figured that I was talking with an underling. My rank is equivalent to what you *foowothips* call Noonbondon."

Bonarain giggled. "**Ooh! He just thought of a bunch of dirty words and names**."

Jeehezhik clenched his gray teeth. "I am no underling! I am the leader of this fleet. I am the one that you will deal with in this…situation."

Soolchakan shook his head and sighed. "The situation is quite simple. We told you to leave and not come back. Why are you back?"

Jeehezhik looked at his communications officer with wide eyes. The officer just shook his head – or at least the head area. He let out a small snarl. "We of the Voonshost Empire cannot leave any star system, in our area, independent. You must join us…or die. Any star system that is not part of our empire and is located in the middle of it…must be one with us."

"We said no," said Soolchakan bluntly. "We mean it. Now go…and don't return." He sent out a general message. "**Does anyone know how many ships these *bimyocks* brought with them this time**?"

Shalam came back with the answer. "**They've got 1,154 up close here to Denhahbon. I've already checked and**

they have another backup fleet of 982 that is about 2,500 Teckfar behind them."

Chyning broke in. "**2,136 ships? Do you think that they mean business**?"

The communications officer stood up. "Fenbondon… we…have…something."

The Commander grinned. "Where is he, Prevsovon?"

The body of the communications officer quivered. "Fenbondon…he is transmitting…from…inside our…Bridge."

The Commander had something in his hand that he dropped, it shattered when it hit the floor and a green liquid splattered in a large circle. He looked around wide eyed in horror and his body was quivering.

Soolchakan shook his head. "**What is a Prevsovon**?"

"**That's an Officer Grade 4**," sent Bonarain.

Jeehezhik once again bared his gray teeth. "Your… communication system is very sophisticated…and quite unique. We would like to know more about it. If you join us…we could trade a great deal of technology…that would be beneficial to both of us."

Bonarain scoffed. "**He's lying. He's stalling for time!**"

"**What a mundane surprise**," send Chyning sarcastically?

Soolchakan nodded. "How could you possibly help us?

You have nothing…that is nearly as sophisticated as what we have. We have no need of your archaic garbage. As I said before, you can take your entire fleet of 2,136 ships…and go."

The body of Jeehezhik quivered again. "I said that we cannot leave. You *must* join us. You have no choice! You will either join us…or die."

Soolchakan hung his head. 'Here we go again,' he thought. "As I remember…in our last encounter…we suffered zero casualties and zero loss of ships. You…lost well over 400 ships and…we can only estimate that you lost around 350,000 personnel. Do you really want to repeat that totally one-sided battle?"

The body of Jeehezhik quivered again. "That battle was over 60 *skonvik* ago. Are you trying to tell me that you were there…at that time?"

"What you call 60 *skonvik*, we call 79 years. My age is 9,345 years. I don't know how many *skonvik* that is, but…it is a bit longer than any 60 *skonvik*. Yes, I was a big part of that battle. I am personally responsible for blasting at least 70 of your ships out of the sky. It would not bother me to…blast another 70…or 80…or more."

There were several of the Voonshost personnel on the Bridge whose bodies were now quivering.

Shalam broke in again. **"I just found out…from reading the minds of one of the Commanders in the backup fleet. There is another single ship that is about 6,000 teckfar behind the backup fleet. If anything** happens to the primary and the backup...that ship is supposed to run like crazy back to their home planet and tattle on us for destroying all these ships."

Soolchakan groaned. "**Another attack ship is out there**?"

"**No. This one is a very small three-seat vessel. It is designed for speed. They get the information required of them and run.**"

Soolchakan did some quick thinking. "**Shalam, find that little vessel and destroy it. Hopefully, at this time, it is just listening and not transmitting. If we take it out, they won't know for some time what has happened here...if we're forced to...take more lives.**"

"**I don't see any choices**," said Chyning. "**They're talking around everything, acting like they want an alliance when all they want is to conquer us and obtain our star system, our goodies and us as slaves.**"

Soolchakan sat there brooding, with nothing but a bitter taste in his mouth. He had tried to get the point across to Shalam and Monaha that negotiation was a good method. Now, this enemy was giving him no choice because they had come here with the single-minded intention of complete conquest. "**Shalam, have you found that single vessel**?"

Shalam came back. "**It wasn't hard to find. I'm currently on the starboard side of it.**"

"**Does it seem to have any kind of shielding**?"

"Yes, it does. I can't use any of the normal pulse weapons to breach."

"Can you get close enough to put the tip of your pulse weapon inside the ship...before hopping it to Home and...taking them out?"

After a bit of a wait Shalam finally answered. "I'm in. I have the pilot and copilot in my sights and can cut them in half before they even realize I'm here."

"Destroy it," sent Soolchakan flatly. "Then everybody listen to see if anyone knows of the destruction of that ship."

A few moments later Shalam called in again. "They're nothing but debris. I cut the two pilots in half and destroyed their console at the same time. Before the communications officer could call out to anyone... well...he's dead as well. Then I blew the thing up."

Soolchakan did some listening of his own. "Has anyone heard anything on their transceivers about that ship being blown away?"

Zina called in. "I'm at the back of the secondary fleet. All I saw was a small momentary flash of light when he blew up that ship. I'm hearing nothing...from any of these other ships...that says that they know anything about it."

Soolchakan shook his head. He did not want to get into any all-out battle again, however, the Voonshost were leaving him no alternatives. "**Jeehezhik...I know what you have in mind. You want to try to sweet talk us until we let you in...then you're going to conquer us, steal our technology and utilize it for yourselves against us**."

Jeehezhik smiled. "What makes you think that we want to do that? We came here hoping to form a friendly alliance."

Soolchakan scoffed. "**You are so stupid, you don't even realize that I am talking to you...in your mind. No one else can hear me, because I'm sending a telepathic message to you alone. Ask your crew if they heard me**."

The body of Jeehezhik really started quivering now. He turned to his communications officer. "Prevsovon! Did you hear that last communication from...that Owlam?"

The officer stood up and saluted. "Yes, Fenbondon. He said that he would not mind blasting another 80 or more ships."

"NO, you stupid *fomp*! The one after that!"

The body of the Prevsovon started quivering rapidly. "No...Fenbondon...there was...nothing...after that."

Jeehezhik looked around the Bridge. "Did anyone hear... anything...after that?"

All of the Bridge crew looked at their commander in bewilderment.

"**Do you see now? I can read your mind and I can transmit my thoughts as well. I know that you came here to conquer. I cannot allow that. I will destroy any ship that intrudes in our star system. There is nothing** you can do about it because you can't find us…but we know exactly where you are and we can destroy any and all ships before you do anything."

Jeehezhik was quivering and his thoughts were running amuck.

Bonarain broke in. "**He's about to declare *Dezhoznon*!**"

Soolchakan was confused. "**What in the flames is that?**"

Bonarain huffed. "**I guess you didn't get the entire language. *Dezhoznon* - "until we are conquered". They do not retreat under any circumstances. If they can't conquer us, they don't have the right to return home with the shame of defeat. If they return home defeated… they are executed for their cowardice, incompetence and negligence.**"

Once again Soolchakan hung his head in despair. "Why do all of these *bimyocks* have to have some kind of idiotic ultimatum decision in their lives?" He scoffed. "**Jeehezhik, if you are stupid enough to declare…*Dezhoznon*…we will kill all of you. We will do so without any remorse. We will not be slaves to anyone. We especially will not be slaves to inferior creatures, such as yourselves. GO HOME NOW OR DIE!**"

Soolchakan warmed up his pulse pistol and aimed it at Jeehezhik. When the Commander opened his mouth to scream the word of total attack, he never was able to utter the word as the pulse beam decapitated him.

Another Voonshost officer waddled up to the Command position. "This is Twekbondon, Iychahoka! Jeehezhik has just been assassinated. I DECLARE *DEZHOZNON!*"

Soolchakan cursed, turned his pulse gun and decapitated Iychahoka. **"All Owlamites! We are now in a genocidal battle with these *doovofts*! They made the decision. We have no choice but to annihilate all of them...NOW!"**

All 2,136 enemy craft started racing forward. They were using only their conventional engines which helped the Owlamites. If they had used their light speed engines, they could have been to Hardooth in a very short time. As they started forward, the leading ships fired some kind of large torpedoes that looked as if they were heading for Hardooth.

Soolchakan cursed as he saw the launches. **"Bonarain, Kiyalee, Chyning...start killing those torpedoes! The rest of us...start killing enemy ships!"**

The only chatter coming out of the Voonshost ships was the attack message. They were repeating that word over and over. When some of the torpedoes started disappearing from their trajectories and not being seen anywhere, the chatter changed to a lot of questions as to what was going on with the "death missiles". 452 of them had been fired and before they reached the orbit of Afkoth, there were only sixteen of them still remaining. Shortly after that, all of them were gone.

Now the chatter changed again. Ships were blowing up. Once again they were so tightly packed together that when one blew up from the corruption of the mixture in the light speed cylinders, several other ships were damaged or disabled.

They were inside the orbit of Denhahbon with 34 ships blown up and 116 helplessly floating in space due to debris damage from the explosions. They blindly charged on. Before they reached the orbit of Afkoth, 342 more had blown up, damaging and disabling another 221.

The backup fleet entered the orbit of Denhahbon…minus 8 ships blown up and 19 others disabled. Shalam and Zina were doing their job from behind.

They charged on in their suicidal rampage. Even though their numbers were somewhat depleted, they still remained tightly bunched up. This continued to make it easy to damage several when blowing one of them up.

A message was sent from one of the enemy ships to the rest of the fleet. They were to wait until they were much closer to the inhabited planet before launching any more death missiles. Since they had seen all of them mysteriously disappear, they wanted to give their enemy less time to destroy or…whatever they did to them, the launched missiles. Soolchakan was very relieved when he heard that. He was hoping that they could disable the entire fleet before it reached the orbit of Ragath and Rogoth.

From the orbit of Afkoth to the orbit of Bri, they were able to blow up another 316 ships and disable 401 more.

All Owlamites in the attack were astounded at the stupidity of these people. How could they be so devoted to an attack when they saw their numbers dwindling so rapidly, while still not being able to see who or what was killing them? It made no sense.

Anybody could give an order of a suicidal attack, however, only the most moronic of fanatical fools would carry it out. The charge went on. Their culture was very strange. Or they were totally so terrified of the law concerning that insane ultimatum, they considered themselves dead already.

By the time the enemy got near the orbit of Makatindi, another 488 ships were gone and 96 more were disabled.

They only had 95 ships left that were still charging. 853 were floating around in space making attempts at repairs in order to get back in on the idiotic charge. Soolchakan knew they were going to have to go back and clean up the mess that was still behind them.

Before they reached the orbit area of Weeloow and Dilhazass, 91 ships were blown up. Only 4 remained. Chyning was tasked with taking out the remaining fully functional quartet while all of the other Owlamites went back to get rid of the damaged ships permanently. In less than half of one mithpell, Chyning had demolished all four and was coming back to assist in the cleanup.

They found that the Voonshost were abandoning eight of the damaged ships. The repairs would take entirely too long. All of the surviving personnel were to be shuttled to a ship that was in better shape and easier to repair. They had planned on turning on the internal self-destruct sequence before the last individuals were off of those ships. They never got the chance. Since it only took four people to engage the self-destruct sequence, all four were hopped out of the ship into the outer space area of dimension #2. Then all eight ships were hopped to #45 and added to the huge collection of stolen spaceships that was already there. The plan was to find a way in their computers and see if they could find the home planet of this particular vermin.

Cleaning up the last 845 damaged ships was finally accomplished. The devastation of the Voonshost fleet had taken nearly an entire day. The Owlamites were rather tired from all of that hopping and Jumping. They all needed some sleep.

Soolchakan did not know if he could sleep at all. They had just killed over 1,700,000 Voonshost personnel in that attack. Before he Jumped back to Hardooth he noticed that a lot of the debris from some of the enemy ships was being drawn to the gas giant Weeloow. It did not bother him one bit that there were numerous bodies floating in that debris field. They had plunged on, regardless of the fact that the losses were staggering even before they got this far. He decided that one of these ships would be an addition to the crashes on the back side of Niygool.

When he got back to Hardooth, he was surprised to find himself waking up the next day. He had been able to sleep in spite of the massive fatalities he had helped inflict on the Voonshost. All of the Owlamites had been able to sleep. They had been more mentally exhausted than guilty.

"Now comes the hard part," said Soolchakan. "We have to get into those computers and see if we can find their home planet."

Shalam looked at him suspiciously. "Are we going to attack…and destroy them?"

Bonarain cleared her throat. "We're going to inform them of the fact that we destroyed their fleet. Then we're going to let them know that if they ever attempt anything as foolhardy as that again…we will show no mercy. We're tired of war. We're tired but we won't back down to anyone. We will *not* surrender."

Monaha was glancing at Shalam and Soolchakan. "Will it be a…search and destroy mission?"

Soolchakan closed his eyes and shook his head. "I sincerely hope that it is *not*."

Zina looked at the computer system of the Voonshost. "How are you going to get any passwords…when we've killed all of them?"

Bonarain smiled. "I did manage to get some command passwords before we got rid of the big commanders. Most of them should work…on something…I hope." She glanced around looking a little worried.

It took almost three months to decipher some of the cryptic writings of the Voonshost. They had a thing for parables and riddles. The only thing that the Owlamites could get from this kind of writing was that it was supposed to confuse anyone who might accidentally obtain this information. It did…for a while.

The final result of all of the information that was acquired was that this so-called powerful empire consisted of only seven star systems. Of course one of them was the one where the Voonshost originated.

The four members of the first generation found landmarks

on each of the seven planets. They were wondering how to go about hurting the Voonshost to a point where they would leave Hardooth alone.

They visited the conquered planets first. They found the damage that had been done to the fleet at Hardooth had totally ruined the power of the Voonshost. The six planets had fought back once they realized there were no longer over 100 attack ships orbiting their planets. The citizens of the planets had won and now it was the Voonshost who were the slaves. The slaves who were rebuilding the architecture and culture of the peoples they had attempted to enslave and destroy.

Since the indigenous races were not trying to breed the Voonshost for an endless supply of slaves, the Owlamites did not do anything about those planets. Soon the Voonshost on those planets would all be dead and they would be nothing more than a bad blemish on the history of the planet.

When the quartet arrived at the Voonshost home planet, they were rather surprised by what they found. All of the foreign slaves had revolted when they found out that the mighty space armada had been demolished. The result had been death for all of the races that had been brought to Voonshost against their will. The result of that was that the Voonshost had forgotten how to do many things they forced the slaves to perform. Now they were having to re-learn all of those menial jobs that were so important to the economy as well as everyday life.

Another thing that had happened was that they had gutted the supply of metals on their planet in order to manufacture all of the spacecraft that had been sent against their enemies. They had one space station and three spacecraft that were orbiting their planet, however, there was no way to repair and/or rebuild most of the circuits and hulls for those ships so the Voonshost were having to invent ways to continue their culture without the use of most of the metals. They had no way of getting supplies to the space station so it had been abandoned. The three spacecraft were abandoned as well because there was no way to update or repair them. Once their orbit decayed badly enough, they were going to enter the atmosphere of the planet and there was a great possibility that some pretty large pieces were going to do a great deal of damage when they landed.

Soolchakan went back to Hardooth to explain to Shalam and Monaha how it was not necessary to commit total genocide on the Voonshost because they were not a threat any more. It could be a very long time before they became a threat again…if ever.

Soolchakan felt some pride in the fact that he did not have to commit genocide on a foreign race. He wondered if this could have ever worked on some of the species that they had totally killed off in the past. He wondered, however, he knew that it was all just speculation and wishful thinking because he had not been in charge at that time.

His main hope was that he was passing on a legacy to his children where you don't have to kill an entire race to survive. Take away their ability to conquer and then leave them alone… unless they become a headache again.

13

Tulivren 6, 321 ATUT, Zina announced that she was pregnant again. Bonarain, Kiyalee and Chyning got ready to perform the fetal repair again. Once again, however, they could find no problems of any type with this new life. They were able to determine that it was another girl. When Zina heard this, she came up with the name Minima (*Kindness*).

During the entire pregnancy, Bonarain continued watching the little Minima develop. Still, just like the other pregnancies of the newer generations, there were no maladies, deformations or mutations of any type.

On Initikoy, 19 Marrem, 322, Minima was painlessly plucked from her mother's womb. They now had the system working so well, they did not get any golden baptism from the new child by getting a diaper on the baby at the earliest possible moment and then changing it immediately after it was "moistened".

Another addition to the Owlamite race was now being watched by all of the older ones. They found that the very slow aging process of the young was consistent. The only difference was between the sexes as to when they started and finished adolescence. The girls matured, at a younger age, before the boys did.

Soolchakan was wondering if they would see a fourth generation. Jada was 108 years old and Peldom was 103. Baktim and Zoya were both 102. They were all physically mature adults and capable of more procreation. He was still feeling a little uneasy about the incestuous part of the mating, however, with Bonarain there to work on the fetus, it did seem to get rid of any of the possible mutations of any children…hopefully.

Miviskoy, 2 Zerbolud, 338 ATUT, Jada and Peldom joined in the Owlamite way. Once again Bonarain, Kiyalee and Chyning were there to try to teach the new expectant mother how to perform any repairs on the fetus as it developed. When they found that it was a girl, Jada named her Mahanee (*Bountiful*).

Mahanee was born on Hartkoy, 20 Roistume, 339 ATUT… after allowing Jada to experience at least one contraction. After going through the contraction, Jada was more than happy to lay perfectly still while the child was extracted from her womb in the painless Owlam manner.

Soolchakan held the new baby in his arms. "We now have a fourth generation of Owlamites," he proclaimed happily. "I hope, that all of them, are born as perfectly as this one is…as all nine of the others have been." He looked at Bonarain. "Keep doing whatever you're doing to keep them perfect. It is wonderful."

Bonarain smiled at him helplessly. She had never informed him that the children of the third generation and now the fourth had all developed flawlessly (from everything she could find) in the womb. She could only sit there confused in wonder as to why the second generation was so flawed while the rest were so perfect.

Soolchakan heard that once again, Jada was pregnant. The new baby was due sometime in late Statichy, 362. It was another girl. Her name was going to be Panami (*Treasure*). He started thinking of how all of the biggest pieces of news lately had been the birth of a new Owlamite. It was not a new invader from outer space. Wonderful!

They still kept vigilance in the monitor room and now they had more Owlamites who could take turns watching the monitors. It was good to be bored while watching the monitors. The only thing that you saw was an occasional comet, shooting star or meteorite. That made it pleasant knowing that no one was out there coming to get you...at this time.

The one thing that Soolchakan pondered was that none of the first generation women had come to him for another child... yet. He wondered how long they were going to be satisfied with the four they had given birth to. They were all so happy when one of the other generations came up with another child - what were they waiting for? He left the thought on the back burner because he had commanded them to come to him without any trickery against him or each other.

They celebrated the new year of 400 ATUT. No new invaders. A total of fifteen Owlamites, only three of them being "underage".

In the year 441, Minima, who had joined with Baktim, gave birth to the first generation 4 baby boy. She named him Zormun (*Integrity*).

At first Soolchakan was a little surprised that Zoya had been passed up by Baktim for Minima. When he asked, Zoya simply smiled and told him that she understood that no one was to join or be joined through trickery. He did not question it further.

Now Soolchakan was wondering if they would see a fifth generation. If they did, were the three women of the first generation going to be able to repair any mental or physical defects of that generation as well?

The day was Miviskoy, the Fall Equinox and beginning of the year 500 ATUT. Once again they had gone another century without any attack from outer space. This was, again, wonderful. The thing that was not wonderful to Soolchakan was the fact that they had now gone 485 years since discovering how to have babies and the population of the Owlamites was still sitting at sixteen. He guessed that pregnancy must be far worse than he thought it was otherwise the women would be more inclined to get pregnant. He had given them the right to decide if they wanted it or not and had used the *Power* to order that no trickery was used - by anybody, so he once again put the thought on the back burner.

On Astekoy, Whegire the 16th, 541 ATUT, the Owlamite population was blessed with a new baby boy named Bendarik (*Fortitude*). He was the third child of Shalam and Aya and the sixth member of the third generation.

On Hartkoy, Lergan the 30th, 599 ATUT, the fifth generation was begun with the birth of Hisang (*Joy*), parented by Zormun and Mahanee.

The next year, 600 ATUT, they were able to celebrate another century without any invaders from outer space.

The day: Astekoy. The year: 658 ATUT. It was not a day but an event. Tulivren 30, 658 was on Leegkoy. Thorinale 1, 658 was on Initikoy. The day between those two days was the Summer Solstice…and the birth of the second child of Zormun and Mahanee, a boy: Zorkeen (*Summer*)

In the year 700 ATUT, they once again celebrated the fact that another century had gone by without any invasions. Of course they did keep a close watch on the Voonshost, just to make sure that they had not come up with a way to build spacecraft out of some kind of hardened wood or ceramics…or any other manufactured materials.

On 12 Inamyon, 728, Zormun and Mahanee presented the world with their third child, another boy, named Banama (*Prize*)

Now there were twenty Owlamites. Soolchakan still pondered as to why the first generation women were still holding back when Bonarain and Kiyalee had been so eager to become mothers and had tricked Chyning into it. Maybe because the trickery was not allowed it was not so desired any more. He certainly hoped that was not the reason. He simply let them have their way as to when they wanted another one. He noticed that no one had to stop Mahanee from having more. Aya and Zina both had three children and Mahanee had caught up to them even though she was more than 200 years younger than either of them.

For a long time there were no more new children. Once again Soolchakan let it go because he had seen what the women went through during their pregnancies. He felt that there should be more desire to procreate, now that they knew how and the fact that Bonarain had invented a way to repair any deformities or mutations due to bad recessive genes.

Then came Hartkoy, 3 Whegire, 889 ATUT and once again, Mahanee came up with another baby girl. Maramee (*Wonderful*). After 161 years, now there was another infant running through the halls making noise.

A short nine years later on Hartkoy, 29 Roistume, 898 ATUT, Aya presented the Owlamites with another daughter – Amma (*Innovation*). Soolchakan was curious as to what the innovation was, however, he did not question her or dwell on it.

The year 900 started with another celebration of another century without any invasions from outer space. The first generation could remember several times when the invasions were several centuries apart, however, it was still nice to be able to not have to fight anyone for Bri, Hardooth or their lives.

On Astekoy, 1 Consoray, 904 ATUT, Jada and Peldom had a new baby boy. They named him Ashak (*Sky*). Now there were three very young children that everyone had to keep an eye on.

Hartkoy, 24 Marrem, 909 ATUT, Baktim and Minima announced the birth of a new girl named Nafee (*Red*).

Soolchakan gave up trying to figure out the mind of women. Here they were giggling and playing with these young children while talking about their own pregnancies and the growth of their children, however, the first generation women were still not making any noises about any more procreation. He guessed that it had to do with all of the repairs that they had to perform on any fetus in the womb.

Before the millennium was over, Mahanee had to do it again. Tadkoy, 19 Strebale, 967 ATUT, she had her fifth child which brought the population to 25. Zormun and Mahanee welcomed their new son, Poolkiy (*Acquire*). Soolchakan was finding it harder and harder to understand some of these names they were coming up with. He felt that some of them were not appropriate, however, he still let the others name their children whatever they wanted... as long as it was not vulgar...or something that would embarrass the child either as they were growing up or in the future.

Hartkoy, the Fall Equinox. The beginning of a new year and the end of a millennium - 1,000 ATUT. Now there was hope for the future in that the population was rising and the monitors still showed nothing untoward from outer space. Soolchakan was thinking of how it had been 1,015 years since the last death of an Owlamite. He was still saddened by the fact that the last batch of dead Owlamites was not because of an invader but because of the stupidity of a bully and the very odd change in that booze.

What will this new millennium bring?

Gosskoy, 21 Zerbolud, 1055 ATUT, Mahanee did it again. Zormun and Mahanee announce the birth of their sixth child. A boy named Sunok (*Capable*).

Soolchakan was not sure how to take it. This was the sixth child of Zormun and Mahanee and also the sixth member of the fifth generation…all children of the same couple. Right now it did not look to promising for a sixth generation. He had made it clear, with an order using the *Voice of Power* that you were only allowed to join with someone in your generation. You will NOT join with a member that is of the exact same parents. There were other members of the fourth generation so…wait and see what happens when they start procreating.

The year 1100 ATUT came along and once again they could be happy that there had been no Owlamite deaths in 1115 years. The first generation could not remember any time prior where no Owlamites had died in that long a time. All of the wars they had been through with other races on the planet and outworld intruders, it was a blessing indeed.

Miviskoy, 2 Roistume, 1101 ATUT, another child is born to - guess who - Zormun and Mahanee. Another boy named Alam (*Signal*). It seemed that Mahanee wanted to repopulate the planet with Owlamites all by herself. She loved children. She loved nurturing them, playing games with them and watching them grow. Some of the other women thought she was insane for having so many. It did not bother her at all. She loved all of her children.

Astekoy, 29 Strebale, 1104 ATUT another child is born to the fifth generation. Finally, however, this little girl who is named Nafena (*Crimson*), is the daughter of Ashak and Nafee. When she grows up, she will have the choice of five different sons of Zormun and Mahanee.

On 21 Strebale, 1108 ATUT, Kiyalee walked up to Soolchakan. She had no expression on her face at all. She reached behind her neck and got a dab of mucus. She sniffed and then sighed.

"Soolchakan…as you said…no tricks. I'm telling you…I want another child."

He looked back at her a little surprised. "You certainly waited long enough to try again, didn't you?"

She shrugged. "I know but…I remember all of the joy of raising Aya and…I'd like to do it again."

He raised his eyebrows. "You're telling me that there is no coercion here, right?"

She squared her shoulders a little. "None at all. I want another child."

He nodded. "Okay. My bedroom…or yours?"

She looked off to the side and smiled. "Let's mess up your bedroom."

Now that Kiyalee was pregnant, Bonarain, Kiyalee and Chyning all got together and went over this fetus. Again they were a little upset over the fact that the second generation children were such a mess in the womb while none of the other generations were showing any signs of any problems. It was a very disturbing and confusing mystery to the three women.

After one of the long sessions of repairing the liver of the fetus, Bonarain leaned back and wiped perspiration off her forehead. "I still don't get it. Why are our children such…crap… while the others are so…perfect?"

After wiping away some of her own perspiration, Kiyalee shrugged. "Is it possible that…when we do these repairs…we are actually repairing them…all the way down to the lowest level? Are we removing…any and all recessive genes…and giving them nothing but good dominant genes?"

Bonarain and Chyning looked at each other in dismay. Bonarain turned back to Kiyalee. "You…might have just hit it correctly. If our grandchildren…and the next generations beyond that, are so perfect…we *are* doing just that…maybe."

Chyning snickered. "Here's to some wonderful corrections then." She saluted.

Bonarain scoffed. "What it really means is that we… genetically…are nothing but garbage. We're repairing…our mess."

"A mess that was caused by someone else," said Chyning bitterly.

Initikoy, 3 Statichy, 1109 ATUT, a new daughter was born in the second generation to Soolchakan and Kiyalee. She is named Momatak (*Declare*). Soolchakan was not very sure what she was declaring, however, it was her choice.

On Momatak's second birthday, Chyning had a talk with Soolchakan. She took him off to the side and had a mental conversation with him.

"**Believe it or not, I've decided that I want to be a mommy again.**"

He gave her a patronizing look. "**After what you went through with Zina, you're actually telling me now...that you want another one?**"

She shrugged. "**It wasn't as bad as I thought it was going to be and...Zina...I so love her beyond anything else ever imaginable and...I want another one.**"

He nodded his head. "**As long as it *is* your choice with no form of coercion from any other...source.**"

She moved directly in front of him with her face close to his. "It *is* my choice!"

He decided to give her the same choice. "**Your bedroom or mine?**"

She smirked. "**Yours.**"

He grunted in disgust. "Of course."

Hartkoy, 22 Thorinale, 1111 ATUT, another new daughter

added to the second generation. Amaree (*Amaze*) was born. Soolchakan did ask in this case about the name. Chyning stated that it might give Zina a bit of a complex if her sister had a name that was drastically different, so a synonym was used to name the younger sibling to try to avoid any awkward questions.

The population of the Owlamites was now up to 30.

Gosskoy, 30 Lergan, 1116 ATUT…surprise…Zormun and Mahanee announce the birth of child number "eight". Another boy named Fomin (*Ocean*). Soolchakan could do nothing but shake his head. Nine people in the fifth generation and eight of them were the children of Zormun and Mahanee.

Once again, Mahanee declared how much she loved children and how she loved to nurture them. Zormun was thinking of claiming a second apartment. When they first joined, Zormun claimed apartment number 1-111. It seemed a little small now considering the size of the family and how eager Mahanee was to keep on having more children. That many small children filled up the other three bedrooms very quickly.

The Fall Equinox came once again. The beginning of a new year. The year 1120 ATUT. Bonarain now came to Soolchakan talking about another child.

Soolchakan sat there chuckling. **"Is this a competition with Kiyalee and Chyning?"**

Bonarain was taken aback by the statement. **"What *ever*

do you mean by that?"

He grinned. "**All this time, you had two children and each one of them only had one. Now...they have two. Are you trying to stay ahead of them**?"

She raised her hand as if she wanted to backhand him. She grunted and dropped her arm. "**The only one who seems to want to stay ahead of everybody is Mahanee. Honestly! Eight children, when no one else has even thought of a fourth or fifth child? If I wanted to compete, I think that I'd be spending most of my life in your bed**."

He shrugged. "**She does love her children. She loves having young children around her**." He shook his head and chuckled. "**In herds!**"

Bonarain just grunted in agreement.

He sighed. "**Your bed or mine**?"

She gave him a sweet smile. "**I think that I should mess up your mattress...for once**."

He gave her a somewhat acrid smile thinking about how both Kiyalee and Chyning had made the same remark. "**Any time you're ready**."

They vanished from the main room of the apartment.

He was in his bedroom looking around for her when he heard a knock on the door. He opened the door to see her standing there.

"I don't have anything landmarked in your bedroom," she

said with a polite smile.

He simply grunted and stood aside as she walked in.

Once again the three women got together to do some repairs on the newest child of Bonarain. They were, once again, rather disgusted at how many repairs they had to perform on each one of their children, yet none on any of the other generations. The positive side was that they now realized that all of the hard work of repairing these children was getting rid of many of their fears regarding a herd of inbred idiots…at least they hoped that was the reason. Only future generations could possibly confirm this theory.

Bonarain was due sometime in the third week of Thorinale. On Hartkoy, 19 Thorinale, Kiyalee and Chyning headed for the main room for another, if possibly the last, session on repairs to the little girl that Bonarain was carrying. She told the other two women that she had named the girl Nadiwi (*Arise*). Bonarain did not show up.

Chyning looked around confused. "I wonder where she went."

Kiyalee shrugged. "I'll call her." She closed her eyes and mentally called out to Bonarain. After four attempts she opened her eyes looking a little worried. "I…can't seem to reach her. Or…she's not listening for some reason."

Chyning frowned and made a few mental attempts as well. Now she looked worried. "I'm not getting anything!"

Now Kiyalee was really worried. "**Soolchakan! This is Kiyalee! Something is wrong**!"

Soolchakan came back. "**Is there some outworld attack coming at us**?"

Kiyalee huffed. "**No! I can't get Bonarain to answer a call out to her. Could you call to her**?"

Soolchakan was a little confused. "**Where are you**?"

"**I'm in the main room with Chyning**."

Soolchakan appeared in the room with a big frown on his face. "What is going on here?"

Kiyalee looked a little desperate. "Both Chyning and I have made several calls to Bonarain. She hasn't responded at all…to anything. She's due…very shortly, possibly today and…I can't reach her…and I'm worried."

Soolchakan scoffed. "If you're worried about her delivering this baby, I wouldn't worry at all. Remember that she was alone when she gave birth to Monaha. She knows what to do."

Chyning cleared her throat. She spoke through clenched teeth. "She isn't responding to any calls. That…isn't like her."

He sighed. He closed his eyes and made a few mental calls to Bonarain. After the third attempt he opened his eyes looking a little concerned. "That…is unusual." He licked his lips and sniffed. "**Bonarain, this is Soolchakan. Wherever you are… answer me NOW!**" He waited for a response. "**Bonarain, this is Soolchakan! Wake up! Let me know where you are!**" Once again there was no response.

Kiyalee and Chyning were even more worried now.

Soolchakan had his hand up to his mouth. **"Does anyone know where Bonarain is, was, or where she was heading...this morning?"**

A response came back from Bendarik. **"She said that she was going to find some ripe *dinsamp* melons. I think she went to one of the hydroponics gardens on one of those ships in dimension 45."**

Soolchakan groaned. "There's over 1,000 ships in 45, with usable hydroponics, right now. Where do we start?"

Kiyalee stomped her foot in anger. "There are only 200 that are fully operational at this time! The rest are there for spare parts. Out of that, there are only 90 that have fully functioning gardens. Those are the ones that we have to search."

"Let's get to it," said Soolchakan. "If she's not answering... she just might have been...hurt...somehow...and...I don't want to think of what might have happened."

The only ones who did not participate in the search were the very young, Bendarik who was watching the monitors and Mahanee who was watching the young. For eight days they searched every nook and cranny of the ninety ships that had working hydroponics gardens. They found an area where several *dinsamp* melons had been harvested, however, Hisang informed them that she had been the one who took those for a big meal with her siblings.

They searched several other ships that still had working atmospheres in them. Nothing. They all mentally called out to Bonarain during the entire ordeal. Nothing.

Soolchakan got with all of the women who had given birth. "Is it possible that if she...Jumped to one of the hydroponics gardens...on any of those ships that...it could have been too much for her...considering she was pregnant?"

Kiyalee scoffed at the thought. "Jumping and hopping to different dimensions doesn't require that much...physical effort. She's in good condition and...she could have done it without a second thought...especially to dimension #45."

Aya shook her head. "The most strenuous part of it would have been...if she did do it that way...would be to pick up one of the melons. She didn't have to do that. After she cut a melon from the vine, just place your finger on it and Jump back to your room with the melon. Harvesting some melons...not a problem."

Soolchakan sat down with his head in his hands. "Jumping is not a problem. Hopping is not a problem. Moving melons is not a problem." He sat up. "What is the problem that would make her vanish...so completely?"

On 21 Consoray, nine weeks after the disappearance, they finally gave up. Even if she were hiding from them all, even though some act of malice, when Soolchakan had used to *Voice of Power* (several times) to command her to come out and show herself, she would have responded. She was gone and no one could figure out where or how or why.

Soolchakan sat there despondently staring off into space

after announcing that the search was over. "When Nadiwi was… supposed to be born…that would have made 32 Owlamites…in the world. Now, with Bonarain vanishing, with the child, we are now back down to 30. This time, we don't even know why."

The names of Bonarain and Nadiwi were added to the very long list of names on the wall of memory. They were the first Owlamites lost in 1,135 years…and one of them could not have been more than a few days old…if even born. There were question marks following both of their names.

The Fall Equinox occurred once again. It was the beginning of the year 1,139 ATUT. Even after nineteen years, the thirty Owlamites still were puzzled by the mysterious disappearance of Bonarain.

14 Statichy, Kiyalee went to Soolchakan. "I think that we've all been despondent long enough…don't you?"

He looked at her strangely. "What makes you think that we're all despondent?"

She sighed. "All of the young ones. This was the first death of an Owlamite they have ever faced. You and I…and Chyning… we…we were at thousands of funeral pyres. We've spread many an ash over the original site of our city. I hate to say it but, we can handle death a lot easier than they can."

He looked off into space. "So what are you saying? What's your suggestion?"

She embraced him. "Another child."

He was not sure whether to hug her back. "By you?"

"Yes."

He put his arms around her. "Do you think it will help… the younger ones?"

"Hopefully. They all have to realize that…death…is a part of what goes on…even if we don't like it. They have to face that reality."

"Along with the birth of any new ones?"

"Yes."

He took hold of her shoulders and gently pushed her back. "I can see some of the logic of what you're saying. It is a…hard lesson…for anyone to learn. But…they do have to learn it." He cleared his throat. "Your bedroom or mine."

She gave him a half-hearted smile. "Yours."

He sighed. "Always you want to mess up my bed…again."

"Better than messing up mine," she said with a facetious grin.

Gosskoy, 4 Inamyon, 1139 ATUT. The new daughter of Soolchakan and Kiyalee is born. She is named Sodona (*Hope or Hopefulness*). The hope that they were wanting was not very enthusiastic. Still, Sodona was here and she was going to be nurtured properly.

Kiyalee did not like the way things had turned out. She hoped that Sodona would end the mourning over Bonarain. It gave a little bit of a lift, however, not enough. She went to Soolchakan again.

"Maybe we should do it again."

He shook his head with a bit of a smile. "Are you trying to catch up with Mahanee?"

"No, but I do see smiles on their faces every time they look at a new baby."

He looked up at the ceiling. "How old is Sodona now?"

"She's five years old."

"And you want another one…that quickly?"

"If it'll put a smile on their faces and end some of this mourning…yes…and in your bedroom."

The morning of Initikoy, the Winter Solstice, 1146 ATUT, Chima (*Innocent*) was born. The newest daughter of Soolchakan and Kiyalee. Once again it did kill some of the despondency, however, it still did not seem enough to Kiyalee.

Having seven young ones under the age of 45 did stir things up a bit, however, since Bonarain had been the first loss that any of the children of Soolchakan had experienced the loss was still there.

They were celebrating the Spring Equinox of 1168. Soolchakan was still disenchanted with the idea of having event days that were not counted on the calendar. The Equinox took place between 30 Marrem and 1 Zerbolud. He felt that the Equinox should be 1 Zerbolud and the next day should be 2 Zerbolud, however, none of his children agreed because it had always been that way for them.

On that day, Chyning got hold of some fruit juice that had been sitting in the refrigerator a little too long (fermenting). Her celebration seemed a bit too wild. Soolchakan just shrugged it off because a few others were acting somewhat crazy as well. During her craziness, she ran a stripe of her mucus across his face and then stood there giggling as if she were challenging him. He grabbed hold of her, Jumped to her bedroom and then striped her forehead with his mucus. They spent the rest of the day in bed.

The next morning Soolchakan woke up before the sun came up. He jostled Chyning to get her stirring. She woke up with a hangover. She looked around the room somewhat confused and then a realization hit her.

She cleared her throat three times before saying anything. "Last night…did I…do something…a little…*rash*?"

He was a little bewildered by her question…at first. "You striped me with your neck mucus…if that's what you're referring to."

She closed her eyes and buried her head under the pillow. "Oh…*h'oolyach*!"

He shook his head and groaned. "Did you do something… that you now regret?"

"Why didn't you stop me," she whined?

"After you striped me, it was a little late for that."

"Oh, shut up!" She covered her head with the pillow again and moaned.

Kiyalee heard the news and now got with Chyning in assisting in the repairs of the fetus. Since Bonarain was gone, the two of them had to depend a lot more on each other for these repairs. They were becoming more adept at it than they thought they could be. Their children were turning out, fully repaired, just like the others.

On Tadkoy, 18 Roistume, 1169 ATUT, Chyning gave birth to a new daughter that she named Sona (*Celebrate*).

Soolchakan quietly walked up to Chyning after the naming event. "Sona? Are you serious?"

Chyning gave him a dirty look. "Would you prefer… drunken stupor?"

He sniffed and turned away. "Sona is fine."

She gave him a strained smile. "Would you hold your new daughter for a few? I need to go to the bathroom. I don't think that anyone will question a daddy holding his daughter… even though she was conceived during a…drunken stupor." She shook her head. "In the future, we're going to have to remember to throw out any fermented juices."

He just smirked and shook his head.

4 Marrem, 1199, an alarm went off in the monitor room. Someone was entering the star system. Soolchakan, Kiyalee and Chyning all got a close up view of the strange ship. They had never seen one like it before.

"It isn't very big," said Chyning.

"Yeah, well I remember that those Zizzys didn't need much room in their ship for a lot of people," said Kiyalee.

"Let's not speculate," said Soolchakan. "Let's get out there and…find out what we've got."

Chyning looked concerned. "How are we gonna understand them? Bonarain was the one…"

"We will have to utilize the lessons she taught us," said Soolchakan sternly. "She was able to get it done quickly. We may be a little bit…or a *lot* slower. Let's go! The sooner we get there, the sooner we get the translation done. Then, the sooner we find out what their…intentions are."

This was the first experience in defending the planet by a lot of the younger ones. There was a lot of fear and anticipation in their minds. Soolchakan did everything he could to calm them, however, he knew that he was on edge himself.

They all got in their fighters and Jumped to an orbit around Bri. The alien ship was orbiting Bri and in all probability the planet was being scanned by the aliens, just like all of the aliens before them had done.

Soolchakan went to the Bridge and started reading the mind of the one he guessed was the Commander. There was a lot of chatter going on as several of the aliens were closely looking at monitors that were examining all parts of Bri. It took a while, however, Soolchakan started understanding some of their language and speech patterns.

Kiyalee called to Soolchakan. **"I'm actually understanding some of this *h'oolyach*! Are you getting it?"**

"Yes I am. Bonarain was more practiced at it and that made us a little lazy. We need to practice a little more but I don't want to do it too often...with other aliens."

Kiyalee nodded to herself. **"Right! The engines... are typical. I guess until someone comes up with a better system, or someone rewrites the laws of physics, everyone is going to use the same setup. It works, so why change anything...other than the exterior design?"**

Chyning guffawed. **"I don't think that these people came up with it because of someone else. I think that... they came up with it on their own. It just shows that... the laws of physics are the same everywhere. If you have scientists on your planet who can figure out how to make a light speed engine...you make it and now you can fly all over the place at incredible speeds."**

Soolchakan thought of pondering this information, however, it got in the way of translations of the language of these people. He was also distracted somewhat by the way these people were made up. They had what looked like a very petite Heyyah body. Their heads made it clear that they were not Heyyah. The head was perfectly round, hairless and pale pink. They had a small mouth that moved when they talked, no sign of a nose or nostrils and two very small eyes. They also had a row of curly tentacles around their head. The row began (if you were looking at the left side) on the left side of the neck, went up the side of the head, over the top and down to the right side of the neck. They all had exactly fifteen of these curls going around the head. He noticed a few of the curls were randomly wiggling on different aliens. From what he could see of their outward appearances he could not distinguish gender at all.

He noticed a few other things about these people (who called themselves: Korpynch). He did a few practice statements of their language and syntax. When he got the sentence he wanted, hopped to Ghost dimension directly in front of the Commander of the ship and screamed at the Commander (in their language). "WHAT ARE YOU DOING IN MY STAR SYSTEM, YOU FOUL INTRUDER?!"

The face of the Commander changed immensely. The eyes were opened to four times the size they had been. The mouth became a much larger gaping hole. All of the curled tentacles now stood straight out with the ends whipping violently. There was a high-pitched scream that came out of the mouth and a rather large, (yellow) wet stain appeared in the crotch of the off-white pants.

Soolchakan started running around the Bridge screaming at all of the crew that was in there. "GET OUT! LEAVE MY STAR SYSTEM! GO AWAY OR I'LL KILL YOU ALL!"

The reactions of the other members of the Bridge crew

were all very similar. They all started screaming in fear. Their tentacles were all standing out straight and quivering. Several of them soiled their pants (both liquid and solid). A few of them fainted.

Mahanee and Hisang had come onto the Bridge to observe how Soolchakan was going to handle these strangers.

Mahanee was aghast. **"Soolchakan, what are you doing**?"

"I'm scaring the *piddleeyanks* out of them! Maybe I can make them go home and not come back."

Hisang hopped to Ghost dimension and started running around just screaming at the crew. She was getting the same reaction that Soolchakan had been getting…except that now there were more of the Korpynch who were passing out.

Mahanee mentally broadcast to the rest of the Owlamites what was going on in the Bridge. Within just a few moments, every Owlamite was in Ghost and scaring any Korpynch they came across, anywhere on the ship.

The Ship Commander finally regained some of his (or her) senses. The order was given to flee from this star system by the most direct route possible. The Korpynch departed, vowing to never come back…unless there were some among them who were much braver (and were wearing diapers) so that no one could observe them soiling their garments.

The snickering and giggling Owlamites got back in their fighters and as soon as the Korpynch ship cleared the system, they all Jumped back to Hardooth.

When they were all back home in the gorge, Shalam called out to Soolchakan. **"Is that what you call negotiations**?"

"No. I call that scaring the *h'oolyach* out of them to the point that they don't come back."

Monaha was still giggling. **"Do you think that it worked**?"

Soolchakan sighed. **"Only time will tell that. For the moment we have ridded ourselves of them. Hopefully is it permanent**."

Kiyalee gave Soolchakan a strange look. She was a little baffled. "How did that crazy scare tactic…work with these people? Why haven't we ever tried anything like that before?"

He snickered. "One thing that was very evident when I was reading their minds, was the incredible amount of superstitions they have. They're terrified of the spirit world and anything that revolves around it. They have all kinds of courage and tenacity against anything corporeal. Hit them with the non-corporeal and… they lose control of their bodily functions…in unison…because of all of their in-bred superstitions."

Chyning scoffed. "Interesting society! Do they have any reason for conquering?"

"Not here," said Soolchakan with a big grin. "Not anymore. All we have to do is show up in Ghost…watch them wet their pants and…they're gone."

Kiyalee sighed. "Why couldn't they all have been that

easy? It would definitely have made life a lot easier."

"No doubt," grunted Soolchakan.

14

In 1208, Ashak and Nafee had another girl, thus adding to the fifth generation. She was named Na (*Scarlet*).

In 1220, it turns out that Monaha ended up adding polygamy to the children of the first generation of the Owlamites. He was of the second generation, however according to him, if the first generation could practice polygamy then so could the second generation. Monaha and Momatak became the parents of a new son on 7 Whegire, 1220, who they named Zar (*Solid or Solidify*).

Zorkeen and Nafena became the first married couple of the fifth generation. On Statichy 28, 1225 they introduced the sixth generation of the Owlamites to the world. A little girl named Xatang (*Image*).

Not to be outdone by his brother, Shalam married Amaree and on 1 Thorinale, 1240, they had a baby girl named Polii (*Honest*).

Once again a sort of competition between the members of the second generation. Zina delivered a new son on Strebale 19, 1252. A baby boy named Zintom (*Passage*).

In the year 1296, ATUT, Soolchakan was now informed that he was *the* longest serving *Voice of Power*. Even longer than Jeejow who had been there for 1,311 years. He took it in a very somber manner, reminding the rest of the Owlamites that it had now been 10,304 years since the firestorm weapons had changed them and that it was not a competition as to who remained in power the longest. It was, and always had been, an unfortunate set of circumstances that changed the *Voice* from one to another.

Gosskoy, the Fall Equinox of the year 1300 ATUT began a new year and a new century. Still there were only 38 living Owlamites...of which they knew. They still did not know what happened to Bonarain or the daughter she had been carrying.

On the High Holy Day, between 15 and 16 Citendali, Kiyalee gave birth. It was her fifth child...but her first son. She named him Loov (*Different*).

The next year on Marrem 20, 1311, the fortieth official Owlamite to exist was born. He was of the sixth generation, son of Banama and Na. He was named Farn (*Vitality*).

Lergan 29, 1320, Xatang got to meet her brand new little brother. Zorkeen and Nafena announced the newest addition. They named him Yumok (*Action*). Soolchakan sat down and figured that since this was number forty-one, born 1,304 years after Shalam, it might be 2700 ATUT before the population reached 100.

Monaha and Momatak announced the new birth of their daughter on Consoray 30, 1391. She was named Nahama (*Bestow*).

The last child born during the fourteenth century was the second child of Banama and Na. A new baby girl born on Inamyon 13, 1396 named Pomani (*Zeal*).

Leegkoy, the Fall Equinox of the year 1400 ATUT. The

new year and the beginning of the fifteenth century ATUT. Once again all of the Owlamites prayed for peace in the land and in outer space. They had seen a pretty good span of peace in outer space, however, they were hearing of wars that were going on in different countries on Hardooth for inane, insane or stupid reasons. They wanted nothing to do with any of that. Keeping an eye on outer space was a big enough headache. Any babysitting of other countries and races was ridiculous because you just might end up fighting for the wrong people.

It was also during the year 1400 that Soolchakan decided to a new tradition. Since he, Kiyalee and Chyning were the first generation that was the way they would be officially addressed. Soolchakan of the First, Kiyalee of the First and Chyning of the First.

Shalam, Monaha, Aya, Zina, Momatak, Amaree, Sodona, Chima, Sona and Loov were all of the Second.

Jada, Peldom, Baktim, Zoya, Minima, Bendarik, Amma, Zar, Polii, Zintom and Nahama were all of the Third.

Mahanee, Panami, Zormun, Ashak and Nafee were all of the Fourth.

Hisang, Zorkeen, Banama, Maramee, Poolkiy, Sunok, Alam, Nafena, Fomin and Na were all of the Fifth.

Xatang, Farn, Yumok and Pomani were all of the Sixth.

All were to be identified by their generation and according to an earlier edict by Soolchakan, you could only marry in your generation. That way he would be able to keep track of it easier (maybe). He was waiting for the day when there would be too many to keep track of and he hoped that it would be soon. The women were not cooperating. They were not giving birth fast enough for that phenomenon to occur. He once again shrugged it off as the rigors of pregnancy were a bit much on the body, mind and soul, so he left it up to the women as to when they wanted to procreate.

The first child of the fifteenth century was another girl. Kiyalee of the First gave birth on 1 Zerbolud, 1407 to Zelok of the Second (*Daring*).

Loov and Sona of the Second married and shortly after that Sona gave birth to a baby girl on Strebale 23, 1416, Tonat of the Third (*Picture*).

Loov and Sona wasted no time in producing another child. Another baby girl was born by the pair on Inamyon 7, 1418. She was named Sanapin of the Third *(Emotion)*.

Farn and Xatang of the Sixth married and now a new generation was born. On Whegire 22, 1419 a boy was born. Sab of the Seventh (*Happy*).

Loov and Sona cannot keep their hands off of each other. Or Sona is trying to catch up with Mahanee. Their third child in six years comes along. A baby boy is born on Whegire 2, 1421. His name is Machek of the Third (*Proclaim*).

Once again the bug bit Chyning. A new baby boy in the second generation was born on Roistume 16, 1422. His name is Jotsoom of the Second (*Kinship*).

Kiyalee found out what the count was and she decided that she wanted to be the mother of the fiftieth Owlamite. On Statichy 24, 1430, another girl was added to the second generation. Hamar (*Festive*).

For some reason, Chyning was feeling a little left out, or left behind. Kiyalee now had seven children while Chyning only had four. On Statichy 12, 1436, Chyning gave birth to another girl. Her fifth child was Zhontam of the Second (*Melody*).

Chyning learned a valuable lesson about CHANGING YOUR BED SHEETS. She had not been in her bed in quite a long time because, of course, Owlamites really do not need much sleep at all – unless they have been really exerting themselves. She decided to lay down for a while and asked one of the younger women to watch her two young ones. Zhontam was still just a baby while Jotsoom was in his teen years. She found some strange substance on one of her pillows. She thought it might be something left over from a meal in the bed...she tasted it...and immediately went into heat. It just happened to be some of the mucus left there (accidentally) by Soolchakan. She made a desperate mental call to Soolchakan. He showed up in her bedroom to find out what the problem was and she striped his forehead with her mucus. The result of this accident was a baby boy born on Strebale 1, 1437. She named him Molkan of the Second (*Cleansing*). Soolchakan and Chyning were the only ones who knew the symbolism of his name - change your nasty bed sheets more often – a *lot* more often. From this they found out that the Owlamite mucus could remain effective for a very long time – even dried and rotting on a pillowcase.

The second wife of Shalam, Amaree, decided to have a second child. She gave birth to a baby boy on Thorinale, Summer Solstice, 1450. She named him Sodek of the Third (*Greeting*).

Yumok and Pomani of the Sixth got together and gave the Seventh generation another member. On Inamyon 5, 1498, she gave birth to a daughter that she named Mymin of the Seventh (*Green*).

Soolchakan started feeling more optimistic. They closed out the fifteenth century ATUT with 54 Owlamites. Maybe they would be able to hit the 100 mark before the year 2700 ATUT. He was very glad that most of the new additions to his memoirs were the birth of new Owlamites…even though more than one of them was a complete (or idiotic) accident.

Farn and Xatang, the parents of Sab gave him a little brother on Consoray 5, 1525. They named their new son Korpem (*Persist*).

Jotsoom of the Second ended up getting married to both Sodona and Chima. The thing that made this different was the fact that this was only the second time that two new baby Owlamites were born in the same year. That had not happened since the year 220. On Whegire 9, 1530, Sodona gave birth to a boy named Balak (*Expand*). On Lergan 22, 1530, Chima gave birth to a girl named Ino (*Perky*).

Zoya of the third finally got married. She was born in the year 220. Her husband Machek was born in 1421. Finally she got to get in on the procreation and she added to the phenomenon of more than one child born in the same year…and the same month.

On Lergan 28, 1530 Zoya gave birth to a boy named Mobor (*Endure*).

Bendarik and Nahama of the third wedded and became the parents of a new girl in the fourth generation. On Strebale 18, 1532 Sazha was born. (*Ability*).

In the same year, Chima of the Second, who had given birth to her first child in 1530 became pregnant again and on Zerbolud 6, 1532, she gave birth to a girl she named Zhytash (*Yearn*). Zhytash now put the population at 60.

Zintom and Amma of the Third joined and now there was a new baby boy born to the fourth generation. He was named Bymin (*Robust*).

Zar and Polii of the Third joined. They gave birth to another fourth generation baby boy on Statichy 16, 1538. They named him Ozar (*Contain*).

Yumok and Pomani of the Sixth gave birth to a second daughter on Statichy 22, 1541. They named her Na-Ima (*Hazel*).

Molkan and Zelok of the Second married and on Thorinale 3, 1549 gave birth to a baby boy they named Borim (*Emanate*).

Sodek and Tonat of the Third entered the bonds of matrimony and on Citendali 21, 1555 gave birth to a baby boy. They named him Bak (*Look*).

In the same year, Baktim and Minima of the Third also gave birth. A baby girl was born on Tulivren 1, 1555. She was named Alamet (*Landmark*).

Loov of the Second obtained a second wife in Zhontam.

On Marrem 11, 1566 she gave birth to a new baby boy. She named him Lorib (*Achieve*).

Molkan of the Second obtained a second wife as well – Hamar. On Inamyon 29, 1567 she gave birth to a baby girl that she named Yaming (*Alert*).

The second wife of Shalam, Amaree decided to have another baby. She came up with another baby girl on Citendali 12, 1580 named Anda (*Answer*).

Sixteen years after her first child, Zhontam decided to have another child. On Lergan 8, 1582 another third generation baby girl was born. She was named Neea *(Music)*. Soolchakan was getting even more optimistic about the future when this brought their numbers to 70.

Zorkeen and Nafena of the Fifth came up with their third child. On Roistume 25, 1586 a baby girl they named Araba (*Natural*).

Molkan and Zelok of the Second had another child. On Consoray 30, 1591 a baby girl was born named Bana (*Impart*).

Not to be outdone by the first wife, Hamar of the Second, second wife to Molkan gave birth to a baby girl on Marrem 13, 1593. She was named Yamang (*Siren*).

The sixteenth century ended with 73 Owlamites living on the planet. Soolchakan hoped that this would continue long into the next century.

On Strebale 18, 1606 Loov and Zhontam of the Second gave birth to their third child. A girl named Sowee (*Portray*).

Jotsoom and Sodona of the Second announced the birth of their second child. On Zerbolud 16, 1607 a new baby girl was born named Mila (*Temperance*).

Molkan and Hamar of the Second announced the birth of their third child. A boy was born on Roistume 17, 1608. He was named Bidge (*Stamina*).

Molkan's first wife Zelok did not want to fall behind. On Citendali 7, 1608 she gave birth to a new daughter. She was named Eeama (*Resolve*).

The second wife of Monaha, Momatak announced the birth of her third child. On Tulivren 5, 1611 she gave birth to a boy she named Naban (*Favor*).

The second wife of Loov of the Second, Zhontam gave birth on Statichy 26, 1612. Her fourth child. Another baby girl named Chera (*Adept*).

Just seven years after her second child, Sodona of the Second gave birth to her third child. On Lergan 1, 1614, a boy was born named Polgothon (*Pioneer*). This child brings the population to 80.

Another momentous occasion happened. Sab and Mymin of the Seventh announce the birth of the first member of generation eight. On Thorinale 28, 1619, a boy is born named Za-Ing (*Leader*).

Soolchakan is pleased that a new generation has entered the world and (thank the Great Maker) is showing no sign of inbred mutations. Kiyalee and Chyning were busy teaching all of the mothers how to repair anything wrong with their child in the womb, however, still, none of the other generations needed very much, if anything, in the way of repairs to their children.

Just under eight years later, Sab and Mymin of the Seventh announce the birth of another baby boy. On Marrem 10, 1627 the new child was named Or (*Go*).

On Inamyon 11, 1630, Zhontam of the Second announces the birth of her fifth child. It is a baby boy she named Mayakton (*Reliable*).

Panami of the Fourth finally weds. She chooses Mobor of the Fourth and on Lergan 9, 1631 she gives birth to a baby girl that she names Oanin (*Smile*).

Mahanee of the Fourth will not be left behind or challenged. On Whegire 30, 1632 she announces the birth of her *ninth* child. A girl named Nesh (*Gracious*).

Balak and Sanapin of the Third unite. On Consoray 7, 1633 they announce the birth of their new baby boy Bikaropin (*Academic*).

The second wife of Jotsoom, Chima announces the birth of her third child on Strebale 24, 1634. The new baby girl is named Nasahan (*Haste*).

Mobor of the Fourth now has a second wife. Sazha unites with him and on Marrem 30, 1636 she gives birth to a girl that she names Bawa (*Speech*).

The second wife of Molkan, Zelok of the Second gave birth to another child. A son who was born on the Summer Solstice of

1638. She named him Baka (*Positive*).

The second wife of Shalam, Amaree gave birth to her fourth child, a boy on Citendali 18, 1644. She named him Odan (*Growth*).

Soolchakan had some inner pride that he did not let the others know about because he did not want to make anyone think that there was any favoritism. The birth of Odan brought the population to 90 and it was the first son of Soolchakan who was the father of that child.

Borim and Ino of the Third joined in matrimony and on Whegire 14, 1649 she gave birth to a girl that she named Inorim (*Playful*).

Jotsoom and Sodona of the Second announce the birth of their fourth child on Zerbolud 3, 1650. A son named Azar (*Uphold*).

Machek and Zoya of the Third announce the birth of their second child on Inamyon 15, 1650. A daughter named Maga (*Essence*).

Bymin and Alamet of the Fourth joined together. On Tulivren 23, 1657 they announced the birth of their son Galem (*Foundation*).

Korpem and Na-Ima of the Seventh married. On Marrem 12, 1680 they announced the birth of the third member of the eighth generation...also the third male in the eighth generation. They named him Joz (*Turn*).

Peldom and Jada of the Third announce the birth of their

fourth child. On Statichy 27, 1691 a girl is born named Shashy (*Tranquil*).

Lorib and Zhytash of the Third join together. On Strebale 19, 1699 they announce the birth of their son. They named him Porim (*Future*).

Lorib quickly ended up with a second wife – Anda. On Roistume 20, 1699, she announced the birth of her new son. She named him Batar (*Sanction*).

Soolchakan was wondering about some of the names and what they symbolized to the parents, however, he remembered that he was going to leave it alone...unless it was something completely awkward, insulting, rude or vulgar.

Lorib became the first (other than Soolchakan) to obtain three wives. He also obtained all three wives about the same time and became the father of three sons all in the same year. Yamang was the third one to join with Lorib and on Thorinale 4, 1699 she gave birth to a son that she named Eerok (*Emblem*).

Soolchakan held a brand new baby in his arms with pride. He finally saw one thing that he had been hoping for. On Consoray 1, 1700, the population of the Owlamites hit 100. Banama and Na of the Fifth announced the birth of their third child. A boy named Majim (*Continue*). Soolchakan had originally figured that the way things were going, they would not reach that plateau until around the year 2700. Most of the women were not that eager to get pregnant. It was now near the end of the seventeenth century and Majim was here...now. Maybe by 2700 the count would be... who knows? If they could stay out of planetary squabbles and the outworlders stayed away, then there was always hope.

By the year 1700 the population was at 100. By the year 1800 the population was now at 126. Things were definitely looking up.

The year 1800 was uneventful. The year 1801 started out normally…up until the month of Tulivren. Meffin and Araba were the only ones who were with child. Meffin was due in Statichy of 1802 and Araba was due in Whegire of 1802.

15

Then came Tulivren 18, 1801. Xatang made a desperate mental call to all Owlamites everywhere. She had found her husband Farn...dead...and gutted. The two of them had been seeing some sights along the coastline in Peegruch. She had gone to check one thing, he another. She had called to him mentally and received no answer. She had searched for almost half the day when she found his body hidden between two boulders near the beach.

Soolchakan ordered all personnel to Peegruch to look for anything that they could find at the scene of the crime.

The body of Farn had been badly desecrated. It was obvious that his body had been rolled over several times during the grisly dissection. The area was a bloody mess. The liver, the heart, the kidneys, the brain...and a large amount of skin of his back had been peeled off. The missing internal organs and the skin were not to be found in that area at all.

Kiyalee and Chyning were sadly planning another funeral pyre. Soolchakan was now adamant that this tradition would cease. He had never liked the idea of burning a body as if it were useless trash. Instead, he had the body placed in a sealed coffin and taken to one of the vaults on Zhagool. Most of the bombs that had been stored there had been used so the majority of the vaults were now empty. There they would be able to keep the evidence intact and no one, not even some professional forensic pathologist, would be able to get to the body without the permission of an Owlamite.

After six days of searching the area, they could find nothing that helped figure out who had attacked Farn or why.

Eleven days later, Tulivren 29, 1801, Machek called out to all Owlamites. His wife Zoya had been killed and her body desecrated in the same manner as Farn. This time, however, the crime was committed in Jebeltau. Now Soolchakan and the rest of the Owlamites were really worried. Peegruch was part of South Chilamte – Jebeltau was in Ficara. The exact same crime, committed on two different continents only seventeen days apart and no one had ever heard of anything like that happening before.

Then on Thorinale 14, 1801, a few friends were in Ekogib on the Aerisau continent. They found one of their party, Nesh... murdered in the same manner as Farn and Zoya.

Who could be doing this...and how? Soolchakan was ready to stop all travel of any type until they could figure out what had happened. Kiyalee and Chyning argued that they had to be able to do some form of investigation in order to determine the who, what and why. Soolchakan reluctantly allowed it. He knew that among the Owlamites Bikaropin seemed to be the only one who was intelligent enough to perform any form of investigation.

Inamyon 11, 1801, the body of Shalam of the Second is found - in High Country - on an east coast beach at the bottom of the cliffs. He has been murdered and desecrated in the same manner. Now what do we do?

One murder is tragic. Two murders...coincidence (?). Three murders is a pattern. Four murders is absolutely the work of a serial killer (or killers)...who so far has only struck against Owlamites...of which they are aware.

Who is doing this ritualistic killing and why? Why are the murders so alike, but spread out so far? Is any other race suffering this same indignity? So many frustrating and unanswered questions. Not to mention the fact that no current living Owlamite had ever been in the situation where they had to investigate a crime of any sort.